The Devil's Own

Maria McDonald

Waterford Christmas 2022

Waterford city at Christmas is a treat. Twinkling lights adorn the streets. Shop windows beckon shoppers with tinselled displays of colourful gifts. My favourite bookshop excelled this year. Situated right in the middle of the shopping district, "The Book Centre" has a myriad of children's books, adult thrillers, memoirs and the classics, all interspersed with boxed candle sets, novelty mugs, key rings and board games.

Stepping inside, my heart lifted at the sight of the display directly in front of the door. The banner above the exhibit of new releases said "Bestsellers". There it was with a sticker across it reading "Book Club choice of the month", and above the tagline on the intriguing cover "A tale of two soldiers". I lifted it as delicately as if it were a precious jewel. It felt lighter than I expected, considering its size. I flicked through the pages to the acknowledgements at the back then smiled at the signature inside the front dust jacket.

The shop was overheated, packed with Christmas shoppers wearing coats and hats damp from the earlier rain. But nothing could mask that unmistakable yet elusive smell of new books. Beside me, a tall broad man wearing a disposable mask, under crinkled leathery eyes, picked up a copy of the book. He read the inside jacket cover before tucking it under his arm and heading to the checkout.

A young woman, early thirties with short spiky hair and red Doc Marten boots, waved her copy of the book at what may have been her mother, who nodded back.

An older man picked up a copy and turned it over to read the back cover with shaky arthritic hands. His features were hidden behind thick-framed glasses steamed up over an oversized black mask covering most of his face. I can't help but wonder what they would all make of it. Would they be touched by Edith's story, upset by Arthur's upbringing? Would they care?

The touch of my wife Jean's hand on my arm startled me.

"Penny for them," she said.

"I'm considering buying this book. What do you think?"

"Too late, love. I beat you to it."

Jean handed me the branded paper bag, and I grinned like a schoolboy. She linked her arm in mine. Together, we left the bookshop and walked towards the restaurant where our adult offspring were meeting us for a celebratory dinner.

It had been quite a journey, a revelation of sorts, of kindred spirits, and the bonds that bind us to friends and family. The many tentacles that make us who we are.

Chapter 1

Brian

Monday 21st September 2020

I t all started when we were clearing out the old house in the Curragh Camp. After forty years of service with the Irish Defence Forces, I was due to retire. Jean and I had spent all our married life in the Curragh Camp, rearing our three children in married quarters, twenty of those years in this house.

The attic had been full of the usual accumulated rubbish, Christmas decorations, suitcases, the kids' old toys. Most of it was going in the skip or to charity, and I had nearly finished when I noticed the cabinet. In fairness, its presence in the farthest corner of the dimly lit attic was expertly camouflaged. Covered entirely by a moth-eaten army blanket, it was shrouded in a labyrinth of cobwebs. Layers of thick dust fluttered in the air when I lifted it, causing me to sneeze in violent outbursts.

On closer examination, I realised it was an old British Army metal cabinet. They were standard fixtures in the company office when I first joined the army: a throwback to the days of British rule. The British were long gone. Someone must have commandeered this one at some stage over the past one hundred and forty years. Brought it into the house for their own use and abandoned it in the corner of the attic.

Curiosity got the better of me. I tried to open it, but it was locked. I looked around me at the roof beams, still as solid as the day the house was built. The dim glow from the overhead bulb didn't cast enough light. I needed a torch. Walking back to the entrance, I shouted down, "Jean, hand me up the torch, will ya?"

She appeared below the ladder. "What are you doing? I thought you got everything down from the attic."

"I thought I had, but there's an old cabinet here in the corner. I want to get a better look at it."

I could hear Jean muttering to herself as she stomped down the stairs to the kitchen. We usually kept a torch under the sink, but I wasn't sure if it had been packed away. I was about to climb down to help look for it when Jean's upper half popped up into the roof space waving a torch in her right hand. She cut me short when I lit up the cabinet in the corner.

"No way, Brian. That's not ours. And even if we do own it, which I doubt, there's no way you are bringing that old rubbish to the new house."

Her tone was more of a warning than a suggestion.

"I have no intention of bringing it anywhere. Don't worry about that, love. Look at the state of it. I just want to get a better look at it. I'll be down in a minute."

I could hear Jean muttering again as she went back down the ladder. Her tone, though unintelligible, sounded firm enough to remind me that I needed to get on with the packing. Our move to our new home was only days away, and we were behind schedule. There was a cupboard in the front room that I promised Jean I would get to that day.

I directed the light from the torch towards the empty lock. There was no key visible, either under the cabinet or above it. As I completed one last search by torchlight, something caught my attention on the beam behind the cabinet. On closer inspection of the roof beams, I discovered a noticeably larger pile of dust in one corner. I felt along the beam with my hand. Sure enough, there it was, a large metal key, dust encrusted but functional. I blew on it and wiped it on my trousers, leaving a long grey trail of dust and cobwebs down my khaki pants.

After a concentrated effort, a lot of perspiration and a few expletives, I heard the satisfying click of the lock opening. Adrenalin buzzed through my veins, a flashback to that buzz before shooting practice on the ranges.

Preparing myself mentally for whatever lay inside, I opened the door tentatively but was immediately disappointed to reveal several books. They were hardback, A4-size journals, three of them in total. I carefully lifted them out and blew the dust off them, sending me into another sneezing frenzy.

Jean's voice echoed up from the landing, "Brian, I'm away to work; see you later."

"Bye, love," I shouted, distracted by the journals in my hands.

Moving closer to the entrance, I sat on the edge with my legs dangling over the opening and the journals beside me. I took a cloth from my combat trousers pocket and wiped the cover of the first journal. It was dark green, the colour of wet and rotted undergrowth with the word "PRIVATE" written across the front in large, uniform letters.

The pages inside were loose but filed neatly in date order. The first page was blank, and I flicked through, page after page of a scrawled childlike script. Each page appeared to begin with a date and a place name. I marvelled at the headings of Malta 1895, Egypt 1896, India 1897, Palestine, Dover, Tipperary. A page with the title Curragh September 1911 caught my attention. I promptly dropped the journal, cursing as it fell to the landing below, shattering the fragile binding and scattering loose pages across the floor.

Scolding myself for my clumsiness, I picked up the next

journal. It appeared to be a dull beige colour under the dust. When I wiped it, I saw that it was decorated with line drawings of flowers and butterflies in coloured ink, long faded. I opened it and there inside the front cover, read the entry:

The personal property of Mrs Edith Torrington
Warrant Officer Quarters
Curragh Camp, Co Kildare
And formerly of India and England.

The handwriting was elegant. Large flowery strokes, each letter perfectly formed and aligned with little drawings in the margins.

"Wow." I hesitate for a second, mindful that this was the diary of a woman I didn't know. I shrugged to myself. Mrs Edith Torrington was probably dead a long time at this stage. It would be doubtful if anyone would object to me reading her journal. However, I hesitated to invade her privacy, so I put Edith's journal aside and picked up the next one. It was a dark red with lines in black ink on the front underlined with military precision:

Warrant Officer Torrington A.
Connaught Rangers (disbanded)
Eire National Army

My curiosity was ignited. On a recent trip to Galway to visit an old army friend, he'd given us a guided tour of the museum in Renmore Barracks. It was full of paraphernalia brought back by the Connaught Rangers from the Boer War and India. Even Jean was fascinated with the collection. There were many British regiments raised in Ireland, such as the Connaught

Rangers, who earned the nickname The Devil's Own for their bravery in battle. The British disbanded them in the early 1920s. So many of those Irish men who had served in the Rangers died in the First World War.

After Ireland achieved independence, there were no new recruits to replenish their number. I had never even thought about what had happened to those still serving with those regiments at the time. They had been through the horrors of the First World War and maybe even the Boer War before that. I wondered how many had travelled back to Ireland and joined the newly formed National Army under Michael Collins.

I opened the journal and skimmed through page after page in uniform handwriting. Each page had a heading with a country and a date, similar to the first journal, but the script was neat and tidy. I couldn't help myself. I had to read it, so I got comfortable and opened the first page.

Chapter 2

Arthur's Journal

Sandes home, Curragh Camp: 21st September 1923

The Sandes Soldiers' Homes saved me from myself. Wherever the British Empire positioned their army, Ms Elsie Sandes set up a soldiers' home and that is exactly what it is. A home away from home. A sanctuary where alcohol is forbidden, where good Christian living is actively promoted. My attendance in the Sandes home keeps me sober, but lately my dreams are haunting me.

The lady in the Sandes home told me that it might help if I wrote down what had happened to me. That writing the horrors I have seen might be "cathartic" as she put it, although she had to explain to me what that word meant. It made sense, so here I am, sitting in the reading room of the Sandes home, with my journal and a pen, and I do not know where to start. I asked Mrs Magill, and she said, start at the beginning. So here goes, I will begin with that day forever etched in my brain, 21st September 1880, and my last memory of my father.

Manchester, September 1880

He was weaving his way down the alley, stumbling like a toddler, muttering to himself. I ran to warn my ma. When Ma had her paying customers over, I learned to make myself scarce. The bedspring's rhythmic creak and the muddy boots peeking out from under the curtain that surrounded the bed meant she was still busy. Unsure of what to do, I stood still, trying to stem my growing sense of panic.

Then I ran, slamming the door three times behind me, hoping she would recognise the signal that her drunkard of a husband was on his way. In some vain hope of slowing him down, I ran towards him and slammed into him, knocking him flat on his back. His breath left his body with a giant oomph, and he did not get up again. Fear took over then. I thought I had killed him or maybe hoped I had. How different my life would have been if I had killed him at that moment before he killed my mother.

Standing over him, breathless and scared, I prayed for the first time in my twelve years.

"Arthur," I heard my ma behind me. She had dispatched her customer; the coins were in her hand, and she gave them to me to hide in the secret pockets in my britches. Warning me to be silent by putting her index finger to her lips, she bent over his prostrate body. We both sighed when we heard his grumbling start up again. Ma signalled to me to take his right arm, and she took his left. Together we led him to what we called home.

One room in the basement of a dilapidated, overflowing hovel that housed twelve families with one toilet between us out in the backyard. At least there were only three of us in that room if you discounted Ma's customers. Other families had five or six children, all cooking, eating, and sleeping in one room.

Our basement room was convenient for my ma's paying customers. Without her earnings, we would have starved. Some days my da went on a rampage, wrecking our room until he found her stash and those days, we went hungry. Ma learnt quickly. She got into the habit of giving me the money to hide about my person.

Ma was clever about it though. She still left a small amount under the mattress or tucked in behind the pipe under the sink. At least then, when he had his fit of rage, he found something, and he would leave us alone. When he was sober, he was a gentleman, or at least that's what my ma said. I wouldn't know; I never saw him sober.

We led him to the bed in the corner, and he flopped onto it, fully clothed, like an overstuffed rag doll. He groaned and dribbled and turned on his side. Within seconds he was snoring, so we tiptoed away.

"Give it to me, Arthur." My ear stung from the clip she gave me as a warning not to cross her.

I handed her back her earnings. She counted the coins, nodded as if satisfied and gave me a farthing.

"Get yourself something to eat, now get lost."

I watched her walk away. My ma, not yet thirty, was bent over, her bones protruding through her clothes. Lately she had become fond of the gin and showed it with the hollow cheeks and sunken eyes of a woman twice her age.

The shiny farthing was burning a hole in my hand, and my stomach was rumbling, so I made my way to the bakery on Simons Street. Just before closing, they sold off any leftover bread and cakes for little or nothing. Sometimes the baker's wife took pity on me and threw in something extra. On those days, I slept with a full belly.

I was in luck. The lights were on, and I could see Mrs Beasley through the large window wrapping up the last of that day's merchandise. I went to the back door of the bakery as I always did and gave a hesitant knock. Mr Beasley must have been in the storeroom, for she handed me out a parcel with a finger to her lips. She would not take my farthing.

"Go, quickly now. Save your money for another day," she whispered as she waved me away from the door as if she were shooing pigeons away from breadcrumbs. I didn't need to be told twice. Pocketing my farthing, I ran and didn't stop until I reached the riverbank.

Glancing furtively around to check no one had seen me, I made my way to my secret place. A tree stump under cover of an old oak tree tucked away in the corner of the forest that bordered the river. I could hide there, out of sight, safe, with only the burble of the water and the birds in the trees for company.

The parcel was warm in my hands, and I gingerly opened it and cried out with joy. Two meat pies, still warm. A whole crispy loaf, that yeasty smell still emanating from it. My mouth watered, and I licked my lips in anticipation. The first bite was like manna from heaven, and I sighed as I chewed the highly seasoned meat pie. It had been a long time since I had tasted anything resembling meat.

The taste danced on my tongue as I savoured every single bite. I ate as slow as I could. First a morsel of meat pie, then a bite of bread. Between bites, I chewed and smiled and surveyed my world like a king looking out over all he owned.

It was just getting dark as I finished my pie. I carefully wrapped the second pie and half the bread to give my ma when I got home, in case she forgot to buy food again. She did that when she drank gin, forgot to buy food, forgot to eat, forgot who she was. Not even the thoughts of her could dampen my spirits.

Whistling as I walked, I made my way home, happy with my world.

My peace was short-lived. I could hear my parents screaming at each other from the far side of the alley. There was no point in going home to listen to them tearing each other apart. I loitered for a bit then walked around the block a couple of times. Eventually, silence reigned. I made my way down the alley to the basement door and slipped in as quiet as a mouse.

Ma was sitting on the bed silently weeping and nursing an eye that would be purple by the morning. My da sat in the corner, his back against the wall, rocking himself. His arms were wrapped around his torso as if he were afraid that if he let go of himself, he would lose control and hit her again. Both sets of eyes snapped on me. I could feel my insides tremble, as I looked from one to the other, not sure who to be more afraid of.

The rough table stood in the middle of the floor, and I dropped my parcel of pie and bread into the middle of it. I got a knife and cut the food into two portions before separating them and placing a portion on each side of the table. They started to move, like two rabid dogs circling the table, watching, salivating, wondering who would pounce first. I backed away, towards the door, without saying a word.

Ma stopped circling. She pounced on the food, grabbed the bread, and stepped back, nibbling without ever taking her eyes off my da. He watched her as if startled that she should be so bold as to eat in front of him. Then my da edged forward with the stealth of a hungry animal, grabbed his portion of the pie, and stuffed it all into his mouth, his hand under his chin to catch any crumbs. I marvelled that he had thought to do that, that his whiskey addled brain could give him that level of instruction as it struggled to keep him upright. He swayed as he stood, his cheeks full of the pie as he masticated with gusto.

"Pig," she muttered, but he heard her. With a roar, he bounded towards her and pushed her backwards. She fell with him on top of her, squashing what little breath she had left in her body. He rolled off her, and she started to pummel him with her bony fists, raining blows down on his fat stomach that brought howls of rage from deep within him. He rolled away from her and used the bed to climb back up to his feet. I could see his eyes fall on the poker beside the fire, and I instinctively knew what he was going to do. I rushed forward with no clear thought of how to stop him.

"No, run, Ma, run."

I ran at him, but he pushed me back, and I fell, winded, and hit my head off the corner of the bedpost. When I woke, I could smell the metallic heat of blood and taste it on my cheek. I felt my head warily before I struggled to stand up. I looked down and saw the pool of blood at my feet, and my eyes followed the trail of it to my ma's body, lying in the middle of the room. Her head and torso a bloody pulp, my da standing over her, the poker raised above his head, ready to rain another blow on her limp and broken body.

"Stop," I tried to shout, but only a croak came out that did not even sound like me. Da looked over, his eyes wild and bulging out of their sockets. He lowered the poker slowly and took a step toward me. I shook. Twenty drummer boys were playing in my brain. He raised the poker as he took another step. I closed my eyes, ready to accept the inevitable and retreated so far into my own little world of pain that the shouting did not even register with me at first.

It was only when someone touched my arm that my nerve endings jumped, and I opened my eyes. The men from upstairs had disarmed my da and surrounded him while the women were keening around my ma. I stumbled, suddenly weak, and was led away by gentle hands to a room upstairs.

The police were called, and I had to talk to them, tell them what I heard, what I saw. But not before I heard the neighbours talking. How they had heard my ma screaming and knew it was different. I heard one woman tell the others that her husband had broken down the door and saw me da edging towards me, the poker in his hand dripping with my ma's blood and bits of her brain. I wondered then why that woman felt the need to add that detail. I was silent, standing in the corner, awaiting my fate.

They took care of me that first night, but what could they do? They all struggled to feed their own families; they could not take on a waif and stray like me, so I left.

The following morning, I packed up my meagre belongings with my bandaged head and my damaged soul. I walked out the door, down the alley and away from Manchester, swearing to never set foot in the place for as long as I lived.

Sandes home, Curragh Camp: 21st September 1923

I still remember how determined I was that day that I would never return. At least I kept that promise to myself. I did not keep the others. That morning I swore that I would never touch alcohol. I did not keep that promise, not for many years, but I'm a teetotaller now. Thanks to the Sandes Soldiers' Home.

Chapter 3

Brian

Monday 21st September 2020

I put down Arthur's journal. Such a horrific event in a young boy's life. To see his mother murdered by his father. I wondered how any child could recover from that. An incident from my childhood in Waterford resurfaced instantly from somewhere deep in my memory.

Ballyfair was more of a townland than a village. If you were passing through on your way from Waterford city to Dungarvan, you might have noticed the church. It's a sizeable stone-built edifice dedicated to the Sacred Heart and situated opposite the T of a T-junction. The local pub doubled as a shop and was tucked in the corner behind a large hedge across the road as if trying to hide from the wrath of the passionate and thunder-voiced Father Devlin.

He hated the demon drink and wasn't afraid to use the pulpit to denounce anyone who chose to partake in it. We lived in a row of houses uphill from the shop. My family were farm labourers, little people in the general scheme of things, but great neighbours who pulled together when they had to.

On the day of the incident, I was at home, too sick to go into school. Some childhood illness that came and went, I can't even remember the exact one. I was sitting in the window with a book. The travelling library had been around, and I was deep into the adventures of Robinson Crusoe when I heard the knock on the door.

I looked up as the door opened and Mrs Power from next door walked in. She held a carving knife in front of her, blade side down, with blood dripping from it onto my mother's polished linoleum floor. My mother screamed and dropped the cup she had been drying. It bounced once and rolled onto its side unbroken. I remember I was fascinated. Why didn't it break? I was so busy looking at it I didn't see my mother take the knife out of Mrs Power's hand and place it on the table.

"He wouldn't stop, Sarah," Mrs Power mumbled.

There was a cut under her right eye, and her lip was bleeding.

"Are you okay, Pauline? What happened?"

"He wouldn't stop," Mrs Power repeated, tears trailing down her haggard face and dripping from her chin.

My mother led Mrs Power to the chair by the fire and knelt in front of her.

"What do you mean? Tell me what happened."

I could hear the tremor in my mother's voice, sense her fear in asking the question, the fear of hearing the answer. Mrs Power started to wail. Loud, keening wails filled the house and spread outwards towards the fields. My mother ran out the front door and into Mrs Power's house with me on her tail. I didn't get very far, for I slipped on a mound of buttery potatoes lying on the floor just inside the door. My mother grabbed my arm, breaking my fall, swung me round and chased me back outside.

"Go, get your father, quickly now."

I did as I was bid without question. The one stolen glance I got of the cottage's interior before my mother swung me out the door was of blood-spattered walls.

Mr Power was a drinker. All that the other kids and I knew about him was that he was cross, he smelled terrible, and every night, the sound of his dinner plate or some other object hitting the wall of the mid-terraced house reverberated across the fields. It was all the women, and the men, spoke about for weeks afterwards. Overly fond of the *poitín*, they whispered at the funeral. They said Mrs Power had finally had enough of his beatings, worn down by his constant snide remarks and cutting ways.

That day she had picked up some work at the church hall and earned enough to buy butter and eggs to supplement her meagre larder. Delighted with herself, she had presented his dinner with an extra dollop of butter melting into the spuds. He demanded to know why she was wasting money on butter. When he picked up his plate and flung it at her, she picked up the knife and stopped his tirade. But she couldn't stop. Once she had stabbed him, she did it again and again, like some sort of vindictive robot. All the years of beatings and abuse poured out of her with every movement of the knife.

For all his fire and brimstone, Father Devlin spoke up for her with the police, then presided over the funeral and pontificated generously about the deceased. That he wasn't an evil man, just a man possessed by the demon drink. Father Devlin said that gave Mrs Power no right to take her husband's life, and she would go to hell for her mortal sin. I overheard my mother tell Mrs Enright that it was Mr Power who should go to hell.

Still, when I repeated that to my brother at the kitchen table the next day, my mother gave me a clip across the ear and made us all pray for my forgiveness. We prayed for Mrs Power's soul too. The police arrested her that day, but even then, her mind had gone. She went meekly like a lamb to slaughter. There never was a trial, for she took her own life, some sort of sharp object to her wrists while sitting in a cell in the local police station waiting to be charged.

My mother and the other local women went into the house and scrubbed the blood off the walls and the ceiling. Whenever Mrs Power's name was mentioned, my mother's eyes would tear up, and she would bless herself. We learned not to mention her name or what happened in that house ever again. Within weeks another family moved in next door. Their need for a home more important than the violent history contained within its walls.

I think a lesson was learned by everyone in our neighbourhood. In those days, it was legal for a man to beat his wife. Like a plaything or a shovel, she was his possession, something he owned and could do with what he liked. For a long time afterwards, we rarely heard raised voices in our neighbourhood. The women who would always have sported a black eye or bruised arms no longer hid themselves away for days on end, for they had no injuries to hide. Maybe the men of the parish thought twice before they lifted a hand to their wives. So, in the end, Mrs Power was a beacon for change in our neighbourhood.

Father Devlin still preached his fire and brimstone from the pulpit. One Sunday morning, he told the women of the parish that it was their duty to fulfil their marital obligations. Their husbands were the head of the household, and they should remember their vows to love, honour and obey. I was amazed that some of these strong women around me didn't take him to task over that. How could a man promise to love a woman, then beat her to within an inch of her life?

I often thought about it afterwards. Did Mrs Power have any choice? Did the constant beatings, the put-downs, the slavery, destroy her soul until she could no longer function as a normal human being? How much misery can the human mind cope with before it snaps?

That thought brought me back to the journals. Arthur's parents should never have been parents. An alcoholic and a prostitute. He had been dragged up. It's a wonder he survived childhood. He must have made it to adulthood and became a soldier and a good one at that if he attained the rank of warrant officer. I wondered what had saved him and lifted his journal to find out more.

Chapter 4

Arthur's Journal

Sandes home, Curragh Camp: 21st October 1923

Writing this journal is proving more difficult than I originally thought. Putting down on paper what happened to my ma and da filled me with a strange darkness that took me a while to shake off. Unable to think any more about my past, I put aside my journal for a while. I have since banished that darkness with hard work and physicality. I think I may have excised my parents ghosts enough to continue.

Leaving Manchester, Autumn 1880

I was barely a child the day I left the room I had known as home, with no idea of where I was going. I was small for my age, undernourished after years of infrequent meals. But I was wiry and street smart, a city brat. I knew how to forage in those streets and alleyways. The first few days were fine. I robbed apples from market carts and bread from windowsills. I probably ate better than I had in my short life up to that point.

With no clear objective in mind, I found myself outside Manchester Central station. The big coal engines swallowing shovels of coal and spewing black choking smoke out through their funnels as they left the station raised the noise level to deafening. There were signs outside on the concrete walls, but I could not read at that stage of my life. Schooling was not high on my parents' priorities.

There were drawings, though, of a train winding its way from the city to the sea. I stared at it transfixed, and for the first time since it had happened, I formulated a plan. I figured if I could get to a large port on the southern coast, I could work my way on a passage to anywhere in the empire.

For the first time, I felt something like enthusiasm. It did not last long though, once the realisation hit me that train fares cost money, and I had none. Once again, clouds of dejection surrounded me, and I made my way across the street, reluctantly pulling one foot after the other. I leaned up against the railings of a tall concrete building and stared back at the station.

There were beggars outside the gates, young boys like me, caps in hand and eyes downcast. I felt sympathy for them, telling myself that I had not yet succumbed to begging. Then laughed, for I had been stealing food for the last few days, yet here I was feeling sorry for beggars. From around the street corner, I watched the boy beside the gateway carefully for a while.

Every time a passer-by threw a coin into the offered cap, the boy gave a deferential smile, and a whispered thanks. As far as I could see, begging was pretty lucrative, for very few people walked by without contributing something. Figuring it was worth a try, I made my way over to the station wall, positioned myself further down the street from the boys, and took off my hat.

Maria McDonald

A shadow fell over my cap, and I looked up expectedly, but it was not a well-dressed gentleman or a lady with a fur-trimmed purse who cast that shadow. I gulped as I stared into the rheumy eyes of the thinnest man I had ever seen. He was dressed in rags, and as his body odour hit my nostrils, I felt my stomach curdle.

"What do you think you're doing, me boy?"

His words were accompanied by foul spittle that wet my cheeks and smelled of stale tobacco and whiskey. My stomach heaved, even though it had been empty since the day before.

"Think you can muscle in on my lads, do ye?"

I shook my head vigorously, unable to speak.

"What's up, cat got your tongue?" and he cackled. The hairs rose on the back of my neck as he pushed me on the shoulder with his bony forefinger. He took my chin, pushed my face upwards, then studied my features, concentration etching his eyebrows, which had more hair than his head.

"Hmm, you'll do, I suppose. You can stay for today...once you pay your Freddie tax."

"But..."

"No money? You can pay from your takings, boy."

He pushed my chin away as if I were a piece of rubbish that disgusted him and walked off. I rubbed my chin where it still pinched from his touch and looked around me. The boy on the other side of the gate was watching, a look of weary resignation on his face. I nodded, and he nodded back, and there we stood for the rest of the day, like two sentinels guarding the gateway into the train station.

No one spoke to us; no one even looked at us. Every so often, the satisfying clink of a coin hitting the base of my cap on the ground made my heart lighten a little. By the time dusk surrounded us, quite a few pennies were waiting to be counted.

As I bent down to pick up my cap, Freddie appeared in front of me and snatched it from my hands. He poured the contents into a dirty cloth holdall and cackled as he flipped two pennies in my direction before walking away.

"Same time tomorrow, boy."

Twin waves of dejection and disbelief washed over me as I watched his retreating back.

"Freddie will always leave you enough so you can eat."

I jumped out of my reverie and turned to face my begging buddy. He was about the same age as me, only broader, sharp blue eyes wise beyond their years set in an open face.

"Who...what?"

"Freddie." He pointed at his retreating back. "The trick is to slip some extra coins into your boots but separate, so they don't clink. I got caught once, and he beat me stupid."

"Who is he?"

"Freddie runs all the boys around here. He's okay. We just pay him his share, and he leaves us alone. Have you got somewhere to stay?"

"No...I don't know anyone around here."

"Come with me. A group of us stay in an abandoned warehouse. It's not much, but it's a roof over our heads. Come on, I'll introduce you...what's your name?"

"Arthur, my name's Arthur."

"Isaac. Pleased to meet you. Come on."

Isaac shook my hand and led me away from the station. We stopped at a market, got some food, and ate as we walked in the gathering darkness. I followed Isaac down a narrow laneway between two buildings so tall that they appeared to reach into the clouds. He pushed open a battered door and ushered me inside.

Through the darkness, I could see a dim light further down a hallway and could hear the mumble of conversation interspersed with the odd peal of laughter. Isaac led the way, and we rounded a corner to a room full of boys of all sizes. An oil lamp sat on a rickety table in the centre, casting a dull glow that barely illuminated the room. Against the walls were makeshift beds, fashioned out of crates and threadbare blankets. Around the room, groups of boys sat eating and talking.

"Evening, everyone, this is Arthur," Isaac said to no one in particular.

There was a general murmur of hellos, and then they turned back to what they were doing. It was as if a new boy was introduced every evening, and this evening was no different.

"Here, you can share with me, if you want." Isaac moved towards the far corner to a pile of old clothing sitting on sheets of wood. "You can't have my bed, but I can spare an old overcoat that'll keep you warm tonight at least."

I accepted Isaac's offer with gratitude. It was the best I'd had since I had left home. He handed me an old overcoat, and I settled myself on the floor beside his makeshift bed. Fear kept me watchful, fidgety, but I trusted Isaac and reasoned that the other boys had no interest in me. I had nothing worth stealing and judging by the snatches of conversation I overheard, we were all in the same boat. We were all begging by day to pay Freddie tax and buy some scraps of food.

Pulling the overcoat tighter around me, I snuggled into it as much as I could, rocking myself as much for comfort as for heat. Looking back on it now, I realise I was still in shock, still reeling over the violence I had witnessed. Every night I had curled up in a doorway or in a disused building, exhausted from my day's activity but terrified to fall asleep. Fear of my dreams where my mother's blood-soaked body screamed at me to help her. Exhaustion eventually took over, rendering my sleep that night, dreamless.

When I woke, I didn't know where I was, and it took a minute to get my bearing in the darkness. All around me were the nocturnal sounds of dozens of boys sleeping, some peacefully, some fitfully. I nestled back into the overcoat, fell asleep again, and dreamt of trying to climb aboard a large boat and being held back by bony fingers clad in rags.

The next day Isaac and I made our way back to the station. I was prepared that day with hiding places around my person, determined that "Freddie" wasn't about to get away with my takings again. The pickings were good, and I was happy with my stash by the end of the day. My cap was nearly full, but I had at least six halfpennies and a couple of pennies secreted around me. As the dusk fell and the last train blew its whistle, I lifted my cap from the ground and turned to call Isaac. The street was empty, the gates to the train station locked, and Isaac was nowhere to be seen.

Suddenly I was upended. My scream stuck in my throat as I felt a thump on my back and a hand on my ankle. I swung, practically upside down, as Freddie shook me from side to side like a rag doll. My coins dislodged from their hiding places and fell to the pavement, zinging their presence as my head bounced perilously close to the cobblestones. My head and shoulders smacked off the ground as he dropped me in a heap, laughing maniacally.

"Thought you would cheat me, eh?"

Instinct kicked in or maybe habit after years of being beaten by my father. I curled up in a ball to protect myself as he beat me about the head and shoulders with his ebony walking stick. The rain of blows stopped as he ran out of breath. He stood over me, wheezing and holding his chest. I crept onto my hands and knees, afraid to make any sudden movements for fear of setting him off again. His face was contorted, and as our eyes met, he fired another blow aimed at my head but missed. The act of moving propelled him forward, and he stumbled. I saw my opportunity and pushed him as I scrambled to my feet then fled, but not before grabbing my cap and its precious cargo.

With no clear idea of where I was going, I ran as fast as my legs could carry me. I kept running, then slowed to a jog, staying in the shadows as much as I could. The outlying trees of a dense thicket appeared in front of me. I ploughed straight ahead into its midst until I found myself facing an ancient oak tree that conjured up my old safe place in the woods back home. I stopped and listened, but the only sound I could hear was my own rasping breath pounding in my ears and the hoot of an owl in the distance. Exhausted, I bedded myself down with my cap as my pillow and slept fitfully until dawn.

I woke with a start, memories of my dash to freedom flooding back to me. My cap was curled up under me, and I checked its contents. I still had quite a haul. Enough to pay for the train fare to get me as far away from where I was as possible. I could not go back to Manchester Central station, but there were other stations, so I set off walking, praying I was going in the right direction. I reckoned I would make my way to the sea and decide what I would do from there.

It was simple enough to get a ticket in third class. Before long, I found myself winging my way through the English countryside, cheek by jowl with men and boys like myself looking for work. But it did not get me as far as the coast. I ended up in the rural countryside with no clue what to do next.

Sandes home, Curragh Camp: 21st October 1923

Looking back on it now, I have no idea how I managed to survive those days. I was scared, penniless, and so totally alone. Fear put wings on my feet the day I ran from that ruffian Freddie. I have never experienced fear like it since. Even during the war years. At least then I had the support of my comrades. I had Henry.

Chapter 5

Brian

Monday 21st September 2020

I closed Arthur's journal and lowered the books to the first step of the ladder before descending with great caution down to the landing. Pausing to gather up the scattered pages I had dropped earlier, I tucked them back inside the green journal and went downstairs and into the kitchen.

The kettle was still on the countertop along with the toaster. Just two of the items which were going to charity the day we move. The new appliances were already purchased and waiting for us in the new house. It would be the first home we owned, not rented from the army, and Jean wanted the latest and the best appliances in her dream kitchen. I was looking forward to it myself. The new house, that is, retiring from the army, not so much.

It was a warm evening, the remnants of a sunny day, and our last week living in army married quarters. We had almost finished the packing and had hired a van for the move, although there wasn't much left to bring. We were donating our furniture; it was old and well used at this stage and wouldn't suit the new house. The last six years had been a hard slog. Years of dreaming and saving, weekends and holidays spent turning the site my parents had left us into our dream retirement home. Most of our possessions were packed into boxes and ready to go. The pangs of apprehension at the thought of the move were playing havoc with my stomach.

I wandered into the front room as I waited on the kettle to boil. The view from that window was something I would miss when we moved to Waterford. Countless soldiers and their families had lived in this house, and I felt the weight of the generations before me and wondered if they had stood in the same place and admired the same view. It wouldn't have changed that much.

As far as I knew, the transport yard wouldn't have been there, and neither would the housing estate at the edge of the Curragh Camp. They would have had uninterrupted views across the plains as far as Maddenstown. Mind you, the view is impressive even today. It was something that we had always taken for granted since the day we had moved into Warrant Officers married quarters twenty years ago.

I was hit by a wave of nostalgia and sighed. We had some good memories in this house. "If only walls could talk," I said out loud as I looked around me. The day we had moved in, the kids had raced upstairs to see their bedrooms. I had spent the week before the move painting the rooms and getting the house ready.

We painted the walls in the girls' room a delicate pink, Jenny's bed made up in Bratz purple and Sinéad's with pale Barbie. We kitted out Conor's room in Man United colours, although Jean drew the line at painting the walls red, relying instead on colourful posters. Jean and I had stood in the hall, listening to their enthusiastic shrieks of delight. This house was much bigger than the one we had at the other end of the Curragh Camp. It was a new chapter in our lives, and I could still remember that feeling of optimism, of being on the brink of something new and exciting.

Over the years, the design and colours had evolved as the children grew, and interior design fashions changed. Still, the familiar homely feeling was the one constant. We had celebrated birthdays, Christmas, positive exam results and champagne-filled New Year's Eve parties with friends and family.

The red-brick exterior exuded a warm glow, even on the coldest of days, which felt like a welcome home. For the first time, I acknowledged that I would miss that, that feeling of safety and security that engulfed me every time I closed the front door. It was the end of an era, but life goes on. We learned that hard lesson when our firstborn, John, died. When one door closes, another one opens.

My military career had come to an end which meant my time in the camp was over. Our home was rented from the Defence Forces, and we had to move on. We were prepared, more so than most, with our new home furnished and ready for us. Our final chapter waiting to be written, and I felt the tug of optimism for the future, despite the past six months.

The advent of Coronavirus had changed the way we live. The lockdown had been hard on Jean. No non-essential travel meant we didn't get to see the kids for months at a time. Now that was the hardest to bear. While she didn't miss the factory, she missed her workmates, missed her routine. She was stuck in the house, only able to go out to shop for food. At least I was still at work, going into the barracks every day and helping the community.

In fairness, we thought the pandemic was going to be much worse. The Defence Forces were prepared to step in to fulfil civilian roles where they were needed. The lockdown meant we "flattened the curve", as they say, and the Defence Forces were stood down albeit temporarily until the next wave. We were called on to run the test centres and then the vaccines centres when they opened. I knew Jean was worried about the future.

When we went into the shops, we wore masks, carried hand sanitiser everywhere, and kept our distance from everyone, still do. Jean says that's what she missed most, human contact. I have to agree with her on that one, but at least we could hug each other.

I made my way to the kitchen. Instant coffee would have to do. The coffee maker was packed away. The kettle clicked off the boil, so I lifted my favourite mug out of the cupboard, the one the lads got me for Father's Day, made a paste with two spoons of coffee and a drop of milk, added the water, and sat at the table with the journals in front of me, anxious to find out more about Arthur.

Chapter 6

Arthur's Journal

Sandes home, Curragh Camp: 7th November 1923

Why is it so hard to put my past onto paper? Writing about those days after my da killed my ma compares to pulling teeth, in my mind. It took me a few weeks to get over that. Then to replay the fear that choked me when I lived on the streets. Well, that was nigh on impossible. Mrs Magill from the Sandes Soldiers' Home said it would be good for me. It hasn't. It has dragged up memories long buried. They were buried for good reason. I told her as much, said I had a mind not to write anymore. She handed me my journal from the locked drawer she stores it in and told me to keep going. It would get easier. I hope she's right.

England, 1880

My problem was I knew how to forage in the city streets, not in the country lanes and hedgerows I ended up in a few days later. I had headed south, hoping to pick up work along the road and put as much distance between myself and my family and the fearsome Mr Freddie as possible.

At night I slept in barns buried in hay and sneaked out at dawn, sometimes chased by a farmer or his helpers. It was an adventure for me, and I was enjoying it. That was before the rain started. I welcomed it at first, turning my face to the sky and opening my mouth to relish the soothing drops that quenched my thirst and freshened my skin. By the third day, all pleasure had dissipated.

It was relentless – a steady deluge from a moody sky that enveloped me. In the distance, clouds swallowed the grey stone of the town buildings that started to appear on the horizon. The rain had penetrated my coat and inner clothes; my skin was damp and clammy. Exhaustion swept over me. My bones were chilled, teeth chattering, and the nearest town was too far away. I could just about make out a series of small wooden buildings ahead of me. There was a dim light which drew me to it, like a bee to honey. As I drew closer, I realised it was a lantern, held aloft by an elderly man assisting a woman into a cart. They took off, oblivious to me watching them from a discreet distance.

When they were out of sight, I crept to the shed door and was surprised when it opened on the first turn of the circular brass handle. I fell inside, immediately warmed by the heat coming from a potbellied stove in the corner – a dull red glow from the dying embers cast an eerie light over the interior of the shed. A massive stack of logs rose as far as the ceiling in the corner of the rectangular room. I cautiously opened the stove door and carefully placed one of the smaller ones on top of the embers. I tried to blow some air in to help it ignite, but my breath turned into a wheezing cough that brought me to my knees. I carefully closed the door on the stove and knelt in front of it.

A flicker of orange licked the log, and I gave a sigh of relief. There was a rocking chair on either side of the stove, both covered with colourful crochet blankets. I peeled off my soaked clothing and wrapped myself in a blanket before draping my sodden coat on the back of the chair. I hung the rest of my sopping clothing over various gardening implements. My jumper hung on the arm of a shovel, while my underpants and vest hung from a shelf over the stove held in place by two heavy candlesticks.

The heat made me sleepy, and the rocking chair looked inviting. I sat and stared into the flames as if hypnotised. My hands outstretched until I had to withdraw them after their pasty whiteness turned a mottled red, and pains shot up and down my fingers. I curled back into the chair and buried myself in the blankets.

I tried to stay awake, promising myself I would dry off my clothes and leave by first light, but I was bone-weary, and my lids grew heavy. I thought I was dreaming at first. My world was hazy, blurred around the edges with an angel of light moving around, humming gently. Tongues of red in the old potbelly stove sent light to the far corners, and the crackle of wood burning seeped into my dreamlike state. The sharp, unexpected whistle of the kettle coming to the boil sent me shooting upright, my nerve ends tingling.

"Hush, boy, hush. It's just the kettle for the tea."

The sing-song voice emanated from a large grey-haired man with soft eyes, the colour of a rain-filled sky. He moved in slow, easy slides across the floor to lift the singing kettle from the top of the stove. He poured the boiling water into a teapot stained from years of regular use.

I found my voice. "Sorry, sir. I'll be out of your way."

"No rush, lad, give the tea some time to draw."

His voice was surprisingly gentle, given his size, but it was his eyes that spoke volumes. I found myself sitting down again without argument and I huddled back into the blanket, relishing the heat and the comfort. He poured hot black tea into two tin cups, stirred two spoons of sugar into both and a dash of milk he had brought in a pewter flask.

He passed me the cup handle first, and I accepted it gratefully. I sipped the hot sweet tea and watched as he cut two thick slices of bread and slathered them with butter. I was drooling when he handed a piece to me, my stomach rumbling in anticipation. I bit into it without hesitation. He sat on the chair opposite and ate his bread without another word. I followed his lead and ate and drank, still curled up in the blanket, but with one eye keeping a constant watch on him.

"Eamon's my name. What's yours?"

"Ar...Arthur."

He nodded and took another sip from his mug.

"You're far from home. What brings you around here?"

My parents were Irish, and there were many Irish around our area when I was growing up. I liked the accent – the gentle sing-song of it. I had also heard it turn to fire when riled or full of alcohol or both. I sat up a little straighter and looked around me. My clothes were still draped on the various gardening tools around the shed. I was naked under the blanket and vulnerable. My eyes met his, but I could see no threat there, only compassion and maybe a sadness of sorts.

"I'm on my way to the coast."

My voice sounded small and childish to me. I cleared my throat, held my head higher and forced a deeper tone to my voice. "I'm hoping to pick up some work."

"Are you now? And what type of work would you be looking for, lad?"

"Anything, anything at all."

He stood, and I retreated into the blanket, my heart beating in my throat. He lifted my clothes from where they hung, one by one, shook them and folded them, then handed them to me with a smile.

"Get dressed now, lad. I have tasks outside. Come out to me when you're ready."

I dressed quickly, determined to make my escape as soon as I could. I peered out the window to see neat rows of earth, ready for planting, and Eamon digging methodically, his head bent, intent on what he was doing. I stepped outside.

"I can do that if you pay me."

Eamon stopped what he was doing and leaned on the handle of the shovel.

"Pay you, you say." He smiled. "No money for that, lad. No, hard work keeps this allotment going, and this allotment keeps me and my Mary fed."

He went back to his digging, and I watched, fascinated by his slow, steady movements.

"I owe you for breakfast. Let me work it off."

Eamon stopped again and gave me that slow smile. "Why, thank you, lad."

He wiped his forehead with a grubby handkerchief and handed me over the shovel. An old barrel to one side had been fashioned into a seat, and he made his way to it, lowering himself onto it with an "oomph" and a sigh.

I dug with gusto, powered by the bread and the hot sweet tea. Eamon talked as I laboured, and before long, the sun was high in the sky, and I realised it must be noon at least. Eamon watched as a carriage approached, and the lady from last night stepped down and into the allotment. She carried a wicker basket with a checked cloth on top and a warm smile to equal Eamon's.

"What have we here?" she asked. "Have you found some help, Eamon?"

Eamon introduced me to his Mary, who immediately offered me food. We followed her into the shed, where she set bread and cheese on the table and proceeded to make tea. I was struck by how openly affectionate they were with each other. I had never seen that before. Well, not in such close proximity.

My parents hated each other. When they were in the same room, they fought or ignored each other, both in equal measure. I knew the other residents in the house did not fight in the same way my parents did. Most of them seemed to have some sort of relationship, but I had never seen a man treat a woman with such tenderness as Eamon treated Mary. I had never seen a woman look at a man with such love, and it was mesmerising.

I ate quietly, watching them as they chatted, answering them as they gently asked me questions about who I was and where I came from. As I blurted out my story, I saw the horror on their faces. For the first time, I wondered how my life would have turned out if my father had not drunk all his earnings or my mother had not sold herself to earn money to feed us. I could not suppress the sigh that escaped me, and both pairs of eyes turned towards me – both grey, both compassionate, both with a sadness that seeped through the kindness.

"I need some help here on the allotment, lad," Eamon said, after a nod from Mary. "I can't pay mind, but I can give you bed and board if you are interested."

I accepted gratefully. Let's face it, I didn't have any other options. My only possessions were the clothes on my back. There was nothing to entice me to return to Manchester. Eamon and Mary showered me with affection. Eamon taught me how to grow vegetables, get the soil ready, dig in the manure, aerate the soil, plant the seeds, tend the fledgling plants and then the harvest, the abundance in the autumn followed by the planting of the winter vegetables.

Eamon found work on the allotment all year round, and I loved every minute of it. When the sun went down in the evenings, Mary taught me how to read and write and left me books to while away my nights.

They made me up a bed in the corner of the shed, and Mary fashioned a curtain around it. She took my meagre belongings and washed and mended them, and even replaced them at times. I fell into bed each night dog-tired but with a full belly and heat in my bones.

Sandes home, Curragh Camp: 7th November 1923

Even writing about Eamon and Mary gives me a warm feeling. That couple had more compassion in their calloused little fingers than any other person I have met since. They took me in and shared what little they had, without hesitation. For the first time in my life, I received kindness which meant more to me than the food and shelter they provided in exchange for helping Eamon on the allotment.

Chapter 7

Arthur's Journal

Sandes home, Curragh Camp: 21st November 1923

It is easier to write about my time with Eamon and Mary. I stayed for six years. They were the happiest years of my young life. Even now, more than thirty-eight years later, I can hear Eamon's voice as he recounted his stories about Ireland. I can still smell the fresh soda bread Mary brought every day, still warm from the oven. It is such a pity those days had to end but end they did.

England, 1882

It was a while before I learned what had caused the sadness in Mary's eyes. It was my second spring with them, and Eamon and I dug out farrows for the spuds. I had never heard about a famine in Ireland. It was before my time, so how could I have known about it? I listened as he talked about his life in Ireland and how he and Mary had to leave. Times had been hard in Manchester. Poverty stalked the streets, and I knew, better than most, how hard it was to get enough to eat. But I had never heard anything like the story Eamon told me about what he called the great hunger in his native Ireland.

"My son, our boy, well sure he was only a little thing. When the crop failed, I could not pay the rent, you see. I sold everything I could, I re-planted, and I prayed, and I worked hard, but I could not feed Mary, could not feed my son. He was born too small, too early, and then Mary's milk dried up. She was starving herself. How could her body produce milk to feed our baby?

"I got us our passage out of there, and we sailed to England. I found work straight away, and we found a place to live, but it was too late for him, you see. He was too sickly. He died, and Mary nearly died with him. She lost her hope, her joy; she never got over it."

I did not know what to say to Eamon. The grief was written in every line on his weather-beaten face and the grey of his eyes. I was barely past childhood myself, and I had no words to express how sorry I was.

I hugged him. A short, tight hug, but he did not let me go. He put his arms around me, and his bear hug enveloped me. I had never experienced a hug from another human being before that day. I froze. I just stood there as this bear of a man wrapped his grief around me and melted me from the outside in. He stood back, his hands on my upper arms, and looked into my eyes.

"Thanks for listening, lad. It is good to talk. God never blessed us again with another child. Me and Mary, all we have is each other, and I thank God for her love every day."

We talked every day after that. He spoke about the "old country" with an affection that surprised me, considering what they had been through. He talked about his adopted home and the friends they had made, but he spoke about the earth most of all.

He spoke about the pleasure of growing your own food, the joy of watching a tiny seed grow from the size of the top of a pin to a plant you can fill your belly with. I often thought he talked about food, thought about food, all the time. But then his famine stories would come up, and I realised how much this allotment meant to him. It was important to him to grow food, produce food, and feed his family, including me.

Working the allotment built up muscles in my growing frame. The practice of digging and weeding and eating good food made me strong. I would never be a tall man but I grew muscular and sinewy, and by the time I turned eighteen, I was a force to be reckoned with.

And then Eamon died. I was heartbroken, shocked, even though I had watched his decline. That autumn, he was slower, weaker, and I had taken up the slack. I had helped him up the steps into the shed and brewed tea, strong and sweet, the way he liked it. The winter was harsh, and he succumbed to influenza. Mary followed him only weeks later. It was as if they were two parts of one person, and one could not survive without the other.

I went to their funerals and paid my respects. And then I despaired. I locked myself away in my shed, and I drank the *poitín* Eamon kept hidden in the back of the press under the sink. He had used it as a rub for bruised knees and pulled shoulders, and occasionally I had seen him down a thimbleful, never any more than that. I downed a lot more than a thimbleful.

That was when I broke my promise to myself never to drink alcohol. I think, in my own twisted way, I reasoned with myself that *poitín* was medicinal, but in my heart of hearts, I knew my father would have used the same excuse.

I woke, unable to lift my head from my bed and an army of blacksmiths beating anvils directly in my brain. My throat was closed, my breath rancid, and I thought I was going to die. I stuck my head under the tap and drank greedily for five minutes, then ran to the door to throw up over the last vegetable bed that Eamon had ever dug.

The men from the council arrived shortly after that day, and I had to move on. Eamon no longer held the right to the allotment, and the authorities reallocated it. Another man took possession of his shed and his precious tools. I left with only my clothes in a bag and the St Christopher medal Mary had given me the previous Christmas. She told me how she had prayed to him as they travelled over the Irish Sea, how she believed that it was he who had kept them safe from harm when others around had fallen foul of the black death. I put the medal around my neck, tucked it inside my shirt and took one final look around the place in which I had been so happy.

Sandes home, Curragh Camp: 21st November 1923

Mrs Magill was right. In writing about those years with Eamon, I realised that they were among the best years of my life. Eamon planted in me an idea of the type of man I could be if I set my mind on it. He showed me how the love of a good woman can save a man, can keep him on the straight and narrow. Why didn't I spend more time copying Eamon's example rather than my drunkard of a father?

Chapter 8

Brian

Monday 21st September 2020

I was so engrossed in Arthur's journal I didn't hear the front door open that evening.

"Brian, did you get the attic finished?"

"Jean, Jesus, I didn't hear you come in. How was work?"

I got up to put the kettle on while Jean hung up her coat.

"I'm glad it's over, let's put it that way. I can't wait for next week. Imagine, not having to get up and go to that place every day. Roll on retirement."

Her eyes crinkled with a smile as I drew her close in a hug.

"Yeah, it'll be great. Tea?"

"Please. What have you been up to?" She gestured at the journals.

"I found them. Locked in that cabinet in the attic. They make for some interesting reading," I said, picking up Arthur's journal. "This guy was a Connaught Ranger and...he was in the Irish National Army. He lived in this house, as far as I can tell. I'm only a few pages in but he had such a hard life, and I haven't even got to the part where he joins the army."

"Well, enjoy. I'm going to bring my tea to bed with me. That shift really wrecked me. Good night, love. Don't sit up too late."

I kissed my Jean goodnight and lifted Arthur's journal, curious to find out what Arthur did next.

Chapter 9

Arthur's Journal

Sandes home, Curragh Camp: 21st December 1923

My wife resents the time I spend in the Sandes Soldiers' Home. She has never understood how important my attendance there is to me. It was the mother in the Sandes home in India who first saved me from the evils of alcohol. I may have slipped on several occasions, but the Sandes home always rescued me. There is no judgement here. Only respect, strong tea and an understanding of a soldier's life.

Farm Labourer to Soldier

Like a lost soul, I moved from place to place, working odd jobs for farmers along the way. Eamon had passed on a lot of his knowledge, and I enjoyed working the soil. But it was hard, dirty work for small pay and no privileges. Most of the farmers treated their dogs better than they treated us casual labourers.

Some of the accommodation they gave us as part of our pay was not fit for human habitation. Money was tight in farming, even I knew that. On every farm, the men I worked with, and the men I worked for, complained about cheap American grain destroying our livelihood. But I did not think that gave the farmers the right to treat us the way they did.

I did not stay long in any one place, just moved from farm to farm, following the crops. I slaved by day and drank by night. Week ran into week and month into month, and by winter, I found myself near a small town, the name of which I cannot remember, but it was there my life changed.

I stopped outside a small shop. In the window, battling for attention amidst the bags of tea and adverts for cigarettes, was a recruitment poster for the Connaught Rangers. Although I did not know why, for I knew nothing of military life, it caught my eye, and I was intrigued. It promised a wage and an adventure, and I gave it serious consideration. Something in that poster reminded me of Eamon and his ruminations about the family he had left behind in Roscommon. Maybe because the Connaught Rangers was an Irish regiment, or perhaps he had mentioned them. What did I know? It just appealed to me.

On that day, I had no work lined up and no plan of where to go or what to do, nothing to leave behind, no strings of any type to hold me. I knew no one in that area other than the acquaintances I had made along the way. Most of them were farm labourers who would slit my throat for a chance of work and a roof over their heads. It did not take me long to make my decision, and within the hour, I was on my way to Portsmouth.

Signing up was easy. The recruitment office did not ask too many questions. Before I knew it, my hair was cut, my uniform issued, and training started. Most of the other recruits were young men the same as me; single, hungry, and bootless. For the first time since Eamon and Mary died, I ate three meals a day. It was like I had finally come home, and I loved every second.

That first year of training, I can safely say, was the best year of my life. My boots were bulled to a shine you could shave in. My uniform was immaculate. I fulfilled every duty, learned how to strip my rifle, and reassemble it, how to march, how to be a man. The peppery smell of boot polish brings me right back to that billet and a sense of peace.

It was there I first came across Henry. Like me, he was a street urchin. We took to military discipline as if we had been born to it. Every cross-country run, we pushed each other to the limit, always finishing ahead of the rest of the platoon. On the ranges, we were the best shots, in the gym the strongest, on the track the fastest. Our rivalry pushed me to be the best recruit it was possible to be.

By the time we shipped to Aldershot, I had gained my first promotion. Henry and I were selected for the course, and we entered the barracks in Aldershot as corporals. I had my own platoon of privates to look after, taking orders from my immediate superior, Sergeant Wilson.

When we got word that we were shipping to Malta, I was so excited. In the back of my mind, I had always thought that we would be shipped to Ireland at some stage. The Connaught Rangers' main depot was in the west of Ireland, and I was looking forward to seeing the country Eamon had told me so much about. My drunkard of a father was born in Connaught somewhere, I am not sure of the exact location, but I had no desire to track down any of his relatives. Eamon's family would have been a different story, but it was not to be.

Malta was unknown to most of us. We were not prepared for this strange and exotic place, but we also knew it was an easy posting. There was no conflict, no significant flashpoints. Sergeant Wilson was delighted. Along with most of the older men, he had served in South Africa seven years earlier. They had some fearsome stories to tell of bloodthirsty battles against the Zulus. He reckoned they deserved an easy posting after that. Maybe he was right; what do I know?

Early on the morning of 13th July 1889, we embarked on our ship in Devonport and sailed into Malta just short of ten days later. We were quartered at Verdala Barracks, and I had never seen anything like it. Malta was a shock to the senses. The only comparison to Portsmouth was the proximity of the sea. In Portsmouth, even on the warmest of summer days, there was a breeze that refreshed and cooled the air around you. In Malta, the heat melted us, and any breeze from the sea brought warm sandy air.

Boredom drove us to distraction. There were only so many exercises and drills a unit can do. Verdala Barracks was well equipped, with a dry and a wet canteen. Most of us preferred the wet canteen, and every night, we gathered, knocking back pints of beer and telling stories of battles and war honours. There is a camaraderie amongst soldiers that civilians could never understand, even amongst those who have not yet served in a hostile environment. We hung on every word Sergeant Wilson, and his comrades, uttered, and we prayed for the day when we could earn our battle stripes, earn our story to tell.

As young men raised in the British Isles, the majority from the west of Ireland, the sun – and its dangers – was a novelty. No one in charge thought to warn us. We spent long hours in the Maltese sun, loving the warmth of it on our bodies. When the sun dipped below the horizon we poured into the wet canteen and quenched our thirst with porter. Within the first month, half of my platoon had been treated in the military hospital suffering from either sunstroke or alcohol poisoning.

The medical officer issued a warning notice, and Sergeant Wilson read it out at the parade. I listened to the warning about the sun but ignored the warning about alcohol. The attraction of the wet canteen was too much for me. When the canteen opened at eight o'clock in the evening, I was waiting outside the door, my mouth watering at the thought of the familiar nectar hitting the back of my throat. By nine, I had downed a half dozen and was ready to hit my bunk. Sometimes I did not retire; sometimes I stayed on until closing time. On those nights, I did not remember how or what time I got back to my bunk, and occasionally I woke in strange places.

On such a morning, I woke in an unfamiliar bed, semi-naked, with a woman asleep beside me. I had no idea who she was or how I had ended up there. Stale alcohol poisoned my breath and stuck my tongue to the roof of my mouth. Looking around me, I spotted my trousers lying on the floor and my boots near the door. I slipped out from under the covers, pulled on my trousers and lifted my boots. The door was firmly closed, but there was an open window on my left. A glance out told me it led to a back alley, and I hopped through and crept back to the barracks.

The sun was rising as I slipped into my bunk, and I prayed that no one had noted my absence. Henry had noticed. I could sense him, even as I pulled the covers over me. I broke out in a cold sweat, fear clutching my insides as I racked my brain trying to remember how or when I had left the camp.

The next night at eight o'clock I gave the wet canteen a miss. My mouth was watering for a pint. I made several attempts to get off my bunk. Even got as far as the door. But then I had a flashback to the fear I felt when I woke up in that strange bed. I knew Henry was already outside the door of the wet canteen, waiting for it to open, gagging for a pint, but I made the excuse of a dicky tummy. I stayed clear of the wet canteen for months after that.

A couple of mornings with no hangover helped me see what I had been missing. And missing was the right word. Parts of my life were missing, blank holes in my memory that I could not fill no matter how hard I tried. I took up running. It was solitary, but I found some peace in my soul as I ran along the cliff tops overlooking the sea. For the first time since I left the allotment where I had led such a happy life with Eamon and Mary, I felt something akin to contentment.

For nearly five years, I stayed sober while my unit moved from island to island in Malta and Cyprus. Fort Pembroke was my favourite camp; the running tracks had some of the most amazing scenery, although Fort Chambray in Gozo was a serious contender. I felt as close to nature as it is possible to get while still training and drilling as a professional soldier. To my mind, my life was almost perfect. Although at times, when I passed the married quarters and saw the wives of other NCOs, something tugged around the corner of my consciousness. I felt a fleeting yearning for human contact, a need for a softer feminine touch, rather than my self-inflicted lonely existence.

Surrounded by men, I was more alone than I had ever been. Which was stupid when I thought about it. At that point, I had always been on my own. My parents were worse than useless, leaving me to fend for myself from when I was a toddler. Eamon and Mary had given me shelter and instilled in me some human decency. But I knew that it was their dead son they saw in me, not me, not Arthur Torrington. The army was the closest I had to family, and I revelled in it. The routine gave me structure, the ordered life, the precision all appealed to my character. I loved the respect my rank gave me. So why was I feeling lonely?

In February 1895, our new postings arrived, and we set sail for Egypt. It was British controlled at that time, although it felt like the whole world was British controlled. They did say that the sun never set on the British Empire, and as a soldier of the realm, I certainly believed that. Egypt was different and yet the same. One British barracks on foreign soil is much the same as another; the only difference is the climate, and Egypt was hot.

Once again, the wet canteen, and Henry, beckoned. The camaraderie on those nights soothed my soul, and I began to feel less alone, less solitary, and more at home with my comrades in arms. Every evening, after my daily chores were completed and my men were dismissed, I joined Henry in the canteen and drank my fill. Except, very quickly, I started drinking more than my fill, and once again, I woke in my bunk each morning with no memory of how I got there.

Henry was usually able to fill in the gaps, scolding me for drinking to excess and falling asleep at the bar, at least on the nights he could remember. I would promise to curb my drinking, and he would promise to restrain his. Then a few days later, we would find ourselves propping up the bar in the wet canteen before venturing further afield in search of female company.

The sultry attraction of these Egyptian goddesses was just too much for any single man to bear, and we all had our favourites. Henry and I fell for one girl in particular. Named Nour, she did not speak English, but she had eyes you could drown in. Until one night, she disappeared. It was a weekend night, and we had been off duty, both drinking heavily and both in need of Nour's charms. We woke the next morning, battered and bruised after being set upon by locals, rescued by a foot patrol and locked up in the guardroom until we slept it off. Feeling sheepish and highly foolish, I swore to never again imbibe alcohol. This time Henry joined me as we promised our CO that we would never overindulge again. Our promises lasted until nightfall and the inevitable whisper of the hair of the dog. It was just as well we were shipping to India.

Sandes home, Curragh Camp: 21st December 1923

My memories of those days are sparse. Maybe it's just as well. Looking back, I can lay the blame on my youth and inexperience but at the end of the day, I had no excuse. I was a drunkard and a fool. Me and Henry were just starting out on life then. Soldiering together, partying together. All we cared about was having hard booze and easy women. We had a lot of growing up to do.

Chapter 10

Brian

Monday 21st September 2020

Memories of my first trip to Lebanon made me drop Arthur's journal and lapse into thought. Arthur's descriptions of Cyprus, Malta and Egypt twigged my memory, and I was transported back to the eighties. I was only twenty-one on my first trip, a young corporal, totally immersed in military life. There were lots of firsts about that trip. It had been my first time on an aeroplane. Imagine that. My children had flown before they were twelve on short hops to Spain for summer holidays.

Ireland in the eighties was a different country from the one we inhabit now. That trip to Lebanon had been my first time out of Ireland. That's if you didn't count the ferry to the Isle of Man. It was my first taste of what I thought was exotic food at the time as well. I had been reared on bacon and cabbage, served with home-grown spuds dripping in butter, or a good fry-up on a Saturday morning and my mother's Sunday roast with mash and mushy peas. Nothing like that in Lebanon, even though they brought the army cooks with them. I was amazed at the size of the tomatoes. Huge juicy fruits that you could eat like an apple. Couscous, spices, meats I had never heard of, let alone tasted.

The first gun battle was different than I had imagined it would be when we had trained for it in the Glen of Imaal. The crack of a shot as it whistled past your ear is a sound like no other and could induce fear in the bravest of souls. The dance of tracers in the night sky as the Israelis bombarded South Lebanon was a sight that was seared into my memory. But it was the smell that stayed with me. Even now, nearly forty years later, that polished metallic smell mixed with the unmistakable coppery scent of fresh blood haunts my dreams. I had never seen anyone die before. Not like that.

Dead people, yes, my grandmother in her coffin, hands crossed around her rosary beads, her silvery coiffed hair framed in white satin. My cousin in a black suit, eyes closed, waxy skin in a polished mahogany coffin. Those dead people I had seen before that Lebanon trip. Old people, sick people who had died in their beds, but this was different. To see a young man's life snuffed out in front of my eyes, well, that was something else. That was something I had never witnessed before. The memory of it still shook something inside me.

Luke was in the same unit, trained in the same platoon. We met the day we joined the army and were shoulder to shoulder when the bullet hit him in the side of the head. Luke's blood splattered over my face, and I touch my cheek at the thought of it. I can still feel it, that slap, like a spray of seawater when you jump off the cliffs at Newtown Cove in my native Waterford. That smell, that unmistakable smell, it still haunts me, in my nightmares, not so frequent now, just every so often, reminding me of how random life, and death, can be.

That was in the days before counselling. In those days, the army had never heard of Post-traumatic stress syndrome. Once the initial shock had been dealt with, we returned to our billets, transporting Luke's body, covered with a tarpaulin, in the back of a truck. I showered in cold water. Bits of Luke's brain matter and blood swirling down the drain. An image I will never forget.

While the officers dealt with the paperwork, our platoon took shifts to guard Luke's body. Finally, a military convoy came to take him to Beirut International Airport. The army returned Luke to his family in Tramore, where he was buried in his parish graveyard with full military honours. None of his platoon travelled with him. We were ordered to continue our tour of duty with the United Nations Interim Forces in Lebanon as if nothing had happened. Each night we retired to the wet canteen where we downed pints by the gallon. Each pint accompanied by a toast to our fallen comrade. The worse for wear, we retired to our bunks at night and prayed that we wouldn't be next.

My mind still full of my own memories, I picked up the journal again...or so I thought. I picked up the wrong one. At first the scrawled handwriting was difficult to decipher after Arthur's neat script. I was intrigued but within minutes the content of Henry's journal left me horrified.

Chapter 11

Henry's Journal

Egypt: September 1895

They are quite beautiful, these brown girls, these sirens of the empire. Their honey-coloured skin, soft and tempting, under a halo of hair as dark as the night sky and chocolate eyes that promise gratification so intense it will overcome you like molten lava. Their dark clothing dances around them as they move, their feet bare on the dusty pavements, their eyes beckoning us into their lair.

Their numbers vary, sometimes ten, sometimes fifteen of them. Young, beautiful, luscious women who welcome us into their habitats and make men of us. I cringe as I remember the first time Sarge brought me. She was young, sixteen maybe, but so much more experienced than I, although that was easy considering my virgin status and her profession. I could hear her laughter for months afterwards, on my own, in my bed at night. She is not laughing anymore. No, I made sure of that.

The older women were gentle, instructive. One, in particular, a woman in her late twenties, I visited often and plied her with gifts – as well as her payment, of course. I studied at her altar, and when I had perfected my technique, I went back to my first, and I showed her what I had learned. It took me a while to find her.

She had been banished from the site near the barracks, forced back to the village to an uncertain income away from the steady wages of the British forces, but I found her. I paid her, and she led me to her room, a dark, dishevelled hovel behind a filthy curtain where I took her in my arms and showed her that I was no longer a boy. She laughed at me. I massaged her throat as I thrust harder, and she struggled. I rubbed her throat harder and listened as her laughter died, and she begged for mercy.

I could not help myself. I was invincible. I was all-powerful. She felt my power and my rage as I exploded inside her. I watched the panic in her eyes, the fear burning in those mirrors to her soul that slowly diminished to a spark that flickered then died.

I left her where I had found her. No one would look for her. No one would look for me. I was just another uniform in the dark streets. No one saw me with her. No one saw me leave. I slipped in through the back gate of the barracks unchallenged. I slipped into bed, and now I lie here in the dark and relive what I have done. I did not mean to kill her. I did not set out with that intention. I just could not help myself. I relish that moment of power, that feeling of invincibility, and I wallow in it.

Chapter 12

Brian

Monday 21st September 2020

I shut the book with a solid slap as my skin crawled. What the fuck had I just read? And did I want to read any more of it? Did I need to? I couldn't get my head around the words written in that journal. I started to pace the floor; three paces each way took me from one end of the kitchen to the other.

"Hi, anyone home?"

I was so traumatised by what I had read in Henry's journal that my neighbour startled me. Tom lived next door, another shadower just like Jean, born and bred under the shadow of the clock tower in the Curragh Camp. He used the hand sanitiser we always kept on the hall table and came through to the kitchen. I opened the fridge and took out two beers.

"Cheers, Tom."

"Cheers, Brian. Jeez, you'll be missed around here. Just the one mind. I've a taxi on the way."

We clinked our bottles together in salute before downing the first mouthful.

"Are ye nearly sorted?"

"Just about. Jean has only a few more shifts, and then she's finished. Everything is packed and ready to go. Tell me something, have you any idea where I could find a list of everyone who's ever lived in this house?"

"Talk to Pat in Area Records. He should have that information. Why? Found a body under the patio, have ye?"

I laughed, then remembered the chilling words written by Henry, whoever Henry might be, and the laughter died in my throat.

"I found some old journals in the attic, and I'm curious as to who they could have belonged to, that's all."

"Lining up some research for your retirement, are you? I suppose there are worse things you could be doing."

"I need to find something to do. Jean wants me to take up golf of all things. Can you picture me around a golf course?"

"You never know; you might enjoy it," Tom said.

The beep of a car horn was Tom's signal that his taxi was outside.

Tom nodded but he continued speaking, "Are you looking forward to the stand-down parade on Friday? It'll be a bit of craic. It's just a pity we can't give you a proper send-off. It's not everyone does forty years of distinguished service. I know it'll be a bit different from normal. Bloody Coronavirus. Never thought I'd see the day that we couldn't have a social evening in the mess."

"It will be grand, Tom. No point in giving out. It is what it is. I'll be there. I'm looking forward to it. At least the kids will be home for it."

"That's great. The last hurrah in the old house, eh? Something to look forward to. I'd say Jean can't wait. Anyway, I'd better go before the taxi leaves without me. See you tomorrow, Brian."

Tom left, and I got another beer from the fridge. I was looking forward to my stand-down parade. The military life had been good to me. Part of me was looking forward to going back home to Waterford. It's odd how I still thought of myself as a Waterford man, despite living in Kildare for twice as long. I couldn't help but wonder if Arthur felt that way. Was it exclusive to soldiers? This idea that during the time they serve in the military, they are soldiers first, proud to wear the uniform; but at heart was he a Manchester man?

Taking a mouthful of beer, I lifted the dark green journal again. I felt sick as I reread the same page.

"This is one sick bastard."

My stomach turned, and I slapped the journal down on the table. I had to find out who this Henry was, had to report this to someone, but who? The childlike script spoke of horror. That poor woman. How could I go about tracking down the murder of what appeared to be a prostitute in Egypt over 125 years ago?

Henry's journal had disturbed me to the point that I was not inclined to pick it up again. It felt out of place in this house, like a cat in a dog's home. I got out the laptop, but a cursory search for murders in 1895 proved fruitless, and I found myself lifting Arthur's journal again. He was bound to write something more about Henry, or did he not suspect what his so-called friend and comrade was up to.

Chapter 13

Arthur's Journal

Sandes home, Curragh Camp: 7th January 1924

Christmas Day with my family feels like a distant memory. Maybe it would have been different if our sons were still with us. With only the girls for company, I felt outnumbered, unwanted even. My daughters take after their mother. Her well-bred manners have rubbed off on them. The women in my life retain something in their makeup which elevates them above the status of the other women in the camp. I was never my wife's equal. It was India that clouded my judgement. India assaults the senses in a way that no other country can. Its colour, its smell, the intense heat. Life is different there or at least it was back then.

India, 1897

Four weeks, three days and six hours of life at sea, and I couldn't wait to feel solid ground beneath my feet. The first glimpse of the landmass of India enthralled me. I was looking forward to seeing my first elephant and to glimpses of jewel-encrusted women with molten brown eyes.

Sergeant Wilson had told us stories at night in our bunks to while away the hours as we cowered; hundreds of sweating bodies being pitched together in the depths of the ship as the currents of the Bay of Biscay tossed our ship around like a piece of flotsam. The relatively calm seas since had done nothing to abate the seasickness that some were suffering. I stood on deck in the morning light, silently urging our ship forward, closer, and closer.

"Soon now, lad."

Sarge was a veteran and had served in India before. He patted my shoulder and leaned on the railings beside me.

"The food is great, different to anything you have ever imagined in England. Full of spices and herbs you've never heard of. It will give you a dicky tummy at first, but you will get used to it. Be careful of the water."

More soldiers arrived on deck to watch the subcontinent appear before us. We were a mixed bunch. A lot of veterans like Sarge and more like me, nervous, edgy with anticipation. I had a nervous tick in the bottom of my stomach, but my jaw remained clenched and my shoulders straight. It did not pay to show fear in this man's army. I had never learned how to anyway. No, I kept my anxiety hidden beneath a clenched jawline.

Sarge had not prepared us for the smell as we docked at the port. My stomach turned as the stench of rotten fish jostled for prominence over the unmistakable smell of human shit. I had never seen so many people in one place before. The noise, the sheer volume of hundreds, no thousands of human beings, talking, laughing, grunting, racing around doing their business, like ants on a giant anthill, and I was overwhelmed. The colours hurt my eyes, exotic red and golds and bright greens on saris and turban-headed men.

Carrying our bags over our shoulders, we formed up and marched through the crowds. Everywhere I looked, beggars held out skeletal hands, cajoling us in pathetic attempts to garner sympathy as we marched by. I hardened my jaw and kept marching until we reached the train station. If it were not for the relentless heat that pummelled us, soaking our uniforms with pouring sweat, I would have sworn we were back in England. The Victoria Terminus was magnificent.

"English architecture at its best, eh?" Sarge nodded at the building as he ordered us inside to its marbled coolness. My mouth may have fallen open when we entered the Star chamber and saw its magnificent ceiling painted blue and studded with gold stars. For the first time since we docked, I felt a measure of calm as we waited on its decidedly British platform for our train.

The barracks itself was functional. Sarge opened the door to our bungalow and led us inside. Two storeys with bunks for fifty men, and each level surrounded by an outside veranda with urinal tubs dotted along its length. Latrines were at the end of the row of bungalows. Rifles were stored in locked racks at the end of each room.

"Pick your bunk; that's where you will be based for the next few years, lads. Unpack your kit and put it away. Reveille is at six o'clock, and I will personally inspect every kit."

He turned with a click of his polished boots and left us to our own devices. I dumped my kit on the first bed beside the door before someone else could claim it. I did not fancy having a bunk at the end of the room where the air is stale and stagnant with the emissions one would expect from fifty men full of ale and mutton. The room was clean, and the air was partially cooled by the constant motion of the punkah above us fanning the air from the open windows. My bunk was comfortable enough to let me sleep like a baby on my first night in India.

At reveille, the next morning, the door crashed open, and Sergeant Yarrow made his appearance. We leapt out of bed and stood to attention at the base of our bunks. Sergeant Yarrow sauntered up and down the barrack floor, looking each soldier up and down like they were an insect he was about to stamp on. Without another word, he returned to the door and exhaled, shaking his head as if disappointed.

The expectant silence erupted as Sergeant Yarrow roared orders. He was a wiry red-haired Galwegian with a roar that could curdle milk, and we were dressed and ready for inspection in seconds. Lieutenant Nolan made his appearance then. Once again, we stood to attention as he ambled up and down the barrack floor, inspecting each soldier from head to toe. Apparently satisfied, he gave the sergeant the okay to march us to the canteen. British tea and toast had never tasted so good. My stomach was only settling back to normal after the pitch and roll of the sea, and I was hungry.

"Is this it?"

John was a big northerner, built for farming and with an appetite to match. The cook was an Indian man, large framed and cocoa coloured.

"Not at all, sir. This is Chata Hazri, little breakfast. Your main breakfast will be served at nine o'clock."

John gave a sigh of relief. "Thank God for that."

A ripple of thanks went around the tables as we all had concerns about rations in this posting. The good-natured chatter was broken by Sergeant Yarrow's arrival, and I wondered where he had eaten his Chata Hazri or if the man ate at all. We were all curious about where Sergeant Wilson had got to, for none of us had seen him since our arrival the night before.

"What do you think this is, a tea party? Move it!"

His roar was louder than the assembled voices of three hundred men, and we all jumped to it, falling in outside on the parade ground. It was several days later we learned that Sergeant Wilson had been sent to the military hospital in the middle of that first night. A month later, we heard he died, dysentery they said, although it had to be something more, I reckoned.

After he died, we discovered he had a wife and family in India. Samara was a native woman. She had borne him two sons, dark-eyed, olive-skinned versions of him. I wondered what would happen to them, these half-caste children, and their mother. They were frowned upon by those in power and rejected by the natives. A foot in both camps but belonging to neither.

All I know is that Sergeant Wilson was a good sort, and we formed a guard of honour for his funeral and had a whip-round for his family. He was buried in the military graveyard at Meerut, and I am sure his remains are still there, although I have no idea what happened to his family.

Sandes home, Curragh Camp: 7th January 1924

It was an exciting time, those first few months in India. Henry and I settled in like we had been born to it. Our previous postings paled in significance. Writing about our experiences there is easy. Maybe Mrs Magill was right after all.

Chapter 14

Arthur's Journal

Sandes home, Curragh Camp: 21st January 1924

Edith complained bitterly tonight. She is unhappy so I had to explain it to her again. For me to stay away from the evil of alcohol I need to visit the Sandes home. My attendance here in the evenings is my saving grace. Writing these journals is helping me. I have no idea why, only that Mrs Magill said it would allow me to deal with my demons and so far, once I got over writing about the trauma of my childhood, it has worked. I feel better about myself. It's time to write about the next happiest event in my life. Meeting my Edith.

India, 1897

We soon grew accustomed to life in India. It was a great life for a young soldier with no responsibilities. The locals provided services unheard of back in England. A man called to the billet daily and took away our laundry, bringing it back the following day, washed pressed and all for a pittance, not even the price of a pint at home.

Before you woke, the nappy-wallah shaved you. The cleanest, smoothest shave a man could ever want while you slept. That first morning Henry did not take too kindly to it, and in fairness, who could blame him. He woke to find a bearded, wrinkly naked man leaning over him with a cut-throat razor. Being the trained soldier that he was, he slapped the razor out of the nappy-wallah's hand. Then knocked him out with a punch an Olympic boxer would have been proud of. There was quite a commotion, but it seems it was not the first time something like that had happened, and peace was soon restored. After that, the nappy-wallah approached Henry with caution. But there was never a repeat performance; if anything, he was expected. It felt like quite a luxury.

The biggest problem for me, for all of us, was boredom. Reveille was at six o'clock and the roll call, before breakfast of tea and a slice of toast. Sarge ran us through PT, and we alternated foot drill with rifle drill and marching until breakfast proper at around nine. After that, we fell in again for some more marching, but by ten, the heat forced everyone to finish for the day.

We were confined to barracks until seven in the evening. That is when the canteen opened, and we could drink beer and tell stories before we fell into bed in our bungalows. Most of us never left the perimeter of the camp. In fairness, there was no need to. Everything was provided, from the canteens to a bazaar selling everything we needed. The natives came into the barracks rather than the soldiers going out.

Our bazaar sold everything a soldier could want. There was the egg-wallah, who sold fried eggs out of a vast pan. The sweet-wallah sold a selection of sugary delights mixed with coconut, exotic soaps and oils, snacks, and clothes. There was one guy who came around the bungalows in the late afternoons, shouting corn-cuttit wallah. That is precisely what he did, cut your corns as you lay on your bunk. An entire industry existed with the single goal of servicing the needs of the protectors of the British empire.

During the day, the heat in the barracks drained us. When the wet canteen opened, we downed beer, told stories, and fell into our bunks by ten o'clock, comatose until reveille the next morning at six. The dry canteen was open all day, but boredom drove me back to the wet canteen every evening. Henry joined me, and between us, we did our best to drink the place dry. We still functioned, though. Every morning at reveille, I shook off my hangover and executed my duties to perfection. My pride in my uniform never diminished. I was a model soldier.

Our first foray outside the barracks brought great excitement. It was a break from the mundane. Wellington Barracks had been our home for months at that stage under Sergeant Yarrow. The wily Galwegian man took the parade and issued the orders. There had been serious rioting between Hindu and Muslim natives, and our orders were to restore peace.

We marched out of the barracks in formation. Our uniforms were pristine, clean-shaven faces and neatly trimmed moustaches on soldiers' cheerful faces, proud of their appearance. We marched as one, beating a steady rhythm on the road to the village. My heart sang with pride in my platoon and in my regiment.

Nothing prepared us for the noise that awaited us. Muffled by a thick cloud of dust, we could hear the locals roaring at each other and the thud of stones and sticks hitting bone and flesh. We stood back at first, watching, and I wondered why we did not just leave them to fight it out between them, these brown men. Hindu, Muslim, made no difference to me, heathens all of them as far as I was concerned. My army record had me down as Church of Ireland, but I had no idea what that meant.

I had no idea if I had been christened into any religion. My so-called parents had never darkened the door of a church, and when Eamon and Mary had asked me if I was Christian, it was the first church that came to mind. When they told me that they were Catholic, I mentally kicked myself. Irish, I should have known that. I thought I was smart saying Church of Ireland. I did not know it was Protestant, not the Catholic religion of the working classes from the west of Ireland where Eamon and Mary emigrated from.

When they asked me to join them in prayer, I did, to please them more than any belief that prayer would work for me. But I did find solace in it. I felt part of their family, part of a larger community where God was good, and life was something to be thankful for. For when I lived there, in that allotment, close to the soil and to the goodness in the souls of that Irish couple, I felt thankful.

Although I never understood why they asked God for forgiveness when he had stolen their only child from them. I just envied them their faith, their absolute faith that there was a greater being up there who cared for them, and when they died, I did pray. Pray that they did meet their maker, that they found peace and were reunited with their precious son.

But these brown men, shouting in that strange language, in those high-pitched voices, made no sense to me. Sergeant Yarrow said the latest riot had started over a cow, much to the amusement of the unit assembled in front of him. Henry and I had some laughs about that. When the riot was over and law and order had been restored, we retired to the wet canteen to debate the issue with lubricating pints and smokes. I told Henry, and anyone else who would listen, that I understood why Hindus would revere a cow. They are gentle animals with no aggression in their makeup, no need to kill another species to survive. They live on grass and give us milk and doe-eyed calves – the living incarnation of mother earth. Mind you, I also like to eat them. Beef is undoubtedly the best sustenance for a hungry belly, so I do not understand why they refuse to eat their meat, but if that is their belief, so be it.

On the other hand, the Muslims liked to wind up their Hindu neighbours by defiling their sacred animal, eating the flesh that the Hindus venerate. I have since discovered that Muslims do not eat pork. Not because they love pigs but because they believe the animal is unclean. It led me to consider that maybe they all just enjoyed the riots. Perhaps it was a break from the boredom of their daily lives. These brown men in this hot, dusty, riotous, colourful country. What do I know?

The riots settled down for a while after that. Relative peace was restored, and our days fell into a familiar routine. One hot and dusty Wednesday afternoon, I was lying on my bunk, half asleep and daydreaming, when Sergeant Yarrow called me to attention. Captain Hollingsworth needed some papers delivered to the Colonel. I was happy to oblige.

The Colonel's was the largest bungalow. It was situated far enough away from the men to give his family privacy and near enough to allow security and protection from the natives. More natives worked in and around the Colonel's bungalow than worked in the whole barracks. There were lawns in the English style to the front of the house and well-attended flower beds. A large veranda surrounded the bungalow, shaded from the heat of the sun.

She was sitting in the shadows, and I did not see her at first. It was her voice calling out to me. There was a musical ring to it. A softness combined with a warmth that melted something inside me, and when she asked me if I would like some refreshments, I could not refuse. Edith was the most beautiful creature I had ever laid eyes on. Slender with alabaster skin and greenish-blue eyes, framed by a mass of molasses brown hair.

I was at ease in her company, enchanted by the sparkle in her eye and her quick wit. The time flew by as we chatted, and I fell in love with this remarkable woman. Then her mother arrived on the veranda, and I remembered my place in this world. Corporal Torrington was dismissed by the colonel's wife, but her daughter's eyes called out to me.

I stayed away from the wet canteen that night. From the depths of my bunk, I relived our conversation, replayed her expressions in my mind and resolved to see her again. Henry disagreed. He told me out straight that she was way above my station in life. The daughter of a colonel, no less, what was I thinking of? She had probably forgotten all about me or, worse still, recounted our conversation to her friends, laughing at me. The nerve of a lowly corporal to chat to her in such a manner. I tossed and turned for the rest of the night, unable or unwilling to get Edith out of my mind.

Sandes home, Curragh Camp: 21st January 1924

Looking back on it now, maybe Henry was right. I should have stayed away but I could no more stay away from Edith than a moth from a flame. I love her. Always have done. From the first day I set eyes on her until this very moment. I know I am undemonstrative. Some would say I'm cold and unfeeling. Edith is the one constant. The shining star who drags me back from the gates of hell. Edith and the Sandes Soldiers' Home.

Chapter 15

Brian

Tuesday 22nd September 2020

I looked up at the ornamental wall clock and yawned. It was past midnight, and I was tired. Jean had got in from work two hours earlier and had gone straight up to bed. It was about time I joined her. I decided that the next instalment could wait until the following day, so I closed the journals and put them on the counter. The bedroom was in darkness, and I could hear Jean's steady breathing. I tiptoed into the room and slipped into the bed beside her, trying not to disturb her.

Sleep eluded me, and then when I did finally get to sleep, strange dreams haunted me all night. Dreams inhabited by Jean's voice calling me from inside a dense forest, but there was a strange woman in her place when I got close to her. A woman with the same dark hair but with green eyes that begged me to help her.

Every time I got close to Jean, she changed somehow into this stranger. I woke with an unsettled feeling, out of sorts and anxious. I felt around for Jean, but she was already downstairs cooking breakfast. The waft of bacon and coffee banished my anxiety and got me out of bed and downstairs in minutes.

"You look rough. Did you have bad dreams last night? You

let a few yelps out, and you tossed and turned so much I had to go into the spare room."

"Jesus. Sorry, love. Yea, weird dreams, all right."

"Is the move getting to you?"

Jean folded her arms around me and kissed my cheek. My mood lifted. Jean had that effect on me. My wife was the most upbeat person on the planet. Nothing got her down. She rose like a lark and sang all day, and I felt blessed to have her.

"We're nearly there, Jean. Just a few more days, and we will be in our dream home."

"It's been a long-time coming. I can't wait."

"I know, I know, but...I will miss Kildare...miss this house. We've lived here for a long time. Reared our kids here."

"Yes, we have some good memories, but now it's time to make new ones. The kids are adults now. It's *our* time."

"And I can't wait to spend the rest of my life with you."

Our romantic moment was interrupted by Jean's mobile phone. She laughed and moved away to answer it. Conor was coming home for the stand-down parade on Friday, and he wanted to check the details with his mother. Jean chatted away and handed over the spatula to me with a nod towards the eggs she was in the middle of scrambling.

Sitting at the kitchen table, she continued her conversation while I sorted breakfast. She was radiant, always was when she spoke to any of the kids. Conor is our youngest. Twenty-four and working as a garda in the city. She worries about him all the time. We both do. We were so very proud of him when he graduated from Templemore. But when we heard he was going to be stationed in Dublin, we weren't so happy. Organised crime has gotten out of hand in this little country of ours, and Conor is on the frontline. Although on his last trip home, he tried to put his mother's mind at ease by telling her that Jenny, his eldest sister, saw more danger in her workplace than he did.

Jenny specialises in trauma in the Accident and Emergency Department of St James Hospital, while Sinéad is a paediatric nurse, equally stressful. I used to thank God that none of them followed me into the military. But I have come to realise that they all face more dangers in their day-to-day jobs than I ever did during my overseas missions with the United Nations. The pandemic this year added to our worries. Jean is not a religious person, but I know she says the odd prayer to keep them safe.

"Ok, love, bye, see you Friday."

"How's Conor?"

"All good, all good. Jenny's picking up him and Sinéad on Friday morning, and they should be here by eleven."

"That's great. Sinéad managed to get the time off as well. Lord, I can't remember the last time we had all three at home at the same time."

"It's only right, though. The army has been our life as well as yours. They spent their childhood in the Curragh Camp. I've spent my whole life here. I'm glad they all managed to get time off to mark the occasion, for it *is* a big deal, Brian. The end of an era."

She was right, of course. My wife is rarely wrong. It is the end of an era. I first came to the Curragh to sign up with the army the week before my twentieth birthday. My parents hadn't wanted me to go, but I wouldn't listen. One of my mates had signed up two years earlier, and we met over the Christmas holidays. He was just back from an overseas trip to Lebanon and was having the time of his life.

I was barely working, had no money and no future. The military life beckoned, and I never looked back in fairness. My parents came around eventually when they saw how happy I was. And then when I brought home Jean, sure my mother was delighted.

From the moment I set eyes on Jean, I knew she was the one

for me. We met in the local nightclub on a busy Saturday night. The whole unit was in the Curragh that weekend, and a group of us decided to pay Nijinsky's Nightclub a visit. I was standing at the bar with Frank Egan having a pint and looking around me, checking out the talent, and there was plenty of it. The dance floor was surrounded by booths. The seating was covered in red velvet, and the lights dimmed except for the shards that danced off the disco ball.

Ray D'Arcy was belting out the hits from his booth to the front and centre of the heaving dance floor. It was jam-packed – sweaty bodies gyrating to the latest hits. Heated conversations and chat-up lines interspersed with bouts of rowdy laughter around the edges and in front of the booths.

Frank and I were both corporals at that stage, full of our own importance and enjoying the single life. Frank was fair-haired, broad built, tall, lithe, and popular with the ladies. He was one of those guys who could talk to anyone about anything. I swear he could convince you the Pope was a protestant if he wanted to. He still has that ability, mind you, but puts it to a different use these days.

Frank was mid-sentence, telling me about a blonde girl he had met the week before but didn't want to see again when Jean tapped him on the shoulder. Frank threw his arms around her, hugging her like a long-lost friend, and I was gobsmacked. She had beautiful rich brown hair, tumbling down over her shoulders, a narrow waist and a velvet laugh that left me entranced. When he introduced me, I fell for her immediately. Everything about her called out to me. I couldn't get enough of her.

Turns out she had been away in England staying with relatives over there, but now she was back. We talked over the music, and when the DJ announced supper, we moved upstairs and chatted while we sat over chicken, peas, and mash until it grew cold, and the supper room was emptied.

Frank and I walked her home, for I knew that they were related at that stage. She was his favourite cousin, and they had grown up together on the Curragh. Best friends more than cousins. We started double dating. Jean's friend Una hit it off with Frank, and it became a regular night out for us. Nijinsky's on a Saturday night, the Oscar cinema on a Wednesday night. Two years later, we were married. It might have been sooner if I had been able to get her on her own to propose.

One stormy night in October, her father was on duty, her mother was at bingo, and we had the front room to ourselves. Jean had dispatched her two younger brothers upstairs with a bottle of red lemonade and enough Tayto crisps and chocolates to feed a dozen men after a route march.

"Peace at last," she said as she closed the door. "I've warned them."

I stood in front of the open turf fire, my hands in my pockets, trying to look nonchalant and failing miserably, my speech prepared and rehearsed a hundred times.

"What's up?" Jean asked.

"Noth...Nothing. Ouch!"

I jumped away from the fire, beating the backs of my legs where the flames had scorched my denims.

Jean laughed. "Go on, ya eejit. What are you after doing?"

Tears were streaming down her face, and she doubled up laughing as I jumped around the room like a lunatic frantically trying to hold the heavy denim away from my bare skin.

"Take them off ye, quick," she said when she could draw breath.

"I will, yea. Just imagine what your mam would say if she walked in and me with no jeans on."

Her laughter was infectious – genuine, warm laughter that

came from her belly. I have always loved that laugh, strived to hear it, to enjoy its richness, its joy. Before I knew it, I was on my knees in front of her and holding both of her hands.

"Marry me."

"Wha...what did you say?"

"I had this whole speech planned...but it's simple. Marry me, Jean."

She let a whoop out that I was sure her mam could hear in the bingo hall a good country mile away.

"Brian McElroy, I thought you'd never ask. Yes, Yes." She threw her arms around me, and both of us collapsed onto the floor. At that exact moment, her two brothers burst through the door, one wielding a hurl, the other a baseball bat. We both looked up at the boys, both in fight mode, both ready to do battle with whoever was hurting their sister. They stopped, confusion on their faces as the tangle of arms and legs on the living room floor tried to disengage.

I looked at Jean, and she looked at me. We both collapsed again, backs flat on the floor, laughing so hard we could barely breathe. Her brothers ended up laughing with us, and then we swore them to secrecy. I had no ring, you see, knew better than to try and pick an engagement ring for Jean, so the following Saturday, we took a trip to Dublin. An hour and a half on the bus, holding hands, my heart singing, then down to O'Connell Street to the Happy Ring House.

Jean chose a solitaire, and my heart soared as we strolled down to the upmarket Gresham Hotel for a celebratory glass of champagne. Not that I liked champagne. I just thought it was the right thing to do. Every so often, I would look across at Jean as she admired her ring finger and the sparkle as the diamond caught the low winter sun through the plate glass window.

We arrived back in the Curragh after eight that evening. Her parents always met friends in Connolly Mess on a Saturday night, and we had arranged to meet Frank and Una there. We didn't even get to say a word. Jean's mother spotted the ring the second we walked in the door. The celebrations went on all night and into the following week.

We hadn't set a date at that stage, but it was done for us before we even got to tell my parents. We were due to visit them in Waterford the following weekend. By the time we got there, the church was booked, the reception was arranged, and Jean was wedding dress shopping. My parents were delighted. They loved Jean.

Looking back on it now, we were so young. Neither of us wanted much of a fuss, but both sets of parents thought differently. Her father insisted on paying for the wedding – eighty guests in Lumville House after a church service in St Brigid's Church on the Curragh. My parents were so impressed with the church, delighted to see me "settled", as my mother put it.

Thirty-eight years later, we are still together, and I can't get enough of her. We may have gone off the rails along the way a few times, but we have been happy overall. Military life is not easy on the family unit, but we made it through. Intact and talking to each other. Retirement could be a different story. It struck me that I would need to take up a hobby, some sort of interest, to keep me motivated. After all, I was a fit and healthy sixty, not a decrepit eighty-year-old. Jean played golf and wanted me to join her. Maybe I should give it a go.

"Penny for them," Jean said.

I laughed. "They're not even worth that."

Jean didn't know I was worried about retiring, and I wasn't about to tell her. She was so excited about the move, about the new house, about taking early retirement herself. We had so much to look forward to. I didn't know why I was so nervous about it. Maybe it was just as well I had those journals to distract me until I got those last few days over with.

When Jean left for work, I got stuck into packing away the army memorabilia, just like I'd promised. I couldn't get Arthur and Edith out of my head. Eventually, I gave in and picked up Edith's journal. Arthur had written about meeting Edith, and I was curious to find out if she had written about meeting Arthur. I hesitated for just a second before I opened it and started to read.

Chapter 16

Edith's Journal

30th September 1924

It is nearly midnight. My last night in Warrant Officers Quarters in the Curragh Camp, Ireland. Tomorrow my new life begins but first I need to leave a record of sorts of what occurred. It is important that the truth is told. Just not by me. Not yet anyway. My life has been no better or indeed no worse than anyone else's but there are events that I have only recently become aware of that need to be explained. I should start at the beginning.

India, 21st September 1898

My mother told me that the life of a woman in British India is a good one. It was the only life I knew; therefore, I cannot judge. My father was an officer of the empire, and I was born in India. My brother was sent back to Dublin to our grandparents so that he could have a suitable education. As a woman, that option was not even considered for me. However, I was happy with the knowledge I learned from my mother as well as from the other women in the community. Needlecraft was my forte, and I was excellent at croquet. The club had an extensive library. I read the classics as well as the other books Mrs Shortall kept hidden in her bag and rented out to those with broader literary tastes. Oscar Wilde and Bram Stoker were my favourites.

I could have had any number of suitors, but all were kept ably at bay by my father's rank and his supercilious attitude to the men he commanded and the wider community we socialised within. My mother said that if he continued with his ways, I would be left on the shelf, an old maid of twenty. Not that any of my mother's candidates for my hand held any attraction for me. They were all just carbon copies of my father, destined to live out their lives and careers in India while I dreamed of high society in Dublin and London.

Then I met Corporal Torrington. He called in the early evening with papers for my father. It was his accent that caught my attention. The men who serve in my father's regiment are primarily Irish. The clue is in the name, the Connaught Rangers. Invariably the men's accents are lyrical and sometimes Gaelic. Some only learn to speak the King's English when they join the Rangers. The officer classes' accents are different, more refined, more like my own, and they bore me if I am honest.

That evening I was sitting on the veranda with my fan and my book. While I saw him approach the bungalow, I dismissed him as just another ranger. When he spoke to my father's man, the unmistakable English baritone accent carried along the veranda and called to me like an invisible line reeling me into him. It was as if I could not help it, as if God was pushing me to introduce myself, so I did.

I offered him lemonade and was astounded when he accepted but managed to hide it well as I invited him to sit in the shade. His hand touched mine as he took the glass from me, and I smiled at him. A smile that was returned, a thousandfold. What sunshine was contained in that smile? Electric-blue eyes that crinkled at the corners, and I fell in love, there and then with Arthur Torrington. He sat, and we talked, and before I knew it, darkness had fallen, and my mother was approaching me, along the veranda, a curious smile on her face. Her expression changed as she came closer and noticed the rank markings on Arthur's uniform.

"Edith, supper is ready."

She nodded at Arthur, who jumped to his feet and saluted as if my father stood in front of him. That was when I realised how nervous he was. That insecure part of his personality made its way into my heart and stayed there forever.

"Mother, I would like you to meet Corporal Torrington. He delivered papers for Father, and I offered him some refreshments before he returned to his quarters."

"Very good, dear, but now it is time to retire indoors. Thank you, Corporal Torrington."

Arthur rose and said his polite, formal goodbyes. I followed my mother inside, but not before checking behind me and confirming that Arthur was watching my retreat. He took off his cap and bowed, deep from the waist, and when he rose again and gave a slight wave of his cap, my heart sang.

And so, it began – my affair with Arthur Torrington. My mother was not best pleased. She had higher aspirations for her only daughter. She had ambitions for me of marrying a lieutenant at the very least, someone of the rank of captain preferably, certainly not an English-born corporal.

As for my father, I am still unsure which offended him more, Arthur's rank or the fact that he was English born. My father placed great store in our ancient Irish roots. Their outlook on what was Irish would be viewed very differently now that part of Ireland has gained its independence from the empire. But at that time, that was how they viewed our heritage. My father saw himself as an Irishman, loyal to the king, to the empire, and he was proud of that heritage.

Hiding my relationship with Arthur was relatively easy. I rode out every day, usually accompanied by my ayah or her son. Bikram was a strange boy, two years my senior, who rode behind me and never spoke. Looking back on it now, I wonder if Bikram could speak, for I never heard him utter a word in my presence, to me or anyone else. He always looked stern yet intelligent, an accomplished horseman who treated animals with a gentle firmness that demanded obedience from them.

During my more fanciful days, I imagined he had been born a prince, for he had that regal bearing. I imagined he had told grievous lies, and as his punishment had his tongue cut out and banished to a lower caste to live out his days in silence. My imagination did run away with me at times. Before I met Arthur.

I chose a new route, one that took me close to an area where Arthur just happened to be walking, most days, after the heat of the midday sun but before evening duties began. We walked, and we talked for hours, and I fell deeper in love with him.

He was quiet and mannerly with an inner streak of steel that showed in the set of his jawline. His eyes were the same shimmering blue of the Indian sky, and I could see humour tinged with sadness every time I looked at him. In my eyes, he was an enigma, strong yet gentle, so noticeably quiet but when he did speak, what he had to say meant something.

My Arthur did not suffer fools gladly. I saw him once bawl out a young private. Arthur had not seen my approach. I was early and had been into the bazaar beforehand, so I arrived from a different direction than was my habit. His tongue cut through that young private as sharply as any knife, reducing the young man to a stuttering fool. Arthur dismissed the private, took a deep breath and turned. That was when he saw me, still mounted and sitting open-mouthed, after hearing his verbal battering. He did not even blink, just dazzled me with that sincere smile he has that shouts sunshine and blue skies.

Bikram was beside me, one hand on my reins, as if ready to take control of me and my mount, like some silent guardian angel. He was rigid, tension buzzing out of him, and Arthur's smile did nothing to dispel his fight-or-flight stance.

"It's okay, Bikram," I said, and I touched his shoulder.

Bikram jumped as if my touch had burned him. He dropped my reins and turned his mount away, retreating to his usual position some hundred yards behind me. Far enough away so that he could not hear our conversation but close enough so that he could be at my side in seconds if need be. Sometimes I wondered if my father had instructed him to guard me. I even put that question to Bikram many times. He never answered, not even with a look. He was like a handsome, somewhat arrogant but always silent blank page.

Occasionally I managed to sneak away without my bodyguard on my tail, usually after dark, when Bikram had retired for the night, and the household was asleep. I could not stay away from Arthur. He was my drug of choice. I craved his company, the sound of his voice. When he first kissed me, I nearly swooned; I was so overcome, so enthralled by this man. The night he told me he loved me, I cried with joy. And then we made love. I had no hesitation, for I was ready. While I feared the repercussions, I no longer cared.

When I fell pregnant, my father was furious, my mother

apoplectic. My condition threatened their social standing, their plans for my future. I was thrilled that, at last, I could marry the man I loved. They would not, could not stand in my way, for I was now spoiled goods, not suitable for marriage to someone of their choosing. So, I got to make my own choice, and I chose Arthur.

We were married on 21st September 1899, and our son Arthur Junior was born on 21st March 1900. Tongues wagged, but my mother told everyone about our son's premature birth and how tiny he was. That part of the story was genuine. Arthur Junior, or Arty as we quickly nicknamed him, was a sickly child, perfectly formed but tiny and prone to coughs and bouts of sickness that frightened me and made me watchful over his crib.

Chapter 17

Brian

Tuesday 22nd September 2020

"Anyone home?"

"In here, Jean."

I greeted Jean at the door with a kiss and an offer of a cup of coffee.

"Yes, please, I could murder a cup. Did you get the rest of the packing finished?"

"Oops! Sorry, love, I'm just so tied up with these journals. I can't put them down."

"Brian, we've only a few days left. You need to sort out what you want to bring with you. Surely those journals can wait."

Jean flopped onto the armchair, dumping her bag on the floor. She looked tired, her pallor brought guilt sneaking through me and the realisation that I wasn't pulling my weight. I should have insisted she didn't go back after the lockdown but there again, I couldn't stop her. She wanted to finish out her time there on the date that she had decided, not one that was dictated to her by this pandemic. I handed her a mug of coffee and a chocolate biscuit with an apologetic smile.

"You needn't think you're going to sweeten me up that easy." She tried to scowl, but it turned into a reluctant smile.

"I started reading Edith's journal. I think you'd enjoy it," I said. "She was born in India, the daughter of a British Colonel."

"Interesting." Jean took the journal from me and flicked through the pages. My wife wears her heart on her sleeve. I sat entranced watching her facial expressions as she read the first few pages of Edith's journal. She became completely engrossed.

"Edith's diary is a totally different kettle of fish to Arthur's," I said. "His early childhood makes for horrific reading although he was rescued in his teens by an Irish couple. He joined the Connaught Rangers after that. And then he met Edith."

"She was besotted by him," Jean said, pointing at Edith's journal, "according to this."

"They were besotted with each other."

"I need to read on. She's just had baby Arty, but he doesn't seem to be thriving."

I left Jean to read Edith's journal as I prepared the dinner. She was so engrossed she didn't even notice when I placed her meal in front of her.

Chapter 18

Edith's Journal

India, 1901

Life was vastly different for me after I married Arthur. We were lucky to be allocated a bungalow, thanks to Arthur's promotion. His rise to sergeant had been rapid and well deserved, and I was so proud of him. I immersed myself into life as a sergeant's wife and a new mother and loved every second.

When my husband returned to quarters each day, I rewarded him with a smile and freshly made lemonade. Our son, Arty, took up all my attention. I adored that child. So did Arthur. He only left our side to go on duty or for his twice-weekly visits to the Sandes Soldiers' Home. At first, I queried him on why he would want to spend time there instead of with us, his family, but Arthur was adamant.

"I was very fond of alcohol, Edith, too fond. The mother in the Sandes Soldiers' Home rescued me. Going there means I stay out of the wet canteen."

"But, Arthur, I thought those soldiers' homes were for single men. Why do you need to go to there when you have a perfect home here with the baby and me, your family?"

"It is my only social outlet. We drink tea, play board games, have conversations with like-minded men who prefer tea to beer."

"But, Arthur..."

"Enough." Arthur slapped the table with the flat of his hand. "This is not open for negotiation. I go to the Sandes home twice a week, and that is the end of it."

I was suitably chastened and dropped the subject. In fairness, I learned to enjoy the solitude on those two nights every week. After Arty was settled for the night, I worked on my needlework and produced some fine embroideries. A few months living amongst the enlisted men's families taught me just how many soldiers spent far too much time and income in the wet canteen. I was grateful that my Arthur was not one of them.

My father kept his distance, and I suppose he had no choice for the sake of his rank, and I understood that. His career was his life, the only life we all had known, and it had given us a good standard of living in India. But my marriage to an enlisted man did not sit well with him and his peers.

My former friends shunned me. The long line of officers who had sought me out in my single days now pointedly ignored me. The young women of my own age who had been my friends and confidants were actively discouraged from visiting me in my home. How could they? The daughters of the officer classes could not be seen visiting the enlisted men's quarters. As the wife of a sergeant, I was not welcome at any of the soirees I had previously attended.

I did not care. Life with Arthur was wonderful. He was kind and gentle, and he adored me and worshipped our son. He introduced me to the other NCOs and their wives, but I did not need anyone else. All I wanted was my husband and my son. My life was complete.

On the eve of Christmas, we were invited to my parents' bungalow. I was astounded when the invitation landed on my doorstep. That astonishment was soon replaced by anxiety and fear as I wondered why now? Why, after all these months, was my mother officially inviting me back into the home I had been reared in. And at a time when my father was at home. Arthur put my mind at ease.

"You're their only daughter." He waved the card at me. "Your father has missed you. How could he not? Your mother has finally talked sense into him, and he wants to see his grandchild."

He was right, of course. My parents paid a visit when Arty was born. My father was abrupt, as was his nature. Once he knew I was recovering from the birth and that the child was fine, he nodded and left, calling my mother after him. It was the first time I had ever seen her ignore his wishes or instructions. She was cradling her grandchild, and I could see the love reflected in her eyes as she stared down at his soft cheeks and tiny hands.

Another roar from my father, who was pacing on the veranda, brought her to her feet. Her eyes were bright from unshed tears; she placed my son back in my arms, then hugged me so tightly I thought I would break. That was the last time I saw my father for quite a while. I called to visit my mother on days I knew father was not at home. She adored Arty. He was a constant source of joy to her, but this invitation signalled something new. My heart trembled at the idea that my father might get to know my husband. In my ignorance, I was confident that once he allowed himself to get to know Arthur the man, and not Torrington the sergeant, he would respect Arthur. I wanted him to know his kindness and his wisdom and witness the love he had for me and Arty.

That evening was cooler than usual for that time of year.

Born in India, I was accustomed to the constant heat and humidity. Arthur suffered terribly during the hot summer months, but this December, temperatures hovered around the seventies, which felt extremely pleasant and a massive relief after the hot summer.

We approached the familiar landscape of my parents' home, the gardens laid out in the formal English lines my mother favoured, although the small patch of grass struggled to maintain the slightest shade of green despite my mother's constant insistence to the gardener that he water it regularly.

My insides trembled at the thought of facing my father. It had been nine months since I had set eyes on him – nine months since he had spoken a word to me. I glanced at Arthur and caught his encouraging smile. That gave me the confidence to step onto the veranda and into my father's world. My mother must have been watching out for us, for she swept towards me and greeted me with a hug and a grateful smile. She put out her hand to Arthur, who brought it to his lips for a respectful kiss that she accepted with a welcoming smile.

"Come, come, your father is inside." She ushered us through the open doors.

Father stood as we entered, clearing his throat as he glanced in our direction. He nodded before continuing the conversation he was having with a fellow officer. It felt like a slap, but my mother put her hand on my arm and gently led me to the opposite side of the room, where several wives and daughters were seated. I knew them all, of course. Had dined with them and shopped with them, but none of them had left their calling card in my postbox since I married Arthur. Several women had spoken to me during visits to my mother and had met my baby, but none asked after my husband. Yet now that I was in my father's bungalow, an invited guest, like them, they were full of questions.

"And your child. How is he doing?"

"Poor boy was premature, I believe. How worrying for you."

"I hope you have found a good ayah to help look after your son."

I answered them all with what I hoped was a pleasant smile, aware that I should not embarrass my mother, but my stomach churned inside. I had indeed found an excellent ayah, for she was mine when I was a child. When she heard of my condition, she volunteered to help me, and I accepted her help with gratitude. I knew that she cared for me and that she would care for my baby, no matter what rank his father was.

Pleading that I was needed in the dining room, I escaped their attention to look for Arthur. I found him, standing awkwardly just inside the door, a glass of whiskey in his hand and his face devoid of all expression.

"I am so sorry, Arthur. We should leave, now, before dinner..."

Arthur put up his hand to interrupt me. "Edith, it is fine. We have been invited for dinner and dinner we shall have. I have no need to speak to any of these people. My own company suits me just fine."

I looked into those crystal-clear eyes, and my heart filled with love for this man. Any other man would have stormed out of that bungalow, angry and humiliated. For that is what they did that night. They humiliated my Arthur. They left him standing there alone, not speaking to him, not acknowledging his existence, and my heart broke for him. But he bore it with such humility, such grace, that it showed them up for the boring snobs that they were. Of course, most of the officers were wary of crossing my father, their commanding officer. Others realised that if Arthur was invited to dinner, he was accepted by my father. Therefore, by extension, he should be accepted by them, but they just did not bother.

As the evening progressed and conversation flowed around the dinner table, Arthur was eventually included, and some of my anger started to dissipate. But I remained angry at my father most of all. A simple handshake on our arrival would have set the tone for the rest of the evening. He knew that. I knew that. But he made the decision not to make that gesture. He chose to make Arthur an outcast, and I do not know if I ever forgave him for that.

I could feel my mother's eyes on us all evening, on me, on my father and on Arthur, and every so often, I gave her a reassuring smile, for she tried so hard that night. Her hosting skills were put to the test on a grand scale, and I am sure she was quite worn out by the end of the evening.

We did not linger. When the men retired to the veranda for brandy and cigars, we took our leave, saying we were anxious to return to the baby. Our excuse was accepted, perhaps believed, and we made our way back to our home under cover of darkness. I held Arthur's hand the whole way home and tried to tell him how upset I was for him.

"It was fine, Edith. You fuss too much. It was a lovely evening. The food was excellent, the conversation interesting, and I was with you. What more could a man want?"

"I love you, Arthur Torrington."

"I love you back, Edith Torrington."

I kissed him then, under the stars on that Christmas Eve night and swore I would remember that kiss forever. He tasted of apples and musk, and his touch sent a tingle down my spine that hastened our pace back to the privacy of our own home.

Chapter 19

Edith's Journal

India, 1902

It was another three months before I saw my father again. He was the last person I wanted to speak to, and I treated him the way he had treated us when we were invited to dinner on Christmas Eve; I ignored him. It was my mother who told him he had to call. My precious son Arty was ill. He had always been a sickly child, and he was slow to develop, still tiny at a year old. My ayah had done her best, helping me source the best foods and medicines, but it was no use.

The day before his first birthday, Arty died in my arms.

I was inconsolable. My mother did what she could, but no one could reach me, not even my beloved Arthur. Although looking back on it, I wonder did he even try. Was he so grief-stricken himself that he could not help me, could not comfort me? He took long solitary walks, and I resented him for that. Hated that he could just walk away, for that is how I felt about it. I felt that he was walking away from me, from my grief, from us, and I started to hate him for that. My arms felt empty without my son. My heart was empty without my husband, and I felt totally alone, abandoned, bereft.

For months I could not function. I slept through the night and halfway through the day. My bungalow was neglected as I ignored my wifely duties and the natives took full advantage, except for my ayah. She stood by my side and kept me alive, spoon-feeding me, washing me, her touch the only comfort I had for Arthur took to staying out at night as well as during the day. Most nights, he arrived home in the early hours, barely able to walk, stinking of beer and tobacco, and fell into bed in the spare bedroom, the one we had planned for Arty.

"I'm sorry, Edith." His bloodshot eyes were sorrowful as he looked down at me.

"Stay with me, Arthur," but he always walked away. I always turned back into my pillow and cried until the mercy of sleep overtook me again. I dreamt of our son lying contently in his father's hands, and when I woke, the pain of knowing that they were both gone drove me mad once again.

The first day that my ayah managed to persuade me to get washed and dressed and sit out on the veranda was at the start of the monsoon season. The rain was pelting down that day, washing away the dust of the earlier months in red swirls around the veranda. The heat was relentless, and I wondered where Arthur was, for he could not possibly be out walking through those rains, and in this intense heat, it was surely in the nineties.

I sat and stared out at the coppery red puddles and did not hear the carriage approach until it was practically at my door. The whinny of the horses caught my attention, and I looked up to see my father approaching under cover of a large black umbrella provided by a native who struggled to keep up with my father's aggressive pace.

"Edith." He nodded at me, and I stared at him, too surprised to say anything.

"Your mother said you had been unwell. I am here to take you home. This nonsense has gone on long enough."

My mouth fell open, and I could feel laughter bubbling up in my throat. It came out like the bay of a donkey, and even I was taken aback by the sound. I cleared my throat and sat up straighter.

"I *am* home, Father."

He slapped the side of the veranda and started to pace along its length, one hand behind his back, the other gesticulating widely as he spoke. "This, you call this home. Look around you, girl. This is not for you. I brought you up to be better than this. You could have had your pick of any of the young officers, but oh no, not you, you prefer to defy me, to embarrass me, and your mother."

"Embarrass you! I love him, Father. Arthur is my husband. I promised to love, honour and obey him, and I intend to keep that promise."

"I can get you an annulment. You can start again, Edith."

"But I do not want an annulment. To do that would be akin to denying that Arty ever existed...and he did. Can't you see that? Arty is...was my child. I will always be his mother, and nothing can change that."

Tears threatened to overwhelm me once again, and I swallowed them back with great gulps of hot air. My stomach turned, but for the first time since my baby died, I felt the stirring of hope mixed in with the release of grief. I did love Arthur, and we could get through this if we pulled together.

My father's face turned puce. His eyes were almost popping out of his skull as he clenched his fists, fighting with his tribal instincts. I imagined he wanted to punch me, throw me over his shoulder and drag me to his carriage kicking and screaming. The struggle within him was apparent until he eventually managed to restore his upper-class English gentleman to the fore. He opened his mouth to speak, but he had no words, just air that came out as an "oomph".

"You will regret this, my girl."

He turned and marched back to his carriage like the hounds of hell were on his heels. Without a backward glance, he sped away, and that was the last time I spoke to my father. He did me a favour, really, for I resolved to get Arthur back on that day. I chose to live again. To process my grief and reach out to Arthur, for it was grief that had torn us apart.

I knew I could fix that for, at the end of the day, I loved him, and he loved me.

Chapter 20

Jean

Tuesday 22nd September 2020

I closed the journal. "Christ almighty!"

Grief swiped me sideways. Even after all these years, it was unbelievable that it could erupt inside me like a dormant volcano just waiting for an opportune moment to gush out and engulf me. On a typical day, it was there, in the background, this grief, this longing, never fully buried, but never visible to anyone, except maybe Brian. He felt it too, probably as much as I did. It had been thirty-three years last week since we had buried our firstborn son.

At times I couldn't remember his face, and it shook me. It was on those days that I would take out the photo I carried in my purse and remind myself of those baby features I had loved. As our other children came along, those features were mirrored at times in their faces or in their movements, and the stab of grief would sting me again, just for a second, made all the more tragic by the knowledge that baby John would forever be a baby in my heart and in my mind.

We watched Jenny, Sinéad and Conor grow up to be good people. Adults with jobs and partners and responsibilities who loved and lived life to the full. The thought of my children brought a smile to my lips. We have been so incredibly fortunate.

When we first got married, we lived in a flat in Newbridge. Two rooms and a bathroom with a constant greasy smell in the hallway from the Italian chipper below. We loved that place, but when I became pregnant, we realised it wasn't suitable for a baby, so Brian applied for married quarters in the Curragh. They were plentiful at that time. I had been brought up in the camp, my parents still live there, and everyone helped us get the house in Pearse Terrace ready. We moved in when I was six months pregnant. There were two bedrooms, the large one at the front was ours, and we decorated the small back bedroom as a nursery. Both grandmothers-to-be were knitting furiously. The excitement was palpable.

And then John was born. I have never felt such love for another human being as I felt for that child, the second I set eyes on him. As for my husband, he was hooked from the first glance. Men like Brian have a reputation of being alpha males, totally patriarchal. To the outside world, Brian gives that impression but when he is at home with us, he is a gentle giant. A teddy bear of a man. He couldn't do enough for me and the baby. Those first few weeks he was constantly at my beck and call.

John was perfect. A healthy bawling 8lbs who took to my breast greedily and slept through the night within two months. John was perfectly normal, perfectly healthy, and then he died. Cot death. Sudden. Shocking. Awful, and I don't think we will ever get over it.

That night I had put him down at his usual time, nine o'clock, just as the news started on RTE1. His cot was in our bedroom, so we both checked on him at eleven when we went to bed. He was sleeping, his little chest rising and falling under the blanket. I remember we shared a moment when our eyes met over the cot, and we smiled at each other, then smiled at our perfect baby boy.

Brian was on escort duty the next day, an early start and woke at five thirty. For some strange reason, I woke with him. In those predawn hours, the outside world is silent. The only sound is the house's natural creaking as wood expands and contracts and the steady breathing of those still asleep. It was the absence I noticed as if the house was holding its breath, as it too noticed the absence of tiny movements. I jumped out of bed without turning on the light, but I knew before my fingers touched his cold little body that our baby was dead.

Those early days were so hard. I moved around in a haze. I watched Brian suffer, and while I wanted to help him, I couldn't. Brian lost himself in his military life, losing his pain on mountain hikes and venting his anger on the shooting ranges. Anger was a large part of that grief. It's a cliché to say no parent should bury a child, but there is a good reason for that. It must be the hardest cross to carry to witness this tiny life snuffed out before he got to live, the lost opportunity, the potential. It never leaves you, gets easier, yes, but never leaves you.

I understood how Edith felt, felt her pain and I knew Brian would too.

"Brian, the baby died."

I could see the grief strike him, just as it had me. We hugged each other tight, memories rushing back to haunt us both.

"It never really leaves you, does it?" Brian said.

"No, it doesn't. We didn't deal with it very well."

"I don't think there is a right way or a wrong way, love, there's no set of instructions on how to deal with grief."

"I chose alcohol, and you chose overseas."

"But we got through it."

He's right of course. We did get through it but oh my God it was so hard. Alcohol masked the ache for me. I hid it from public view and for a while, that's how I survived. Brian didn't even notice at first. I didn't notice myself. Alcohol became my crutch to get me through the nights. I know that now, but at the time, I just wanted to dull the pain.

I thought no one could understand how I felt, not even my husband. In concealing my grief I was lonely but I hid it well. Brian even went overseas, thinking I was fine. Fine. How could I feel okay after burying my child? I remember thinking that I could never feel normal again.

"At the time I resented you so much for leaving," I said. "With hindsight, I now realise I resented you because I thought you were coping. I thought you were getting on with your life when I felt so hopeless."

"And I thought you were fine. I couldn't understand how you could just get on with the everyday when I felt so lost."

"In fairness, I never told you how I felt. I buried my pain deep inside and nourished it with whiskey, usually on my own. Until you rescued me."

"I'm only sorry it took me so long to realise what was going on."

"Well, I'm glad that part of our lives is over. It was a horrible time, but we got through it. It was a lesson learned. Talk to each other."

We did eventually confide in each other. We both still grieve for baby John. I can see it in him at times. He carries a photo in his wallet, the same one I carry in my purse. We pay a visit to John's grave on his birthday and anniversary, and at Christmas, we always lay a wreath. But we don't talk about it anymore. Until now. Maybe we should talk about John more often.

"Did Arthur write about baby Arty?" I asked.

Brian picked up his journal and flicked through to the next entry.

Chapter 21

Arthur's Journal

Sandes home, Curragh Camp: 21st February 1924

My firstborn should be turning twenty-four next month. If he had lived. My son, Arthur junior, or as we called him, Arty. He was a puny little thing. Cried constantly from the minute he was born until the minute he died, just one day short of his first birthday. It was a cruel blow.

No parent should have to bury their child. So hard for Edith to cope with. As for me, well, it was as much as I deserved. It's hard to put down on paper how I felt about Arty. How broken I was, how scared I was. My Edith deserved so much better. She tried to keep that child alive and when he died, she fell apart. I should have been there for her. I wasn't.

India, 25th March 1901

My son died. From the day he was born, I had always known that he was not long for this world. He was always sick, cried almost constantly and wore us both down. The only time he settled was in my hands. His frail little body relaxed in my huge, callused farm labourer hands. It was as if he felt safe there, sheltered, sure of his place in the world. My Edith was not sure of hers, and I felt guilt over that. Before she met me, she had a position in society. The daughter of a British colonel, she was courted, fawned upon even.

Now, as the wife of a lowly sergeant, her life has changed irrevocably. No more fancy dresses shipped over from the best shops in England, no more soirees or croquet matches. Although she seemed happy at first. Looking after baby Arty took up her whole day and most of the night, even with her ayah's help. Edith blossomed in my eyes anyway. She was content, full of life and laughter, and our bungalow overflowed with joy. And then baby Arty died. Not even my strong hands could save him, and Edith disintegrated in front of me.

I walked for miles, going over in my head his short time on this earth and trying to figure out how I could have saved him, saved us. Edith had no reason to stay with me now. It was baby Arty who had kept us together. I could see it in her eyes every time I returned home. She looked at me with such hate, such resentment, and I knew she blamed me. Did my son inherit my lowly lineage? Was that what made him so sickly, so unprepared for this world? Was it Torrington blood from my alcoholic father that poisoned his little body and caused him such pain? Or was it something passed on to me by my prostitute mother that I, in turn, passed on through my loins to my beautiful boy? I walked, trying to outpace my demons, but they tortured me. They followed me and told me how useless I was, how badness was in my core, and I had passed those evil characteristics on to my son, that innocent child, and I hated myself.

Henry accompanied me on my walks. He listened to me,

day after day, as I poured out my fears, opened my heart into the humid air, trying to release this physical pain in my chest. I still put on my uniform every morning, still fulfilled my duties, smartly dressed, boots bulled to a shine you could shave in.

When the parades and drills were done, instead of returning to the bungalow I lived in with my wife, we walked for miles and miles as I talked, and he listened. The walks did not help me sort out in my head my grief for my child. Nor did they help me deal with my grief for my marriage, for I was sure that Edith no longer wanted to be with me, and Henry agreed.

Every evening I returned to my bungalow and felt Edith's accusing eyes as she lay on the couch, not moving, not attending to any of her duties, sleeping and crying in the dust and the heat. Her mother was a frequent visitor when I was not there. I knew that. But even she was unable to shake Edith from her grief. Her mother might have guessed that it was all my fault. In fact, I am sure she did. She had never approved of me as a husband for her only daughter, and who could blame her. Look what happened.

I stopped going home for dinner. Henry suggested that we go to the wet canteen for a beer to wash away the dust that invaded our throats while walking, and eventually I agreed. After all, there was nothing to go home for. No smiling Edith, waiting to make me laugh, to fill me with joy. No baby Arty to babble and cry and rock in my arms until he slept. So, every evening the wet canteen beckoned, and Henry and I resumed our friendship.

Every night I stumbled home and crept into the room we had planned for baby Arty, the room he never got to sleep in. Edith's ayah had put a cot in there for me, and there I fell into it in a drunken stupor and went unconscious.

When I woke, hung-over, haggard and at death's door, I dragged myself out of that cot. Edith's ayah handed me tea, and my man pushed me under a makeshift shower and into my uniform. It was the only thing that transformed me. The second the uniform went on my back, my persona changed, and I became Sergeant Torrington, a force to be reckoned with, an excellent soldier, a man of discipline and strength. But most of all, he is a man in control of his own life and the lives of those under him.

So, on that morning, at the start of the monsoon season, when I woke in a strange bed, and there was no ayah with my tea, or shower, or clean uniform, I was forced to look at myself, and I did not like the man that I had become. The hovel I woke in was dark and dirty, and my head hurt as I pried my eyes open to look around me.

My uniform was on the ground, like a cow pat in the midst of the red dust. I shook the worst of the dust out of it. It was crumpled and dirty, but I had no choice but to don it and sneak out, hoping that no one would see me. I was not too far from my bungalow, and I skirted around the perimeter, slipping from cover to cover, praying I would not be seen. Out of nowhere, Henry was at my shoulder.

"What did you get up to last night, Arthur? Was she any good?"

I could not answer him. I felt sick to my stomach. Was that why I had woken in that hovel? My memory was a total blank. I remembered staggering out of the canteen arm in arm with Henry, but nothing more after that.

"What do you mean?"

"She was a looker, all right," and he slipped away.

I could feel my stomach start to heave, and I threw up, right there at the back of the private's bungalows. I slithered to the ground; my jelly legs unable to keep me upright any longer. I groaned as I landed on the muddy red earth, welcoming the blackness that enveloped me. Vague memories plague me to this day of being carried unceremoniously to the medical hut, of hours of slipping in and out of consciousness as they fed me water and fruit and mutton broth.

As I gradually came around, humiliation overwhelmed me. I wanted to sink back inside myself, like a turtle into its shell, and never poke my head out again. My pride in my uniform and my sense of belonging to my unit were tarnished. I felt the men were laughing at me. In my head, I could hear them, Old Arthur Torrington, the drunkard, the low life, and I cringed, curled up in my cot.

Sweat dripped from my body in copious amounts, sweat that told stories of alcohol and sex. I prayed for death to take me, to reconnect me with my son. At least I deserved to die. Not my innocent little boy, my child. And I remembered Eamon's grief, that he carried with him to the day he died, the sorrow for his dead boy and I prayed to Eamon to help me.

"Arthur?"

I struggled to open my eyes. Edith stood in front of me, sorrow and compassion in her eyes. Unable to bear looking at her, I turned away from her to face the wall.

"Go away, Edith."

"Arthur, look at me."

Her voice was insistent, firm, and filled with what sounded like love to me, but it could not be. It was not possible. I knew she no longer cared for me now that our baby was dead. She had turned against me, blamed me. Surely that was true. I told myself that was the truth of it for so long that I was convinced of it. But here she was, with her rich velvet voice that promised love and laughter. I had always loved the tone of her voice. There is nothing frilly or shrill about my

Edith. She is passionate and strong, and I could not understand why she was here.

"I am here to take you home, Arthur. We are a family, you and I, and we will get through this together. I am so sorry I ignored you, so sorry I made you bear your pain alone. But it ends now. We are going home. Together."

Tentatively I turned, glancing at her from under my eyelids, afraid in case this was a dream. I thought that if I opened my eyes, there would only be Henry looking back at me, laughing at my distress, telling me to forget Edith and come drinking with him. The hair of the dog and all that. But it was not Henry, it was Edith, and she smiled at me, and slowly I opened my eyes, and she stayed there, still smiling, but now with her hand outstretched to me. I took her soft white hand, and I kissed it.

It took us a while to get ourselves back to some sort of normality. Edith made me promise that I would quit drinking. I agreed, without reservation, for I would have done anything to keep my Edith happy.

Sandes home, Curragh Camp: 21st February 1924

I remember how angry Henry was. He was not best pleased and did not hold back in letting me know. I can say in all honesty that I was truly sorry about that, but my wife deserved so much better from me. It was the first time I put my wife before my career. The next few years were the happiest I had ever been. Despite the pain of losing Arty, we were happy together. We read, we walked, and we enjoyed the beauty of India. It was idyllic. It's just a pity it didn't last.

Chapter 22

Brian

Tuesday 22nd September 2020

"Grief hasn't changed over the generations, especially after the death of a child," Jean said. There was a catch in her voice, a slight tremor giving a glimpse of the pain still there after all these years. I put my arms around her, and we hugged, silently for several minutes, supporting each other as best we could.

"I thought I would never get over John's death. I blamed myself, blamed you, blamed God. How could God take our baby? Grieving parents have asked that question since the birth of Christ."

Jean moved to put the kettle on, bringing a smile to my face. Her answer to every question was a cup of tea.

"There are no answers, love," I said. "At least now we have some understanding of how these things happen but back then, it must have been terrible for them."

"Part of me hopes they went on to find happiness but from the hints both of them have dropped, that doesn't seem to be the case."

"At least Arthur stopped drinking. Maybe the death of the baby changed him, made him take stock of his life. You never know, it could have been the making of him. He got to the rank of warrant officer. I can't see how he could get promoted to that rank if he was a drinker."

I didn't say another word. Jean knew exactly what I was thinking. She made two mugs of tea and we sat beside each other, Arthur's journal open in front of us.

Chapter 23

Arthur's Journal

Sandes home, Curragh Camp: 21st March 1924

The Sandes Soldiers' Homes saved my life. That first introduction in India couldn't have been better timed. I was still reeling after the death of our baby, not knowing how to deal with my inner turmoil. Edith was stronger than me, still is. She pushed me to stop drinking but it was the Sandes Soldiers' Home that kept me off it.

21st September 1903

At about the same time I stopped drinking, Sergeant Yarrow coaxed me into going to the Sandes Soldiers' Home. The wiry Galwegian spent every evening there. Had done since we shipped to India, but I was reluctant at first.

"The woman in charge reads from the scripture, but she's not preachy like some of them can be. They offer tea and cake and a reading room the likes of which I've never seen before."

Henry was having none of it. He preferred the allure of the wet canteen. Henry relished the relief of a cold pint of beer after the heat of the day. Tea was not on his agenda. The scriptures certainly were not. I was torn. But that night had scared me. Sergeant Yarrow confided in me that he had a similar experience a while ago. It was that experience that had sent him to the Sandes Soldiers' Home. I listened, took note and eventually let him talk me into accompanying him.

The mother in the Sandes Soldiers' Home saved my life. Of that, I have no doubt. On the very first night, I listened to her soft lilting accent reading the scriptures, and I was enthralled. I cannot remember what the reading was about, only her melodic tone and the feeling of peace it brought over me. The number of men who frequented the home every night surprised me.

They were of all ages and from all backgrounds. We listened, drank tea and ate cake, and I learned how to play chess and backgammon. I rediscovered the joy of reading, I was not great at it, but I was not long improving. The house mother, as she was known, gave reading classes. They were not the preachy, you are all stupid, not being able to read, type of classes. No, she invited us into a brave new world, where we could lose ourselves in new adventures without ever leaving the room.

Every evening she opened her book and read a chapter. For the next hour, I read and reread that chapter until I understood every word and every sentence and savoured those sentences that filled me with awe. Every evening a new chapter was read out in her gentle, melodic tone, and I went over it and over it until I heard the writer in my own head.

After dark, I went home to my bungalow and Edith and I sat, side by side, on the veranda while Edith read to me until it was time for bed. She had brought some of her books from her parents' house, and now that she knew I was interested in books, she introduced me to her favourites. I had never told her I struggled with reading, only that I did not want to, and Edith had never pushed me on it. Maybe she had guessed, for she read aloud, never asking me to contribute, not that I wanted to. Sitting in the dark, listening to her voice changing from character to character, is one of my fondest memories of those years in India.

Our lives fell into a familiar pattern. I worked hard, still loved the military life, the discipline, and the knowledge that not only was I in charge, but I was responsible for the training and health of those below me. When I was promoted to colour sergeant, Edith was delighted for me.

Her mother sent a congratulatory note handwritten on her violet tinged notepaper, which pleased Edith even more. Edith's face that day was soft and filled with pride, and I swore I would strive to always make her proud of me.

The promotion brought extra responsibilities, but I relished them, and flourished in my new role. I saw less and less of Henry, but I did not miss him. Nigel Yarrow and I spent most evenings in the Sandes Soldiers' Home, and then I went home to Edith. Life was good.

And then, one evening, Edith told me she was expecting a baby. I could feel the familiar fingers of anxiety clutching my insides, but I hid that from her. She was so happy. Maybe she was hiding her fears from me, I do not know, but she did an excellent job of it.

She knitted and sewed and gently stroked her growing belly and offered me the serenest of smiles. I returned her smile while my insides screeched, worry crunching in my stomach until I could no longer eat. If this baby were to inherit my lineage, what chance would it have of surviving? And if this baby did not survive, then what would that do to my beloved Edith?

I could not voice these thoughts to anyone except for

Henry, of course. He was the only one who understood my dark side, the part of me I kept hidden. But he was not interested. His response was to advise me to down a few pints in the wet canteen. Have a whiskey or two to boost my bravado. I listened, of course, for no one knew me better than Henry, but for the best part of four years, I had not touched a drop, and not only had I not missed it, but I also felt happier. Life was good. But my anxiety grew stronger, and Henry's coaxing slid inside my brain, and I thought sure, one night would not hurt.

Edith was not best pleased when I staggered home that night, long after the Sandes Soldiers' Home was closed, long after the wet canteen had closed. My legs wobbled. Barely able to hold my frame, I tripped on the steps on the veranda, landing flat on my face with a hollow thump that drove my nose sideways, and my hands splayed on either side. Try as I might, I could not get up, so I crawled like a wounded animal into the cot in the back bedroom. It was there I awoke the following day with a furred tongue and my head hammering so much I could not open my eyes.

I could feel her disappointment hanging in the air, beyond the pounding in my head, above the stench of stale whiskey and vomit that inhabited the space around me. Disapproval fluttered in the air, and I sank lower in the cot, anchored by my overwhelming shame. The shutters sprang open, and the noise sent my hands to my head as it threatened to fall off my shoulders and roll under the cot away from the light and condemnation.

"Close the shutters, woman," I managed to croak.

"Close them yourself."

I opened one eye and squinted at the figure of Edith standing over me, arms folded above her full belly, lips set in a stern line. Anger glinted in her eyes, and her face was red and sweating.

"Why, Arthur, why now? The baby is due any day. I need you."

I groaned and turned my back to her. Guilt nibbled at the edges of my consciousness, and I felt lower than a slug in a cabbage patch. I heard Edith leave the room, heard her sigh, felt her pain, and I crouched lower in the cot if that were possible. Her ayah woke me sometime later with a potion she called tea but tasted like poison. I drank it, figuring I deserved whatever was coming to me.

Surprisingly I started to feel better, almost human. I dressed and went in search of Edith. I found her on the veranda, knitting a tiny lemon matinee coat, and my heart bled for her. Falling to my knees in front of her, I begged her forgiveness. I swore I would never touch another drop if only she would forgive me. And forgive me, she did.

———

Sandes home, Curragh Camp: 21st March 1924

My lovely Edith. I made her life so difficult. She was so beautiful, still is, although I can't remember the last time I told her so. These days she barely looks at me. Who could blame her?

Chapter 24

Brian

Tuesday 22nd September 2020

Jean looked at me, a faint smile lingering around the corners of her eyes. Returning her smile, I put down the journal and encased her in a hug. The words I had just read had touched something deep inside me. I was so grateful for the love of my wife. We have been through so much together. Raising a family isn't easy. We had more than our fair share of troubles, but there again, I thought, what was a fair share?

Yes, our first child had died, but at least we had him when countless others struggled with infertility. We have three children, now adults, healthy well-adjusted adults when other families cope with serious disabilities and illness. 2020 had been a tough year. The year of Covid-19, but at least none of our family had died. We were lucky. Our home was a happy one, and that was down to this woman I held in my arms. I laughed as a Don Williams song came on the radio, and I spun Jean around and putting on my best baritone I sang to her.

Jean danced with me, her cheek on my chest, and I kissed the top of her head.

"We're lucky, Jean, me and you. I'm lucky, to have you, I mean."

She cuddled in closer, and we sighed, just treasuring our embrace. We hadn't always been so lucky. After the baby died, Jean had gone into a downward spiral. I thought she was coping well initially, or maybe I was just so caught up in my own grief I didn't see hers. So much so that I volunteered for another Lebanon trip. Jean waved me off and reassured me that she was well. I should have seen that she wasn't.

When Jean was by herself at night after her day's work was over and she closed the front door on the rest of the world, she had trouble sleeping. When we talked about it afterwards, she had told me that it had started innocently enough, with a hot whiskey to help her sleep. But by the time I returned at the end of my six-month tour, Jean was drinking a naggin of whiskey every night and still having trouble sleeping. I didn't notice at first.

There was the initial exhilaration around the homecoming. The getting to know each other, all over again. We behaved like newlyweds, rejoicing in each other, basking in love and affection and downright lust. But towards the end of my second week home, when Jean offered me a hot whiskey for the third night in a row, alarm bells sounded in my head. When Jean finished off her third whiskey and poured another, I began to wonder what was going on with her. She said it was nothing, she was just celebrating my homecoming, and I took her word for it.

I went back to work after my leave period, and life returned to normal. My twenty-four-hour duties kept me away from home several times a month, but it was during a three-month-long Portlaoise prison duty I realised that Jean might have a problem. The prison duty meant spending three days in the prison alternated with three days off duty and at home.

I was midway through the third month and on my second day when I came down with the flu. It was a lousy dose that left me shivering with a temperature and a cough that sounded like I was a chain smoker of at least forty Rothmans a day. The unit commander sent for a replacement, and as soon as he arrived at the prison, I was sent home.

It was four o'clock on a Thursday evening. A dark, blustery evening with winds howling across the Curragh Plains bringing huge biting raindrops like bee stings against exposed skin. The military Land Rover dropped me right to my front door. I dragged myself out of the vehicle and looked around, surprised to see the house in darkness. Jean's factory shifts meant that sometimes our days overlapped, but I knew that Jean had been off that day and wasn't due for another shift until Monday.

The house was silent, and I stood for a second in the hallway, puzzled – no hum from the TV, no radio chatter in the kitchen. I called Jean's name as I opened the door to the front room and switched on the light. The room shuddered into brightness and revealed Jean lying on the couch, asleep, with a blanket covering her. She didn't stir, and I switched off the light and backed out of the room on tiptoe so as not to disturb her.

I went into the kitchen, and there on the counter was a quarter full bottle of Paddy Irish Whiskey, half a lemon cut into wedges and a packet of cloves. We usually brought a bottle of Paddy into the house around Christmas for the cake and hot toddies over the holidays. I was sure that I had seen a half bottle in the back of the cupboard when I was looking for snacks to bring with me on duty earlier that week.

I flipped on the kettle to make myself a hot drink and thought Jean must have caught the same flu as me and had dosed herself with hot toddies. The house felt cold, and I shivered as I stood there in the half-light. I decided to light the fire while I waited on the kettle to boil. I opened the back door to get the coal bucket and knocked over a bag that clinked to the ground. I brought it inside and was puzzled to find an empty whiskey bottle. I went back into the front room and shook Jean, a gentle nudge on her shoulder at first, then my whole hand, shaking her, trying to wake her. She mumbled and turned over, and it dawned on me that she was drunk, not sleeping.

It was the next morning before I broached the subject.

"You look worse than I do," I said as I handed her two paracetamol and a glass of orange juice. She winced as she swallowed the tablets and gulped down the juice without pausing for breath.

"You've given me your flu." She attempted a smile but flinched as the light hit her bloodshot eyes.

"It's not the flu you have, Jean."

Jean crumpled onto a kitchen chair like a discarded rag and started weeping. I filled a glass of water and sat it down in front of her.

"You can't keep this up, love. Whiskey won't solve anything. It'll only make matters worse."

Jean's head whipped up, anger flushing her pale cheeks. "What's wrong with a little nightcap. You pissed off to Lebanon, left me here to fend for myself and now you complain because I take the odd whiskey to help me sleep!"

"Ah, Jean, love. There's more to it than that. You were comatose last night. How many nights have you done that? How often do you drink until you pass out?"

"Don't be ridiculous. I was tired, that's all. Work has been tough lately."

"All the more reason not to take a drink."

"I...I know. I just...I miss my baby."

I put my arms around her and felt her collapse against me like a rag doll, her tears soaking my already-sodden and sweaty top. We stayed that way for over an hour until her tears subsided, and I led her back to bed. We both slept. Jean was emotionally exhausted and me wiped out by the flu. The next day we went to our doctor and asked for help.

It took Jean a few months to get back to herself. She had leaned on the alcohol crutch for so long that it took serious commitment on her part to learn to sleep without it. Learning to live without alcohol brought the realisation that we hadn't dealt with the death of our only child. We both went for counselling, which helped to a point, but that raw grief remained, usually well hidden, only to erupt when I least expected it.

Here, in the kitchen that would only be ours for a few more days, I danced with the woman I loved and gave thanks that we not only found each other but lived for each other.

"I love you, Jean."

"Love you back."

The next morning, after breakfast, I sat at the table with the three journals in front of me. I couldn't pick up Arthur's, couldn't face his grief, his pain, nor Edith's either, for that matter. Henry's journal beckoned, but I hesitated. Did I really want to decipher any more of his evil scrawl? But I had to know.

Jean and I had talked about them the previous night and I had sworn to find out who Henry was and if he had ever been brought to account for his crimes. I had to read on, had to find out what had happened to him. Hopefully, there was some clue as to why his journal was in my attic.

Chapter 25

Henry's Journal

India: September 1902

The first time gave me a taste, a longing. My appetite was sated, but very soon, I craved that feeling again. That power. She had been an accident. This one I would plan. I would take my time with her, make sure I get the value for my shilling, the King's shilling. It is incredible what these women will do for a pittance. I saw her, watched her for weeks.

Chandni she was called, a beauty, a tart. When I say a beauty, I mean a beauty within her caste, for she was the lowest of the low. Every night she sold her body for little or nothing. Her poverty showed in her face, her skin pockmarked and oily, her hair dull with a straw-like texture that felt odd on something so dark. But still, she had something, that elusive aura that oozes sex. You looked at her, and your loins stirred.

Sarge brought me to the brothel, picked her out, an experienced hand he said. On my last payday, I decided it was time to visit her. I wanted to see what all the fuss was about. The lads sang her praises in the wet canteen, so I had to try her out. I did that okay. I had her on her back and on her knees and up against the wall.

The second time I went, I pushed her up against the wall, and I brought my hands up around her neck and started to squeeze. She enjoyed it. How strange these brown creatures are, not like our English women at all. I doubt if even their body parts are the same as what English woman would have sex hour after hour, night after night, even with their husband?

I squeezed harder as my passion rose, the familiar stirring in my groin making me groan in anticipation. Her hands rose to pull mine away from her throat, and I squeezed harder. And there it was, that look of sheer terror, that knowledge reflected in her eyes that mine will be the last she ever sees. That, as I eject life into her, my hands will choke all life out of her.

I watch her spirit leave her eyes, I feel her life leave her worthless body, and I burst with exhilaration. It was better than the first. The anticipation heightened my pleasure, and I am at once exhilarated and spent.

Chapter 26

Brian

Wednesday 23rd September 2020

Once again, Henry's scrawl sickened me. Feeling the need for some fresh air, I strode out into the front hall and bound out the door, inhaling the fresh Curragh air in huge mouthfuls that I hoped would clear those words out of my head. I stood surveying the plains in front of me, oblivious to the men in the transport yard scurrying around getting trucks ready.

Their movement caught my eye. I focused on them, telling myself they were getting ready for an exercise in the glen. I went through the sequence in my head of requisitioning trucks to transport the troops, organising food and tents and appropriate gear. Putting my brain through its paces, thinking about everything and anything to try and clear Henry from my thoughts.

When my stomach had stopped churning and my head felt clearer, I went back inside. The rest of the morning went by in a blur of packing and organising as I banished all thoughts of Henry firmly to the back of my mind.

When I stopped for lunch, I felt like the journals were haunting me. I was still baffled about why those journals were in my attic and remembered my neighbour's advice.

"Ring Area Records," Tom suggested, "they would have a list of who lived in this house from us going back to the handover of the camp from the British. The Torrington's must have lived here then."

I got out my phone and rang Area Records. A mate of mine worked in the office, and he might be able to track down who exactly had lived in the house since the Irish army took over.

"Pat, I found some stuff in the attic that goes back to the last century. By any chance, would you have access to records of who lived in this house over the years?"

"Yea, of course. Those records are digitalised. What number are you in?"

"Thirty-five. Can you email it to me?"

My email binged with a new message twenty minutes later. I pulled up the Excel spreadsheet and read through the entries. The first person listed was Arthur Torrington, wife Edith 1923 to 1924. The other names meant nothing to me, other than my own, last on the list, Brian McElroy 2000 to 2020. Twenty years we had lived in this house, and all that time, that cabinet had been in the corner of the attic, untouched, unnoticed, with these stories locked inside. How did Colour Sergeant Arthur Torrington, Connaught Rangers, end up living in Warrant Officers' married quarters in the Curragh Camp? The Connaught Rangers were a British regiment disbanded in the 1920s, along with all the other regiments raised in Ireland.

I racked my brain. I knew that there had been a mutiny in India. Soldiers in the Connaught Rangers had mutinied in protest over the treatment of their loved ones at home at the hands of the Black and Tans, the force the British cobbled together to fight the rebellion in Ireland. They were shipped back to England in disgrace and disbanded shortly afterwards.

I reckoned it made sense that some of them would have joined the new National Irish Army rather than transfer to another British unit as most of them were Irish born. Arthur was not, though. Edith certainly was not. So why would they have even considered moving to Ireland?

"So, you think Arthur joined the Irish National Army when the Connaught Rangers were disbanded?" Jean said.

"It's the only explanation that makes sense," I said. "Why else would those journals be in the attic of this house."

"No idea, love. It might be an idea to bring the cabinet down from the attic to get a better look at it. There might be a unit insignia on it; something to identify Henry."

"Good idea."

I got back onto Area Records to see if we had retained any British records, but they could not get me any information on who had lived in the house before Arthur and Edith. I had asked if he would do a search for Henry, but without a surname, rank, or unit, he could not find anything concrete, not that I expected him to find anything. Henry could have been anyone stationed in the Curragh at the time.

Desperate to find out more, I picked up his journal and read the next page.

Chapter 27

Henry's Journal

India: September 1903

This one was even better somehow. I cannot decide if it was the thrill of watching her life extinguish in front of me that made it so heart-stoppingly good, or was it coming too close to getting caught that gave it that extra edge, that extra flutter of excruciating excitement.

When Chandni disappeared last year, there had been talk, silly rumours, of her running away with a travelling merchant, started by me of course, and they had fallen for it. I was cautious then, for a little while, but I could not resist. My craving started again, stronger this time, and I found myself watching them, picking out my next victim.

These chattels are not worth much in the general scheme of things. They exist to service the soldier and service them they do. Some are better than others. I was careful not to pick the favourite. No, I noticed Ananya because she was in the background, exactly where I needed her to be. Not as pretty as the others, if you can call that caste pretty, but attractive in her own way. Her nose was too large for her face, her breasts small

*and pointy, but she was quiet and obedient, and I knew I
wanted her.*

*It was easy enough to seduce her. She was so happy to be
called on, to be wanted, that she succumbed easily to my
advances. Of course, I waited until it was quiet and most of
the soldiers had returned to barracks. No one saw me leave my
bungalow, and no one saw me arrive at her window.*

*I had checked it out over many nights. She did not get
customers every night, and on the nights she did, they left early
and often. I did not know until afterwards that she had a child,
never made the connection, the leap from prostitute to mother.
Not that it would have stopped me.*

*I appeared at her window as prearranged, and she let me
in quietly with no fuss. She sat on the bed in front of me
dressed only in a sari and waited for my instructions. I told her
to look at me, and her eyes rose from the floor and stared at me,
her focus somewhere on my chest, her eyes hooded. That
angered me, for she was of no use to me if I could not see into
her eyes. One stride brought me in front of her, and she
trembled as I lifted her chin and stared into her soul.*

*Fear radiated out from her and incensed me, fed my
fantasy, and I ripped her clothing from her and entered her, my
heart pounding in my ears. As I reached my climax, I brought
both hands to her neck and slowly squeezed. She heard the cry
at the same time as I did. A child's voice, calling for its mother.*

*I stopped, just for a second, then squeezed tighter, the idea
that I might be disturbed bringing a heightened sensation. She
struggled, her eyes begging me for mercy until realisation
dawned on her that I was not letting go, that it was the struggle
I wanted. To feel her pathetic attempts to free herself from
under my body, from my hands, to feel her attempts weaken,
then fizzle to nothing as the light dimmed in her eyes and her*

spirit left her earthly body. In that split second, I was invincible, full of joy and triumph, and I cried out in exhilaration.

When I was spent, I withdrew from her and let her body crumple to the ground like a discarded rag doll.

Chapter 28

Brian

Wednesday 23rd September 2020

I snapped the journal shut. This person was sick and twisted. I need to track down Henry. Find out who he was and what happened to him. Where did he die, how did he die, was this miscreant ever caught, did he pay for his crimes? Did his victims get justice for the way he callously used and abused them? There were three victims so far, written about on these pages. How many more women were there?

I pushed the journal away, sickened at the sight of it. There was such evil contained within it. Reading that journal made my skin crawl, me, a hardened soldier, a veteran of years of peacekeeping with the UN. Over the years, I've seen my fair share of violence. Innocent civilians caught up in other people's battles, but I've never witnessed anything like the evil contained in those pages. I had to find out who he was and if someone managed to stop him. All I had to do was figure out how to do that.

The walls of the kitchen felt like they were closing in on me. Pulling on my overcoat, I headed down the west road towards the old Sandes Soldiers' Home building. I needed the fresh air to clear my head of Henry's madness. It felt like he was on my shoulder, colouring my world, and I didn't want that, didn't want his presence anywhere near me. It was a lovely night. The moon hung low and bright, with wisps of clouds hovering but not threatening any rain.

The Sandes Soldiers' Home had been partially demolished some years back. The remaining portion had been converted into a gym. It stood at the end of the road, behind security barriers, still regal, overlooking the plains. It must have been a magnificent building in its day. Jean remembers attending social evenings and the cinema there as a teenager under the watchful eye of Mrs Carson.

As I strolled along the west road, I felt the history of the camp around me. After Irish independence, the barracks were renamed after the seven signatories of the proclamation. Steward Barracks became Connolly Barracks, Beresford became Ceantt Barracks, Ponsonby became Plunkett Barracks and so on.

Even back then the Sandes Soldiers' Home was the one constant. I was surprised it was allowed to remain, but its mission was to provide a home from home for soldiers, a place where they could socialise without the temptation of loose women and alcohol. It survived to provide a service to the entire Curragh Camp for generations. Jean certainly speaks fondly of it.

I turned and headed back down Lord Edward Hill, passing two older privates making their way into Connolly canteen for their weekly game of darts and pints. How times have changed in the camp. Forty years ago, when I joined up, the canteen would be full at this time of the evening, as would every NCOs mess on the camp. Now, only Connolly canteen remains open.

The seven NCOs messes have been condensed into Ceantt on the west side of the camp and the hospital mess on the east. But there again, back then, the Curragh was self-sufficient.

Single soldiers lived in barracks, married soldiers in quarters, entire generations of families lived in the camp, and all their needs were served, from shops to schools to sports. Those homes have been demolished, businesses have moved on, and only a shell remains of what was a vibrant community.

My mood had taken an upward spiral by the time I reached the local Centra on the main road. The blast of hot air caught me as I entered the near-empty shop. I did the lotto, bought some beer, and sauntered back.

By the time I got to the house, Henry had been cleared out of my system, and I wasn't about to go back there. Jean was already home engrossed in reading Edith's journal.

Chapter 29

Edith's Journal

India, 1906

George was a bawling, healthy baby from the second he entered this world. Arthur held him in the crook of his arm and beamed at me.

"He's a bruiser, my love. Look at those fists."

We both smiled as George roared and punched his little fists in the air, and my elation knew no bounds. I had been so worried all through my confinement that this baby would be sickly like my poor Arty. My prayers had been answered when George made his entrance into the world. He took his time, arriving a week later than expected, but with such noise and bravado, all fears were abandoned.

A healthy 8lbs with a head of dark hair, he grabbed both our hearts with his little fists and his demanding cries; we were smitten. I barely became reacquainted with motherhood when I discovered I was pregnant again. Ten months after George, our beautiful daughter Rose made her arrival into our world. Our household was noisy and joyful, and our lives were complete.

Arthur was happier than he had ever been. My Arthur

was a lovely man, but he was also a complex one. He did not talk much about his life before the army. No matter how much I asked, I got monosyllabic answers. I knew he had been brought up in poverty in Manchester. I knew that he went to live with an elderly Irish couple on their allotment after his parents died. He spoke fondly of those years and how they had introduced him to his love of the land.

Then he joined the army. In many ways, the army was his family. Until he met me, of course. Arthur loved me, deeply and passionately, of that, I was sure. It was the manner in which he showed that love that troubled me at times. Arthur found it hard to be intimate or to show affection to the children and me, but he was not alone in that. He was a soldier. My father had never shown me any affection as a child. So why did I expect Arthur to be any different?

But Arthur surprised me in other ways. When George was only three months old, he arrived home one day with a children's storybook. *Aesop's Fables* was beautifully bound and illustrated, and every night my husband read a story to George. It was the most soothing, heart-warming sight to behold. My upright, straight-faced husband, reading these stories in a voice so gentle it took my breath away. It was a habit he tried to continue throughout our children's lives when he was sober. Every time I saw or heard him read from *Aesop's Fables*, it restored my love and my faith in him, for it showed the goodness in him, the need to do better, the joy he felt in fatherhood.

I worked hard to keep my Arthur happy. On his return from the barracks, his chair was waiting for him, in the shade on the veranda, his slippers in front of him and a jug of cool freshly squeezed lemonade on a side table. I paid attention to my appearance, making sure I was always suitably attired, and I kept my figure trim and my smile warm, for I had seen other women who let themselves go after marriage. Some husbands did not notice or did not care, but there were others whose husband's had roving eyes and took on mistresses.

I did not know or care which category Arthur fell into. All I knew was that I loved this man, that I had sacrificed a privileged life for him, and I was going to keep him happy. We were going to show my father and his kind that love conquers class. So, I lavished all my time and attention on Arthur. I knew deep down he had a problem with alcohol, but I also knew that he did not feel the need to drink when he was happy, so I resolved to keep Arthur happy.

My ayah was great. She took charge of the children, allowing me the time I needed. My ayah was an older woman who adored my children, and I could not have managed without her. My mother called to see her grandchildren every Tuesday evening when my father was at his club. I do not know if Father knew she called, she certainly never mentioned him, and I never asked. She brought gifts of fruit and confectionary for the children and me. Every month or so, she brought fabric from England and magazines. Sometimes I wondered if she was trying to entice me back to my single life.

"What is this, Mother? Are you trying to show me what I am missing?"

My mother looked aghast.

"Why would you ask me that? Why do you always assume the worst from me?"

"Sorry. I just...I know you disapprove of my choices. But I am happy with Arthur."

"I can see that, Edith. Whether you choose to believe me or not, it would bring me no pleasure to see you unhappy. As for Arthur, he may not have been my first choice for you, but he is your choice, and he is your husband, for better or worse."

She inhaled and drew herself upright on her chair. "No matter who you married, I would have brought gifts. You always loved the magazines from England, ever since you were a small girl. Why would I stop giving them to you now? And as for the confectionary for the children, isn't that a right of a grandmother?"

I jumped up and knelt before her, taking her hand in mine.

"I am so sorry. I did not mean to upset you. You are right; of course, you have every right, and I am incredibly grateful for everything you do for the children and me."

I felt terrible then and tried to make it up to her. Our relationship had changed completely now that I was a mother myself. I do not know if it was because something in me changed or whether playing with her grandchildren changed something within her, or maybe it was a mixture of the two. Relationships mature and evolve through the years, and myself and my mother were no different.

The only person who did not evolve, could not evolve, into this new dynamic was my father. Stuck in his old ways, he refused to acknowledge my happiness. In his eyes, Arthur was beneath me, and in marrying him, I had belittled myself and embarrassed my family. I suppose I was lucky in that he never tried to stop my mother from seeing us. But he never got to see his grandchildren, and that hurts when I think about it. His loss, mine too, for my children have no memory of their grandfather.

Chapter 30

Jean

Wednesday 23rd September 2020

Jean looked up from Edith's journal. "I know times have changed, Brian, but people haven't."

"What do you mean?"

"Our problems may have evolved but relationships have always been fraught. Edith's relationship with her parents was problematic but realistically she just wanted their love and acceptance. As for Arthur, she loved him and wanted to make him happy."

"Isn't that what we all want? To make each other happy," Brian asked.

"I suppose what I'm saying is, back in those days the men were in charge and the women did what they were told but what was important was that the men treated the women with love and respect. Nowadays we've just divided that burden between them. Both sexes need love and respect and always have done."

"There's been a lot of progress made but there still is a certain amount of inequality between the sexes."

"Maybe with our generation, Brian, but look at our children. They're the future. They demand equal opportunities."

"They don't have to demand equality, they expect it. Can you imagine telling one of our girls that they couldn't do something because they're female?"

"Rather you than me." Jean laughed. "Anyway, I'm glad the world has changed although living here in the Curragh you wouldn't think it. Look out that window and you'd swear there wasn't a woman in the army."

"Yea, it's still very much a man's army but that will change over time. It's hard to recruit anyone, sure who would want to join up these days with conditions the way they are."

"It's hard to see the camp decimated like this. The buildings left to rot by the powers that be. The heart pulled out of it. This place was a thriving community years ago. I don't understand why they tore down the married quarters instead of just maintaining them. Imagine the difference they could make to young soldiers, the incentive it would be to join the army."

"We've been very fortunate, Jean. We've reared our family in the camp, but that way of life is gone now. I agree with you. It's an awful shame."

"Just think. A few more days before we start on our new adventure. We're leaving the Curragh Camp. One hundred and twelve years ago Edith and Arthur were moving in."

Chapter 31

Edith's Journal

Ireland, 1908

I suppose I had always realised it was a possibility that Arthur would be posted to Ireland. However, it still took me by surprise when it happened. The children were three and two and were hardy enough, but I dreaded the sea voyage. Four weeks at sea trying to keep their inquisitive little bodies from falling overboard or falling ill was not something I looked forward to.

My mother was sympathetic. She remembered her childhood years in England and had no wish to return. Part of me was hoping that my mother would suggest that I stay in India. After all, I had lived nowhere else. I may call myself an English woman, but I had never set foot on her shores. But my place was with my husband, so I packed up our belongings, and we travelled by train to Bombay to set sail for Ireland. The children cried when we left my ayah behind. Truth be told, I cried a little myself. She had been a constant in my life for all of my twenty-eight years, and I was aware that I may never see her again.

Mother looked bereft as she waved goodbye from her

carriage. She had brought gifts, clothes for the children and me, trinkets to keep the children amused on the voyage and a bottle of brandy for Arthur. She thrust an envelope into my travel bag with a finger to her lips to silence the question I was about to ask.

After she left, I opened it and rocked back on my hunkers in amazement at the roll of notes inside. I quickly hid them in my bag before Arthur saw them. I do not know what surprised me more, the envelope of money or the farewell gift for my husband. Once again, my mother had managed to surprise me, and I felt an ache at the thought of leaving her. I knew I would miss her weekly visits and her English idiosyncrasies, and I wished I could bring her with us.

Despite the heartache of leaving everything I had ever known behind me, I was looking forward to our new beginning. Arthur was assigned to the barracks in the newly built Curragh Camp, and we were told that the married quarters were excellent.

"Are you excited, Arthur?" I asked as our train trundled across the Indian subcontinent, leaving a trail of red dust behind us.

"I suppose I am. I have never been to Ireland either, so it will be new to both of us, although I suppose it can't be that different from England."

"Tell me about it."

"Nothing to tell. It is different from India. Cold for a start. You will never again feel the heat like you are accustomed to in India. But it is green and pleasant. I might even try my hand at growing vegetables again." And he grinned at me.

In that irrepressible grin, I saw my Arthur in a different light. The peasant farmer shone through the edges of the uptight soldier, and I looked forward to seeing more of him.

Ireland, of course, was vastly different for both of us. When we docked in Dublin, the soldiers were separated from their families. My children and I were brought by rail to Newbridge Station, where a horse and cart waited on us with our trunks and brought us the short distance to the Curragh Camp.

Stepping off that cart in the dark in the Curragh was an experience. There was a breeze coming off the plains that seemed to cut through me, sending shivers of ice down my spine. I huddled my children to me, wrapping them in a huge blanket my mother had given me for our journey.

We were led to a large hall where they served platters of bread slathered in thick creamy butter and hot sweet tea. The children ate their fill, their sense of adventure restored as they looked around them at the eclectic bunch of families assembled, all like ourselves, tired from their journey but curious about this new life foisted upon us.

The sound of marching drew our attention to the rear of the hall as the first platoon of soldiers joined us. They were soon dismissed, and suddenly Arthur was by my side, scooping up the children and tickling them into laughter. Arthur's new commanding officer called for silence and made a speech welcoming us to the Curragh Camp.

Shortly afterwards, we were assigned our new home. Our quarters had two bedrooms upstairs furnished with beds and wardrobes and two rooms downstairs. The front room had a fireplace and a couch and overlooked the plains, while at the back, the kitchen had a range for cooking, a scrubbed oak table and two chairs. The backyard held the outhouse and room for expansion.

Married quarters in the Curragh Camp were good. Our terrace of red-brick houses faced south, looking out over the majesty of the plains. Eight houses on one terrace, every two sharing an archway into an outer hall, each front door side by side. Barrack Road was behind us, connecting the row of barracks and their parade grounds towards the prison at the far end of the camp. The children's school was close by, just a short walk downhill, while the market was a few hundred yards to the east.

We settled in quickly despite the cold. Luckily, my mother had forewarned me about the weather and had clothes commissioned for myself and the children before leaving India. Still, nothing prepared me for the dampness which seemed to seep into my skin. I felt permanently cold for the first few months, and I harboured a cough that worsened as the winter progressed.

The children were under my feet all day without my ayah to help me, and I struggled. Arthur's hours of work changed as well. In India, the military trained from dawn until ten am, before the heat became unbearable and were free then for most of the day. In Ireland, Arthur was gone all day, and I missed his company in the long afternoons. Of course, we no longer had a veranda or any inclination to sit outside while the winds howled across the plains and up the hill to our front door.

It was daunting. The first shock to my system was when I saw women hanging clothes out to dry on lines ranged across the back of the houses. In all my years, I had never done my own laundry. In India, the natives had always provided those services to the men and to their wives and families. It had never occurred to me that I would be required to scrub my clothes and those of my family.

My mother had not thought to forewarn me, for she had been brought up in a household with servants who attended to those domestic duties. I am quite sure it never occurred to her that I would be landed with such a menial task. I had been taught needlework, not the practical sewing in buttons and mending socks type, but the decorative style, which was no practical use to me in the Curragh Camp. To say I was shocked was an understatement.

Then there was the range in the kitchen. I had never learned to cook, and my first attempts were laughable. How Arthur and my children survived on my burnt offerings those first few months, I will never know. I was blessed with my neighbour, Betty. She never once laughed at me or teased me about my lack of domestic skills. Older than I, she had seven children; the youngest two were the same age as my own, and she took me in hand, like a project she needed to complete. Betty taught me how to cook and clean, how to keep linens white and delicate items fresh. She was a godsend, and to this day, I thank the Lord for sending her to me, for I would never have survived without her.

"You're coming on, Edith. That stew smells great."

"Thanks to you, Betty. My poor children would have starved if you hadn't taken pity on me."

We were remaking one of my tea dresses from India into a dress for Rose. Thankfully, I had become proficient with a needle. My years of fancy needlework in India were abandoned in favour of more practical skills. Rose was nearly three and growing like a wildflower. I wanted to have her summer dresses ready before the new baby came along. A satisfying kick in my ribcage told me that the next addition to the Torrington family was going to be active.

"Steady there, little one; you'll be out kicking a ball with your brother soon enough."

Betty laughed, her eyes closing to slits in her ruddy face. Seven children had taken their toll on her, and her rotund body shape was a testament to her excellent baking skills. One of her fruit scones was in front of me, smothered in creamy butter and home-made preserves. I licked my lips in anticipation as Betty set the cup of strong tea on the table beside it.

It was early afternoon. Our morning chores were completed. The men had been sent back to work with stew in their bellies and an afternoon of soldiering ahead of them. It was time for our break before starting the evening meal made from leftovers from the midday dinner and my favourite part of the day.

Betty was fascinated by my stories from India. She had lived all her life in the Curragh. First as a young girl on the outskirts of the camp, the daughter of a sheep farmer, and later when she married, as a soldier's wife. I, in turn, loved her stories of Celtic mythology and of the flora and fauna that surrounded us. My children's favourite was the story of St Brigid and her cloak.

Betty told them how Brigid had met the King of Leinster and asked him for land to build her convent. He refused, but when she asked him for only as much land as her cloak would cover, he was amused and agreed to her request. Brigid then instructed four of her helpers to take a corner of the cloak and walk in four opposite directions. The cloak spread and grew with them, encompassing the area that became the Curragh Plains.

I liked the idea of Brigid and her magic cloak, for I had come to love the Curragh; it is rugged terrain, the flat green grass that disappeared into the horizon, the ever-present fresh breeze that clears the mind and soothes the soul.

"Your Arthur has a great pair of hands," Betty said as she admired the new table Arthur had made to sit beside my fireside chair.

"Arthur has to be doing something, Betty. His next project is a doll's house for Rose for Christmas. I picked up some lovely patches of fabric at the market to make doll clothes and furniture."

"How sweet. Rose will love it."

We had a small backyard where Arthur built his shed. When he was not in the Sandes Soldiers' Home, he was in his shed, making something or other to improve our lives. Arthur seemed happy in the Curragh. We all were. He spent his spare time in the Sandes home, and that was fine by me. At least when he was there, I knew he was safe. They drank tea, played billiards, prayed some, but at least they did not drink alcohol. Arthur has not had a drink since that time in India, and I thank God and Ms Elsie Sandes every day for that. It was a bit far outside the camp, just a few miles away down at Lumville, but Arthur says he enjoys walking across the plains.

It is our anniversary tomorrow. Eleven years we are married. Imagine that. Arthur will not forget. He is good like that. People do not see that side of him, that soft side to his nature. Every year he makes me a card and gives me flowers. Each time I dried and pressed one of the flowers and folded one inside the corresponding card to store in my memory box. It's kept underneath our bed, along with our marriage certificate, the children's birth certificates and the little blond clip of Arty's hair. Betty says that James never remembers their anniversary and does not remember her birthdays or their children's birthdays. I am glad my Arthur is not like that.

Chapter 32

Brian

Wednesday 23rd September 2020

It's our anniversary tomorrow. Thirty-eight years married. Bloody hell. Where did those years go? I'm good with anniversaries and birthdays, better than Jean sometimes. I always get her flowers although we don't usually buy each other presents. There was no point. When the kids were young, and money was tight, we thought it was a waste, buying gifts for each other of stuff we didn't need. We buy presents for each other for Christmas of course. But for our anniversary we usually treat ourselves to a nice meal out. Maybe we'll do something special for our fortieth.

Of course, I missed a few anniversaries overseas with the army. A couple of birthdays too. I always picked something up in the mingi shops. Even though Jean and the kids didn't get the presents until I got home, at least in my mind, I had bought them on their birthdays. I had never heard the word mingi until I served overseas. It's a name the Irish put on the myriad of pop-up shops that sprang up in our Irish area of operations selling everything from tape recorders to jewellery to perfumes. Most of them knock-offs.

There was a year I bought Jean a gold necklace and bracelet, one she still keeps for good wear. It was expensive even by mingi shop standards. I bought it the day after that stand-off. That was the day I thought I would never see Jean again, the day I thought to myself, how is Jean going to cope with this? Losing baby John and now me.

Our day had started like any other day in Lebanon. The hills of South Lebanon can be bitterly cold, and that day at Al Yatun was no exception. It was that stillness just after daybreak but before the world wakes, when we were alerted by gunfire. Hezbollah guerrillas attacked a Christian militia position loyal to Israel in a little village called Rshaf. They pounded it with rockets and heavy artillery, and all we could do was watch the destruction.

When we got the order from UNIFIL Headquarters to go to Hariss village and prevent Hezbollah from retreating through the Irish area of operations, we were relieved to be doing something. I do not think I can describe how frustrating it is to be a soldier on the edge of battle, waiting to be called upon. That nervous tension that eats away at your insides, the adrenalin that keeps you on your toes but also keeps you alive.

We sped down to Hariss and set up our checkpoint. Two APCs with gunners, one signal operator, one officer in charge who knew what he was doing, or so I thought at the time, and the rest of us. Our orders were clear. Let no one through. No exceptions.

By that stage, the locals were going about their daily business of bringing their children to school in Tibnine. Of course, we had the road blocked and were letting no one through, so a tailback wound its way down the hill just as the Hezbollah guerrillas finished their rampage and were racing towards us, conscious of the fact that the Israelis were probably tracking their whereabouts and knowing they had to get out of the area and quickly. A shouting match ensued between the

Irish officer and the guerrilla leader. He threatened to blow us up if we did not let them pass, to kill each and every one of us.

Our sergeant put us in defensive positions as the angry confrontation continued. The sound of a heavy diesel engine approaching practically drowned out the shouting as a huge dust-encrusted truck arrived with an anti-aircraft gun on the back. It levered itself into position, its barrel pointing at our APCs.

We cocked our weapons. They cocked theirs, challenging us. The locals scattered, abandoning cars, and dragging crying children behind them. You could taste the tension in the air, like thick syrup, as we eyeballed each other, each conscious that all it would take was one mistake, one quick movement or slip of the foot to rattle one of us into firing one shot, and we would all die. We could hear the muffled tones of the radio operator relaying the ongoing incident to UNIFIL Headquarters in the background.

The officer in charge resolutely told the guerrilla leader that they could not pass. The guerrilla leader puffed his chest out and strutted right up to him, his eyes never leaving the officer's face. He was waving his pistol in front of him like it was a flag at a football match, and I wondered if the cigarette he held between his teeth had something more substantial than tobacco in it.

I remember saying goodbye, in my head, to Jean, and I knew I was not alone. Every Irish soldier there was doing the same, but we stood our ground. They were a great bunch of lads, brave men, who kept cool heads in a situation none of us had ever been in before.

We were put in situations like that time and time again. That one stuck in my head because it was the first for me. The whole experience made me thankful for my lot in life and led me to buy Jean that gold necklace for her birthday.

Maybe this year I should buy her something special for our anniversary. I will book the restaurant, can't beat a good meal out, but perhaps I'll buy something from Newbridge Silverware for the new house. An anniversary present for us both. It is our last anniversary in this house, in this life, when I think of it, for the minute we close this door behind us for the last time, our lives will change irrevocably.

The trip into Newbridge took longer than I thought. I decided against cutlery. Jean would kill me if I added to the two sets we already had, tucked away in bubble wrap, ready for the move. I remembered she had admired the white crockery, the last time we were in the showroom, and had mentioned how she might get some for the dresser in the new kitchen, so I bought the lot.

My car boot was loaded down with boxes, and I carried them delicately into the house and placed them on the coffee table in the front room, along with a large bouquet of fresh flowers. I felt like I was adding colour to a black and white photograph – the flowers in direct contrast to the empty shelves and bare mantelpiece.

In the kitchen, I clicked on the kettle and made myself a strong coffee. The journals sat on the table, calling me, and I made myself comfortable before opening Arthur's journal once again.

Chapter 33

Arthur's Journal

Sandes home, Curragh Camp: 7th April 1924

It's odd to be writing about the last time I served in the Curragh Camp. It was a different world then. Before the war to end all wars. The war that ended the Connaught Rangers. But that's for later. First, I need to write about what happened, and what drove me back into the chains of the demon drink.

––––––––––

Ireland, September 1909

I heard the shot. Everyone did. The sound echoed across the parade ground. For what could only have been seconds we all froze. I swung to my right and took off at a run in the direction of the men's quarters. Private O'Hara was backing out of the door on the top floor and was halted by the railings that ran along the veranda's length. His face was chalk-white, his hands to his mouth as if trying to suppress a scream. I pushed past him, entered the billet, and slid to a halt on the

149

polished linoleum. Sulphur hung in the air, and the coppery scent of fresh blood hit me, making my eyes water.

Private Boland was lying on his back, on top of his bunk, third from the door, on the right side of the room. A revolver lay beside him, shiny steel on the grey wool blanket. His lifeless eyes stared straight at me as the pool of blood under his head expanded second by second – dark red eating up the white sheets.

I did not need to look further to know that the back of his head was missing, blown out by the force of the bullet he had fired through his mouth with the muzzle pointed upwards towards his brain.

This was my second suicide victim to find in a week. The acrid air made me cough, and I turned back to the open doorway for air. The veranda was shaking as the men thundered up the stairs towards me. They had been on their way to the dry canteen for their meal when they heard the shot. I was seconds closer, and my stomach turned as I blocked the doorway.

"Halt." My rank gave my voice an authority I did not feel at that moment.

Private O'Hara was throwing up over the railings, and the men were fidgeting where they stopped, their movements making the steel veranda tremble, and I hoped that it masked my trembling limbs. I cleared my throat.

"Private Boland has had an accident with a revolver."

A low murmur answered my explanation.

"Ryan, get the medic. O'Shea, McCann, stand sentry at the door, no one gets in until the medic gets here. Cantwell, get the military police."

Ryan did not have far to go. Walsh 65, the medic, was already on the way, his bag in his meaty hands. Like the others, he had been on his way into the dry canteen when he heard the shot but ran for his bag before making his way to the billets. He saluted me at the top of the stairs, and I led him in, closing the door behind me.

We both knew there was nothing he could do for Boland, and he confirmed it with one look.

"What's going on, Sarge? That's the second one this week."

Walsh 65 was a burly Mayo man, solid as they come, broad shoulders and a fondness for the *poitín* from his home county. But he was an excellent medic, one of the best. He stood in front of young Boland's body, shaking his head, his forehead crinkled in thought.

"What makes young men like that think they have nothing to live for. No wars to fight, no family to provide for. I could maybe understand if he had been in the Boer War, Christ, we'd all seen some sights in that godforsaken place that curdles the blood when you think of them, but he's too young for that."

I could not answer him. There *was* no answer. Boland was a quiet lad, barely eighteen, reared in the west, the youngest of a large family with no money and no prospects. He had been lured to the Connaught Rangers with the promise of earning the King's shilling while seeing the world. All he had seen was Tipperary and the Curragh.

The image of Boland burned into my brain, and I could not shake it. That night, as I read my children their bedtime story, Boland's face swam in front of my vision. When I went downstairs, I had to have a whiskey to banish the image. One finger of whiskey led to another, and I could see the reproach in Edith's eyes, but I did not care.

As I emptied the last of the bottle into my glass, Edith left the room, disapproval mixed with despair in the set of her shoulders and in the brittle tone of her goodnight. I slammed the door behind me on my way to the wet canteen. The next thing I remember was waking up in my office, draped over my desk, an empty whiskey bottle in my hand and a thirst on me I had not felt since India.

It was still dark, that quiet time just before daybreak, and my head was hammering. I was puzzled at first, my hand reaching out for the warmth and scent of Edith. The absence set me upright, looking around me, trying to figure out where I was. I could not remember how I got there, and I stared baffled at the empty bottle I was still clasping.

Horrified, I jumped to my feet only to collapse back into the chair with the weight of the pain in my head and behind my eyes. I managed to drag myself home, keeping close to the barrack walls, only venturing into the open when I had no other choice. Edith had left the door unlocked, and I crept in, stripped out of my stained and dishevelled uniform and drank coppery water straight from the tap.

I could feel Edith's presence behind me, sense her disapproval before she even opened her mouth.

"Arthur, look at the state of you."

"Shut it, woman. Can't a man even have a drink in peace?"

"A drink maybe, but look at you? Look at the state of your uniform. Your eyes are bloodshot, your hands are shaking so much you can't even hold a glass."

I did not mean to knock her down. Not intentionally. She was just in my way as I pushed past to go upstairs. But I kept on my unsteady path, ignored her cry of pain as her head banged off the wall, my brain still deadened from the alcohol. I did not hear the children rise, did not hear the normal sounds of breakfast emanating from the kitchen. I lay in my alcohol-induced fog on top of the bed, dressed only in my long johns.

When I eventually woke, it was mid-morning, and I had missed morning reveille. I cursed Edith then for letting me lie, and she ignored me. She worked around the kitchen as if I did not exist, as if this man standing yelling at her was in a different room, in a different house, in a different life.

A red fog descended on me, and I lifted the teapot from its stand on the kitchen table and flung it at the wall. It smashed into a hundred pieces and left the remnants of cold tea running down the kitchen wall and Edith cowering against the range.

I was trembling, but I did not know whether it was from the alcohol or the rage that threatened to engulf me. My mouth opened as if on its own accord and the roar that emerged came from my core. Edith sank to the floor, her hands over her ears as I continued to roar incoherently. No words, no recognisable syllables. Just pain and frustration and anger rolled into one and vocalised, like a wounded animal.

It was Edith's gentle touch that stopped my roaring. I felt her warmth, her compassion, as she wrapped her arms around me and held me, all the while making soothing, musical sounds like she did with our children when they were babies. My red-hot anguish gradually extinguished as if wrapped under soothing folds of cotton that dampened my pain and left me whimpering. I do not remember much more about that day. The anguish stayed with me, but it was tempered by Edith's love. It should have been enough. Enough to keep me away from temptation. She tried, pleaded with me to stay with her, to ignore the lure of the wet canteen and its whiskey, but Henry's pleas were stronger.

Maria McDonald

Sandes home, Curragh Camp: 7th April 1924

The pain of that day still hurts me. How did I abandon my Edith like that? She loved me then, wholly, with reckless abandon. I failed her then, just as I am failing her now. Why did I listen to Henry?

Chapter 34

Arthur's Journal

Sandes home, Curragh Camp: 21st April 1924

Before I left Edith tonight, I tried to talk to her about my journals. I tried to explain it the way Mrs Magill explained it to me, but I think I failed. Either my Edith didn't understand what I was trying to say, or she no longer cares. I don't know which.

Ireland, October 1909

That was it. My years of abstinence ended. We fell into a routine after that day. I fulfilled my duties as colour sergeant; no one could ever take that away from me. My military career was never affected by my drinking. At least, to my mind, it was not. I was first in the barracks every morning, clean-shaven, uniform pressed, boots bulled, a credit to my unit.

At dinner time, I went back to married quarters and ate with my family. My wife put food on the table at twelve forty-five, and by one thirty, I was ready to return to the barracks for the afternoon schedule. Henry was ready for me at four thirty, and we adjourned to the wet canteen. Like most military families, teatime was at six pm, but I did not always make it home in time. Whiskey and beer lubricated the tongue, and conversations continued well past teatime and into the night.

Sometimes I did not remember how I got home. Only that I woke early each morning, my brain thick like cotton wool and my stomach churning, and my first thought was never again. But when four thirty rolled around later that day, all memory of my waking statement was forgotten as Henry escorted me to the canteen and called for a pint and a whiskey chaser.

I loved the camaraderie of the wet canteen. There were great stories told there, by men propped up against the polished mahogany bar, elbows on the counter and their jackets stored over the backs of chairs. It was a large room with double doors to gain entry, like the entrance to the grand old houses of the wealthy. Vaulted ceilings and ornate plaster added to the illusion of grandeur. The wrought-iron fireplace housed a turf fire that glowed day and night, fed at regular intervals by the man on duty from a stockpile under canvas, positioned near the building's back door. Upstairs were the quarters for the single NCOs and spare beds for those who imbibed too much whiskey or fell asleep at the bar.

At that bar, stories were told, tales of battles and bravery, the likes of which we had never seen. Corporal Drake Jones, a Boer War veteran, sat on a tall stool, his back to the wall, an old clay pipe in the side of his mouth billowing out the sweet vanilla essence of pipe tobacco, while he told stories of intrigue and bravery in South Africa. When he told us the tale of the defeat at the Battle of Isandlwana, we cursed the Zulus and their savagery. He was in Rorkes Drift the following day for that battle, and his voice shook as he told of the bravery of the men he served with. Stories were told of foreign lands, their food, their people. The sun never sets on the British Empire, and between us, we had served in most parts of it. Between us, we had some stories to tell.

It was late September, I think, that night with Henry, after the All-Ireland Rifle meeting. It was a glorious day, no breeze, bright but not too hot, as we stood on the ranges. The steam bogie trundled out on its single track to bring out the targets; the officer class stood under their tents, sipping cold drinks and clapping after each burst of rifle fire. I was well placed but did not win. That honour fell to a corporal from Tipperary. Upright fellow, he was too. Smart, sharp eyes, nerves of steel. A teetotaller, I would wager. The field kitchen served curry, and we wolfed it down, hungry after hours in the fresh air.

When the presentation of prizes ended, we adjourned to the mess, thirsty and elated after a successful day. It was a great time to be a British soldier in Ireland. The Curragh Camp was a shining light, the best camp in the country, in the empire for that matter. Life was good.

Or so I kept telling myself, every night, as I stood at the bar telling war stories. But during my sober moments, a tiny voice niggled inside my head, "If life is so good, Arthur, why are you drinking yourself into oblivion instead of being at home with your wife and children? If life is so good, Arthur, why did Boland take his own life, why did any of them?" For there had been several suicides amongst soldiers.

But that night, none of those thoughts intruded. My only thought was beer with whiskey chasers and tall tales. Henry and I had an audience, and we played to them and sang with them until the early hours. Or at least that is what Henry told me, for I have no memory of that night.

I woke the next morning, naked and sprawled across a

cast iron bunk in the single men's quarters. Fear clutched my chest as I struggled to open my eyes. It took a few minutes to register where I was. I dragged myself upright and swung my feet onto the polished linoleum floor. My uniform lay in a crumpled heap beside the bed. My body was incapable of normal movement. The act of reaching down to pick up my trousers sent shock waves through my skull.

I collapsed onto the floor, my stomach heaving as the room appeared to spin out of control. How long I lay there, I have no idea. Or how I got out of that room and home to my own bed. No recollection whatsoever. Henry filled in the blanks for me. Well, Henry, and the sight of Edith.

I did not remember hitting her or pushing her around. When I woke out of my stupor, the sight of her bruised face frightened me. The sharpness of her tongue frightened me more.

"Look, Arthur, look at me." Her voice was ice cold as she removed her dress and showed me the imprint of my huge shovel handprints on the delicate white skin on her upper arms. She stepped closer as she dressed and leaned over me. "Look at my face. You did this to me."

I was aghast. Edith's right eye was swollen and was starting to turn purple. Horror filled me at the thought that I had turned into my father. Edith was livid, and who could blame her.

"You may be my husband, but I will not allow you to treat me like something you scraped off your shoe. The drinking stops now."

She walked out of the room, and I was left alone with my guilt and my shame. I could not even answer her. How could I? The fact that I did not remember hitting her was not a defence. She deserved so much more. Despite everything, I loved Edith, and I knew, with utmost certainty, that I needed her. Edith was my one constant, well, Edith and the army, but Edith brought out the best in me, and now I was driving her away. I swore to myself, there and then, that I would never touch a drop of alcohol again.

Henry was having none of it. He pleaded and cajoled me at the end of every day, but I stood firm, even on days when my tongue was hanging out for a pint. I could not risk losing Edith. Eventually, Henry got tired of niggling in my ear and went about his business. Yarrow took me under his wing and accompanied me to the Sandes Soldiers' Home. For the first time in two years, I was sober, and I intended to stay that way.

Sandes home, Curragh Camp: 21st April 1924

How many times over the years did I promise Edith that I would stay sober? I am deeply ashamed of the way I treated my wife when I was drinking. I grew up with the images of my da slapping my ma around the place. The day he killed her is seared into my brain. I swore I would never stoop that low. Yet all it took was hard liquor for me to copy the ways of a man I detested. I cannot begin to describe the loathing I hold towards myself.

Chapter 35

Brian

Wednesday 23rd September 2020

There was a spate of suicides in the Curragh a few years ago. We never got to figure out the reason why. I suppose for soldiers, access to weapons is a significant factor. Why any man would want to put a bullet in his brain is beyond me, but there again, I have my Jean to keep my head straight.

There was one young private I had in my platoon, the life and soul of the party he was, always smiling and quick with a smart-aleck comment. His death shook us all. It affected me for a long time. I just couldn't get my head around it. I thought he had an incredibly positive attitude to life. He was only nineteen, a pup, really, and we had no idea of the mental anguish he was in.

At that time, I was a corporal, and Vincent Roche was a young three-star private. The whole platoon had all drawn their weapons from the stores before going on the ranges. All soldiers are allocated their own rifles, and it is their responsibility to keep them maintained. In those days, they had to sign them out of the weapons store along with their allocation of ammunition. After use, it must be cleaned and handed back over and signed back in.

We marched in formation down to the ranges. It was a grand day, overcast but dry and bright, perfect for shooting. All went well, and everyone was in high spirits as we lined up to march back to the barracks. He stopped, said he had a stone in his boot, so we marched on and left him to sort it and follow us. None of us suspected there was anything wrong. He was his usual self.

We arrived at the weapons store, and the platoon lined up in single file to start the sign-in process. I looked back along the road, but there was no sign of Private Roche. Then we heard the shot. It was faint but unmistakable. Over the years, I have heard people say that a car backfiring can sound the same as a gunshot, but to experienced soldiers, there is no comparison.

My sergeant that day was Jim Quirke. He looked at me and shook his head; we both knew straight away. We ran back along the road we had marched just minutes earlier. Sergeant Quirke got there first. Vincent Roche was lying behind the butts, his head a bloody mess. It was too late to do anything for him. Jim took off his combat jacket and covered his body as best he could while I stopped the rest of the platoon from getting any closer.

It was a terrible time for the whole unit. Professional soldiers have a different attitude to death than the general public. They are trained in the use of weapons, trained to keep the peace in volatile situations. Most of the men there that day had served overseas. They had all been in positions where they faced danger, and they had all come back home to tell the story.

Every platoon has a bond that is difficult to explain to civilians. They train together, sleep together, play together, and form a unit of mutual respect. Every single member of that platoon, privates and NCOs alike felt guilt over his death. Shame that we didn't know how desperate he had felt – that we didn't foresee it in some way, that we couldn't help him, that we couldn't stop him.

We paid particular attention to that platoon for a long time, afraid of a copycat suicide, but they all pulled through eventually. There were a few that drowned their sorrows in the canteen and others who took out their frustrations in the gym. As for me, I was lucky. I had my Jean and still have her. She has been my anchor. I understand how Arthur feels about Edith. It's a relief to read that he stopped drinking. Maybe Arthur and Edith can get on with their lives, provided Henry leaves them alone.

It's as if his journal is calling me as I turn to the next page.

Chapter 36

Henry's Journal

Curragh Camp: 21st September 1911

 I stare at my outstretched hands, palms up. Steady as a rock. Not an iota of a tremble. I bring them up to my mouth and nose and I inhale. They reek of her. The aroma of Pears soap and the innocence of youth mixed with the coppery tang of blood. So much blood. The crimson mess lay in front of me, wide open, entrails exposed to the weather. I had no choice. I had to cut her open to release her spirit like the Zulus did. I have no use for her soul, and I do not want it coming back to haunt me. Now she is free, her spirit soaring into the universe.

 I had forgotten how good it felt, nearly overcome by that surge of power that soared through my veins when I saw the fear in her face. The orgasmic release as my hands tightened around her neck and the light slowly extinguished in those chocolate eyes. I am still panting but I want to holler and scream out my joy. But I cannot. Not yet anyway. I need to get rid of the body. I can relive it over and over in my head. I can treasure the memory of that moment when she knew it was over. When she felt my power: when she felt the life being choked out of her. She was the best yet.

Chapter 37

Brian

Wednesday 23rd September 2020

I shut the journal, horrified, my head pounding. The hall door was open, and I spotted my laptop bag tucked neatly under the hall table. I set it up on the kitchen table and paused, fingers poised over the keypad as I tried to figure out what to search for. Google opened, and I tapped in "murder & Curragh Camp". I clicked through the articles. There were plenty of stories relating to the Curragh Camp, but none could be connected to the journal that lay discarded on the table in front of me.

I tried a different search, "murder + 1911 + Curragh" and felt a flicker of excitement as the first article popped up. The heading was "Former soldier sentenced to life" but when I clicked through to the article, I realised it was connected to a murder in 1979 and couldn't possibly be related to Henry's journal.

For the next two hours, I flicked through Google until my eyes felt scratchy and started to water. As I stretched my arms above my head, my aching muscles were grateful for the release. I glanced at the window, surprised to see how dark it had become outside and suddenly aware of how much time I had wasted on a wild goose chase.

I was about to pack it in when a highlighted tag jumped out at me: "Unsolved murder baffles military police". I clicked, and the article flashed up on the screen, a newspaper report from the *Leinster Leader*. The article was short on detail and heavy on speculation. It was all about the discovery of the mutilated body of a young girl in the Curragh, naming her as Gráinne Delmer from Brownstown.

The writer was critical of the military police and their failure to catch the culprit. There was a lot of speculation that the suspect may have been a serving British soldier. It even went as far as quoting a source who confirmed that the suspect was a serving member of a British regiment that had since relocated. There was nothing to throw any light on what I had read in the green journal.

I glanced at the clock again. Jean would be in soon from work, and I was no further ahead in packing up my military memorabilia collection. Grabbing some bubble wrap and a sturdy box, I went into the front room and opened the cupboard to the side of the fireplace. I had only finished wrapping two brass artillery shells when I heard the front door open and Jean call out. I abandoned my packing and went into the hall.

"I have to show you this, Jean." I led her into the kitchen and handed her the dark green journal, opened at the entry for September 1911.

As Jean read the journal, I busied myself making tea while partially watching her. I saw the initial shock turn to revulsion on her face before she snapped the journal shut.

"What on earth?"

"It's awful, isn't it? Reading it freaked me out. I googled it and found an article about the murder. They never found who did it. Did you ever hear anything about it?"

"No. I don't think so. I'll ask my mother tomorrow. We're meeting for lunch. Maybe she'll remember hearing something about it, even though it's way before her time as well."

I knew she was right but couldn't help but think that such a vile murder would have been talked about for years afterwards, and maybe, just maybe, her mother would have heard something about it.

"I hope so. It sounds crazy, but I'm hooked. I have to find out who Henry is and why his journal was here, in our attic, in Arthur and Edith's attic."

"The thought of that journal, up in the attic all these years, makes my skin crawl. We have to find out who these people were, Brian. Do you think the local history group could help? Reggie Darling might know something. His family barbershop has been here since British times."

"I could do with a trim and a hot shave," I said.

"You need to get that done before your stand-down parade. The perfect excuse to chat to Reggie. For now, pass me Edith's journal. She knows something. We just have to find out what."

Chapter 38

Edith's Journal

21st September 1911

It was teeming that day. The day I first saw Gráinne Delmer. The rain came down in sheets across the grassy plains, making it impossible to see further than a few yards in front of me. The sound of the heavy drops pounding off the hard grass drowned out all other sounds as the sky turned a purple shade of black. There was no sign of her. No sign of anyone. The last of the stallholders had packed up and taken cover. You would not put a dog out in that.

It had started dry enough, a greyish morning with a sky full of dark menace as I left the children at the school gate and sauntered towards the market, musing over my life. The children were doing well in school. The teacher was strict, fond of homework and the strap, but the children did not complain.

Life in Ireland was good for us, until Arthur started drinking again. I prayed he would return to the Sandes Soldiers' Home, dropping hints when he was sober. I thought we had settled in well enough, considering how different life was on the Curragh Camp. Every day I missed the heat of

India, the way of life; I still call myself an army brat. My father served in India, and that was where I was born and spent my formative years. That was where I presumed I would spend my life until I met Arthur. Meeting Arthur transformed everything.

It was love at first sight. At least for me, but I know he felt the same as I did. When Arthur asked my father for my hand in marriage, I was thrilled. This handsome young soldier swept me off my feet, and when his regiment was sent back to Ireland, I followed him. We ended up living in Ireland, eight years and three children later, and sometimes I wished that we were back in India. But my life was with my husband.

This was where we lived because that was where Arthur's career brought us, and the idea of him brings a smile to my face. Colour Sergeant Arthur Torrington. He looked so smart in that uniform, and I remember thinking that I would move to the end of the earth for that man.

The market was busy that morning. Women rushing to get supplies before the dark clouds opened, the promise of heavy rain spitting at us. Imogen, my toddler, took off on me as I was chatting to the stall-holder. Her hand slipped out from mine, and she clutched my skirt as she always did. I was so caught up talking about knitting patterns that I did not notice her release her grip. She toddled off following a bright red ball of wool that had blown off the stall in a gust of wind. The same flurry that made me grab my bonnet and laugh with the stall-holder as she laid her ample bosom over her stand to protect her wares.

I was unsure how long Imogen was missing, only that I glanced down to the rear of my skirts where she usually stood. Imogen was gone. Laughter froze in my throat. I called her name but nothing, only the low hum of conversation and haggling. I called again and heard the panic in my voice.

People turned to look at me; offers of help and murmuring rippled around the market square.

I called her name again and again as I sped along at a frantic pace. Other women joined me, hailing her as they searched under stalls and behind carts while clutching the hands of their little ones. I went back to the wool stall and looked behind it to the trees and the short grasses of the plains beyond. Then I saw her toddling out of the trees. Her blonde curls were bobbing up and down as she babbled incoherently to the young girl holding her hand. She was striking. Raven-haired and dark-skinned, she had an exotic look about her, all wrapped in a scarlet shawl.

As they reached me the girl gave me a radiant smile that stretched to her rich dark eyes.

"She was chasing this." She handed me a ball of red wool.

"She said it was for her Daddy's army coat."

I swept Imogen up in my arms and buried my face in her curls, breathing in her scent. A split second later, I slapped her hard for toddling off and frightening me that way. She howled, and everyone laughed amidst comments of, "All's well that ends well" and "poor little mite", "poor mother, you mean, wandering off like that and frightening her poor mother".

Without further ado, the heavens opened, and the rain bounced off the road. Everyone scattered, and the girl who had brought Imogen back to me was gone. I did not get a chance to thank her. I lifted Imogen onto my hip, lifted my basket in the other hand and with my shawl over my head, scurried up the hill to the house. I stood in the hallway, looking down the hill back towards the market, but there was no sign of her, no sign of anyone. I did not find out her name until the next day.

Chapter 39

Edith's Journal

22nd September 1911

That day I met the children after school. We strode out the west road, up the hill and past the prison, until we came to the spot on the plains that Betty had told us about. Betty said that the mushrooms should be abundant after the heavy rain. And she was right. They were everywhere. I showed the children which mushrooms to pick and which ones to avoid.

You must be careful with mushrooms. Pick the wrong one, and it could kill you or drive you mad. Betty had offered to check them for me before I cooked them anyway. She was born and reared in the Curragh and knew all the best places to find mushrooms and berries.

The wind blowing in off the plains was cold that day and whipped colour into the children's cheeks. George was six and tried to boss it over his sisters. Rose, aged five, thought she was George's equal and competed against him in everything. They tore around, racing to find more mushrooms than the other while Imogen toddled along behind, dropping more than she gathered.

We sang rhyming songs as we picked, songs from my childhood, and we had so much fun. I was so engrossed in their laughter that I stumbled back over what I thought was a tree branch downed by the wind.

I let out a shriek, and my children stopped abruptly, then laughed to see their mother upended with her basket of mushrooms scattered around her. They scampered to my rescue, each grabbing an outstretched hand and hoisting me to my feet. They gathered up my mushrooms into their bags and scrambled away again in search of more.

My skirt was muddied from the fall, and I swore inwardly, for it was only clean on me that day. The area I had wandered into was muddy, parts of it freshly disturbed and all of it strewn with brambles and sticks. I looked closer to see if the berries were ripened yet, but they still had some weeks to go.

A sigh escaped me as my mouth watered at the prospect of the jams I hoped to make. Then I spotted it caught on the brambles. A piece of red cloth, muddied, soaking wet, and shredded from the thorns.

The ground beneath my feet was uneven, and parts of it had been washed away by the rains. I looked around for the children, but they were some hundred yards away and intent on their mushroom picking. I looked closer. There was a shape, an outline of some sort, where the soil had washed away. My heart clenched as a trickle of sweat wound down my back.

I lifted a sturdy twig and dug at the clay around the outline. My heart leapt as if it would jump right out of my chest as the soil moved, revealing a girl's soft white hand. I dropped the twig, my hands to my mouth, and turned and fled, calling my children behind me. By the time we got to the prison, I had started to collect my thoughts, and I stopped running and gathered my children to me. Bending over slightly, I held George by the shoulders. I looked directly into his eyes, so he was left with no doubt that I needed his full attention.

"George, you're a big boy now. I am putting you in charge. I want you to bring your sisters home, now, as quick as you can. Go into Betty and stay there until I get back."

George nodded to me, his big blue eyes solemn and suddenly older than his years. For once, Rose did not argue. She hugged me, took Imogen by the hand, and followed George on the road home. As soon as they were out of sight, I shouted at the prison guards, and they came running from their sentry posts. I told them what I had found, and the younger soldier went back inside to fetch his sergeant.

They asked me to show them, and within minutes we were returning to the spot with shovels and a sense of dread. I watched as they carefully dug out the body of a young girl. They dug around the outside contour and then swept back the muck from over her body, gently as if she were made of glass.

She was lying on her back, her hands by her side and her shawl draped over her body as if she had been tucked up in bed. I recoiled in horror when they pulled back her shawl to reveal her disembowelled body, and I do not think that sight will ever leave me. I started to shake and could barely speak.

There were seasoned soldiers gawking down into the shallow grave, the horror on their faces mirroring my own. The sergeant in charge looked younger than I, and his pallor had turned a strange greenish shade of white. Around me, I could feel the retching of others and then I heard an anguished shout as one young soldier recognised her.

"Gráinne." He turned puce and ran some yards away before he collapsed to his knees and started to vomit. His comrades ran to his aid, rubbing his back as the whispered news filtered through the crowd.

"Gráinne Delmer."

"Mick's younger sister."

"She's a local."

I felt the crowd part behind me, and then Arthur was there, holding my hand, supporting me, telling me that he would take it from there. I felt the burden of finding that young girl's body shift from me onto my husband. I felt him take the mantle upon himself. He took my hand, and he led me home, and when I woke in the middle of the night, shaking and distraught, he took me in his arms and held me until I slept.

I think I must have dreamed about that poor girl, for I woke with a scream and a vision of her body lying in the cold, damp clay. I wanted to gather her up into my arms and carry her to my hearth, but someone was standing in my way. I struggled, and I woke. Arthur was holding me, stroking my hair, whispering to me in his soothing quiet way that everything would be okay, that everything was okay. I relaxed back into his arms and fell asleep again with the security blanket of his bulk curled around me.

When I woke again, Arthur was up and getting dressed in his uniform. The room was still in darkness, and I could hear the wind rattling the windows. Arthur sat down on the bed beside me and stroked my head.

"The fire is lit; take a few more minutes. The children are still asleep."

He only had the words out of his mouth when we heard Imogen shout and a giggle from Rose. My day had started in

173

earnest. Arthur smiled and left me to dress. I listened to his heavy footsteps on the wooden staircase as he carried Imogen down to the warmth of the kitchen. Then the patter of Rose and George as they followed, chattering and laughing.

Arthur had cleaned out the ashes and rekindled the smouldering embers so that the kitchen would be warm for us. He did that every morning. I counted my blessings once again as I went downstairs to start the porridge.

The rain had stopped by the time Arthur left to walk the short distance to Beresford Barracks. I got the children organised and stood in the outer hallway with them to fasten their coats and pull on the woollen hats I had knitted for them the week before.

A noise behind me startled me, and I felt my heart skip a beat before I realised it was Betty's front door, and Susie and Lilly came running out to greet my two. I sighed with relief and scolded myself for being so jumpy. All four went whooping down the hill, racing to see who could get to the school gates first. Susie and Lilly were twins, a year older than Rose, and they were all great friends.

"I couldn't stop thinking about that poor girl," Betty said as we retired to my kitchen for a cup of tea. It was a habit we got into that term – a cup of tea and a chat before we started our daily chores.

"Do you know her family?"

"Yes, I do. Sure, they are from just out the road. Lovely family. Her brothers are in the army, her father was too, although he has been dead this long time. Boer War, as far as I can remember. God bless her poor mother."

I reached over and patted Betty's hand. It was hard to see her so upset. It was hard to *be* so upset. My nerve endings felt like they were jingling all over, and fear gripped me.

"Someone did this to her. Someone local. On Tuesday, I saw her at the market, holding Imogen by the hand, laughing, smiling, and so pretty. Only a day later, I saw her laid out in a shallow grave, her insides cut open and exposed for the world to see. How could someone do that to her, to anyone?"

Betty took my hand, tears sliding down her ample cheeks as we tried to comfort each other. We sat like that while our tea went cold, but our chores were waiting. So, an hour later, we pulled ourselves together, donned our coats and hats and made our way to the army butchers for Friday was the day we collected married rations.

The savings were too good to be missed. It meant I could afford treats for my family that others could not. Every week, I put away a few pennies so that I knew I could treat my children to the little luxuries when Christmas came. Their faces when they opened their stockings to find oranges, chocolate and a shiny new penny were a sight to behold.

The army butchers killed their own meat and hung it, so it was always good quality. Even the cheapest cuts were superior to the meat on offer in the civilian butchers in town. We rarely ventured into Newbridge. Everything we needed was provided in the camp. It was completely self-sufficient. It also had a larger population than Newbridge, but the majority were single men, soldiers of the empire. Once again, my thoughts turned to poor Gráinne Delmer and who could have done that to her.

Every evening, before bedtime, when he was sober, Arthur would read a story to the children. He had started the routine when George was a baby, and all three children hung on his every word, even though they knew every single story by heart. Arthur's copy of *Aesop's Fables* was well-thumbed and frayed around the edges, but the children sat entranced.

That evening, Imogen sat on Arthur's knee while George and Rose took up their places on each arm of the chair. I remember watching them, silhouetted in front of the fire, and trying to find the joy that image usually brought to my soul. But finding that girl's body had disrupted something inside me, and I knew my life would never be the same again.

Chapter 40

Jean

Wednesday 23rd September 2020

I was stunned. Edith's journal lay open in front of me. Her flowery handwriting was slightly erratic as if the memory of finding that body rattled her so much, that she couldn't hold her pen properly. I looked at Brian.

"Edith found the body."

"The one Henry wrote about?"

"Gráinne Delmer. It has to be the same girl."

We both stared at the three journals on the table. In one, Henry confesses to the murder. In another, Edith finds the body of the murder victim. Questions buzzed around my head. Why were these journals in a locked cabinet in my attic? Who was Henry? Was he in the same unit as Arthur? Did a Connaught Ranger murder Gráinne Delmer in the Curragh in 1911? What happened to them all after that?

"We need to keep reading," Brian said, "it's the only way to get the full story."

I nodded. Brian was right. Hopefully, contained in those pages, there was information that would give us Henry's true identity.

"Do you think he paid for his crimes? Henry, I mean."

"I hope so. His victims deserve justice. His attitude to women was appalling; no wonder there was no mention of a Mrs Henry or any women other than those he murdered."

"What about Arthur?"

"Arthur seemed to be a complex character, but I think he may have been a good man, trying his best. He had a problem with alcohol, which Henry seemed to exploit. But he had Edith to pull him away from Henry's evil influence. Well, Edith and the Sandes homes."

"Finding that body must have been so traumatic for Edith. I hope Arthur gave her the support she needed."

Brian moved beside me, opened Arthur's journal and we both read the next entry.

Chapter 41

Arthur's Journal

Sandes home, Curragh Camp: 7th May 1924

Despite the change in jurisdiction, the Curragh Camp remains the same. It is only a short walk to the barracks, one of the great advantages of living in the camp. It is well built and laid out in a logical manner. At that time, I was stationed in Beresford, one of five barracks on the west wing of the camp. In each barracks, red-brick buildings surrounded a parade ground. Accommodation for single soldiers was within each square; long narrow billets with polished linoleum floors and steel-framed beds and lockers. Each barrack has its own mess and meeting rooms for the men and NCOs.

On the other side of Barrack Road lay the family accommodation for non-commissioned officers, the ball alleys, the swimming baths, the gymnasium and of course, the reading rooms. Every religion and none had a place for soldiers to call home, away from the billets, and more importantly, away from the dangers of drink and the allure of loose women. The Sandes Soldiers' Home was my home from home. Why did I let Henry persuade me otherwise?

Curragh Camp, September 1911

I took off when I got the message that my wife had found a body. Private Jones barely had the words out of his mouth before I sprinted off the parade ground with him chasing my tail. He panted out the details as we ran from Beresford Barracks, my inspection of B Company forgotten.

I sprinted down Barrack Road, past Stewart and Ponsonby Barracks. Soldiers stopped to stare, wondering what would cause the normally sedate Colour Sergeant Torrington to run as if the Zulus were in hot pursuit. We sprinted past the prison and onto the plains and skidded to a halt at the edge of a large gathering. I parted the crowd like Moses parting the Red Sea as I made my way to my wife.

Edith collapsed into my arms. I held her head to my chest as I seethed with anger at the sight in front of me. That young girl, her mutilated body exposed to the elements and in full view of my wife and every soldier present.

"Cover her up immediately."

I did not need to shout. My tone was enough, and Sergeant Nolan took off his overcoat and covered the body. The crowd dispersed as the military police arrived. I led my wife away after giving our details to the officer in charge.

When we got home, the children were in the outer hall with our neighbour. Betty took one look at Edith's pale shocked face and ushered the children into her house under the care of her eldest daughter. Betty followed me into our quarters and made hot sweet tea for us all. She sat and listened as Edith cried and told her what she had found while I paced up and down the room.

My wife was traumatised by what she had seen. Women should not have to witness something like that. The damage to the body was too much. It is not something that has been seen since South Africa. I remember the horror stories told in the wet canteen. Stories of recovering our soldiers' bodies after the battle of Isandlwana, every single one slashed open, their entrails hanging out in the African sun. What savage could do that to a girl, a child even, and my stomach twisted as I watched my wife's horrified expression.

"...shock. The children."

I realised Betty was talking to me, and I shook myself.

"Thank you, Betty; we appreciate your help."

Edith sat red-eyed and exhausted. I noticed that her hair was tinged with grey, and I wondered when that had happened. I took her in my arms and promised her that everything would be fine.

"Arthur. That poor girl. It was her; do you remember I told you about the girl who found Imogen? It was her. She could not be more than fifteen. Her poor mother."

"Hush now, love. Do not fret. Our lot will be back any minute now."

Edith pulled away from me, reminded of her family duties. Betty had already stoked the fire, so Edith busied herself preparing the tea from the leftovers from the midday meal. The children arrived back, subdued but hungry. They ran straight to their mother at the stove and handed over their bags of mushrooms.

"Betty sorted through them, Ma. She said these are good for eating."

Edith hugged them each in turn, and I felt the warmth of her embrace. I counted myself as a lucky man to have Edith in my life and to have our children. George was a plucky little fellow. He was inquisitive and outgoing, and I could see a future for him in the military.

Rose was every bit as plucky as her brother. I reckoned

she would need a firm hand to keep her on the straight and narrow while Imogen was too young yet to show any character traits. Imogen simply emulated her older siblings and basked in the affection that everyone lavished on her. I smiled down at her as she climbed up on my knee and cuddled into me. She felt like a hot water bottle glued to my chest – a little parcel of love who needed nothing from me other than a cuddle. I relaxed for the first time that day as the warmth from her tiny body spread through mine and into my heart.

I felt Edith watching me, and when she smiled over at me, my awkwardness returned. I removed Imogen from her position like a limpet clinging onto a rock. Ignoring her whimper at being disturbed from her warm resting place, I set her sitting upright on the linoleum floor, cleared my throat and excused myself.

"I'll get out of the uniform before we have our tea."

I could not fathom the expression on Edith's face. She looked sad, disappointed even. I do not know why. She knows I must take off my uniform, to remove the mantle of military life and to slip into my husband and father role. It was something I looked forward to most evenings. When I removed that uniform, I removed Colour Sergeant Torrington. I could become Arthur Torrington, husband and father, and I treasured those evenings. I could play with our children, hug my wife, and become a real person.

When I came back downstairs, the children were seated around the table, and Edith was waiting to serve their tea. Great steaming bowls of soup with chunks of carrots and onions, fresh from my allotment. The earthy aroma filled the house, and I smiled at Edith. She had learned a lot since we came to Ireland. Betty was a great neighbour and an amazing cook. She had taught Edith how to feed her family on small money and an abundance of ingenuity.

Edith returned my smile, and once again, I said thanks for my blessings. Edith was a good mother and a great wife. I took my place at the head of the table on one of the two kitchen chairs. The children sat on a bench I had fashioned out of old lengths of wood discarded by the war department when they had renovated the barracks. I had spent weeks sanding them and rubbing them down with oil and sweat until they shone.

Every day I looked at that bench with the satisfaction of a job well done. I could hear Eamon's lilting voice telling me that the devil makes work for idle hands; that was always Eamon's motto and one he tried to instil in me.

Edith was waiting on me to say grace before meals, something I had never done before I married her. It certainly was not something my father had ever taught me. All I had learnt from my father's knee was how to run away from a beating. I looked around my table; my "amen" echoed in little voices before they tucked into their food. Edith was feeding Imogen from her bowl, blowing the soup to cool it to suit Imogen's toddler mouth. The room was silent save for the tick of the clock on the mantel and the clatter of spoons against dishes.

George and Rose devoured their food, ravenous after an afternoon of fresh air and exercise out on the plains. They were quieter than usual, throwing anxious looks at their mother in between slurps from their bowls. What happened today was most distressing for Edith and the children. Nothing like this had happened in the Curragh before. Not that I was aware of anyway, and I swore to get to the bottom of it in the morning.

Sandes home, Curragh Camp: 7th May 1924

Writing about the events of that day is so strange. Everything about that day felt off kilter. I don't know what expectations I had of how a mother should behave. All I knew was that Edith was behaving strangely. Her duty was to look after her husband and children first, above anything else. There again she had stumbled upon the body of a young girl. Of course, she was upset. My duty was to protect my family. In that I had failed that day. My wife had been exposed to an horrific sight that no woman should encounter. I have no doubt that image has stayed with my Edith, haunts her still. What would I know? She doesn't confide in me anymore.

Chapter 42

Arthur's Journal

Sandes home, Curragh Camp: 21st May 1924

Summer has arrived. It's easier to stay out of the messes in the long bright evenings. I still struggle. Edith thinks it's so simple to stay away from alcohol. It's not. It is a constant battle even with the help of the mother in the Sandes home. Henry doesn't help. He whispers in my ear every so often, trying to tempt me back. There are times I feel as if I am being ripped from limb to limb, torn between my wife and my friend. Each day is a new battle. Edith is winning the war. For now, anyway.

Ireland, September 1911

I was familiar with the Sandes Soldiers' Homes. They had saved me from myself years ago. Here in the Curragh, the newly built Sandes home was due to open, and it was a credit to Ms Elsie Sandes. The old building was outside the camp at Lumville, a bit of a stroll but hardly far for a soldier who spent his days marching.

The new building had a cinema, meeting rooms, and a huge reading room, quite superior to the one I had attended in England and overseas. Every evening after the children went to bed and Edith was busy with her mending, I made my way to the Sandes Soldiers' Home. It was my favourite place, but I was looking forward to the new one's added attractions.

My orderly jumped to attention as I came into his line of vision, and I could not suppress the swell in my chest, the satisfaction that small action gave me. He had respect for me, respect for my rank, respect for Arthur Torrington. I had come a long way. He held the door open for me to enter and offered a smart salute.

My desk was clean and tidy, the way I had left it, but I knew that would not last long. I placed my baton in the rack in the corner, along with my topcoat and gloves. My sergeant arrived with arms full of paperwork, waiting for my signature, and I gestured to him to place them on the empty desk. After instructing him to leave the door slightly ajar, I started the work in front of me.

I immersed myself in my work, hoping that it would take my mind off Edith. She had a terrible shock to see the body of a young girl murdered like that. It came as quite a shock to me when I saw the state of the body. An image I had not been able to shake out of my head since. The low murmur of voices in the outer office carried through the open door. The men were discussing the murder. It was bound to be the main topic of conversation throughout the camp.

"It has to be someone who was over there. Sure, where else would you see a body cut like that?"

"But that was the Zulus. We don't desecrate bodies like that; it was the savages."

"So, you think there are Zulus hiding in the furze bushes on the Curragh Plains."

"No, that's not what I'm saying. What I mean is that the killer must be a soldier, someone who was posted to South Africa. Someone who saw what the Zulus did to our men over there and copied that...that...I don't know what you would call it."

"Savagery, that's what it is, pure savagery."

I cleared my throat, and they jumped to attention. The men had not noticed me standing in the doorway listening to their conversation.

"That's enough speculation. Leave the investigation to the military police. It's their job to get to the bottom of it. Get on with your work."

They dispersed, their salutes sharp, their heels clicking on the polished linoleum and once again, I felt pride in myself. I only had to speak once, and they obeyed. They respected the uniform, they respected me, and that felt good. I was happy with the team I had built around me. They were focused, career soldiers, men who cared about their regiment, respected the flag and everything it stood for.

I returned to my paperwork with added purpose. Once I got that out finalised, I intended to contact the military police myself and offer to help in their investigation in any way I could.

As it turned out, I did not have to contact them. In the early afternoon, the military police arrived at my office. My orderly intercepted them and knocked on my door to announce their presence. I called them in and shook hands with Captain Peterson and Captain Allen. They were both well-experienced officers but both were as shocked as we all were at the violence perpetrated on that young girl's body.

Captain Allen read from his black notebook. His broad

Kildare brogue somehow softened the air around us as if we were discussing the price of a pint and not the murder of an innocent young girl.

"I believe your wife found the body, sir."

"That is correct. Mrs Torrington is distraught. A woman should not see such horrors."

"True, sir, very true. We will need to speak to Mrs Torrington again this evening if possible?"

"Certainly, Captain. If you would call after eight, the children would be in bed. It is not a topic I want to be discussed within earshot of them."

I had intended to spend the evening in the new Sandes Soldiers' Home, but duty called. My wife and children needed me. My poor Edith was distraught. As her husband, it was my duty to protect her, to look after her. I did not doubt that speaking to the military police about finding the body would upset her again, and I would do whatever I could to lessen that pain.

That evening there was a knock on the door at precisely eight o'clock, and I was gratified that the military police were so prompt. My poor wife had enough to contend with, and I did not want her stressed waiting to speak to the investigators. I signalled to Edith to let them in and stood to greet them.

"Can I get you some tea, gentlemen?"

Captain Peterson and Captain Allen accepted graciously. Edith busied herself mashing the tea and setting out the best cups and saucers. I saw the two officers exchange a look as Edith's hand shook, rattling the cup in the saucer as she handed it over to them. Edith was very nervous and upset and had to make several attempts to get her teacup to her lips without spilling it.

Captain Allen took out his notebook and cleared his throat as if to signal that the time for niceties had passed.

They needed to get down to the real business behind their visit. Edith broke into tears as she described her horror at finding that poor girl's body. While I understood her tears, it was quite embarrassing for her to lose her self-control in front of the military police.

"Really, gentlemen, does my wife have to relive everything again? This is quite upsetting for her. No woman should see a body like that."

"No, Arthur, it's fine. I need to do whatever I can to help these gentlemen find whoever did this to that poor girl. It was quite horrific...and...and she was such a pretty thing."

I tutted my disapproval, but I allowed Edith to continue. Maybe it would ease her mind to tell these men what she had seen. Perhaps it will help her deal with what happened. I certainly do not understand the workings of a woman's mind. Edith talked while Peterson and Allen took notes, and thirty minutes later, there was no more to be said. I escorted the military policemen to the front door, giving my wife some time to freshen up.

"Well, gentlemen, I believe my wife has told you everything she knows. I hope you find the animal that committed this murder, sooner rather than later. The women in the camp are scared, and rightly so."

Peterson and Allen appeared to take what I had said on board. I walked them to the door and watched as they turned the corner on that damp evening. A misty rain glistened on the grass under mutinous grey skies, and I felt a chill blowing up from the plains.

Returning to the kitchen, I opened the press and felt around for the bottle of whiskey that Edith kept for medicinal purposes. Pouring us both two fingers of the golden liquid into the glasses her mother had given us as wedding presents, I brought one over to Edith. We sat staring into the flames of the fire, sipping our drinks and trying to put the past few days behind us.

Sandes home, Curragh Camp: 21st May 1924

As far as I can remember, I had a drink with my wife on three occasions. The first was a glass of champagne on our wedding day. The next was at a Christmas Eve dinner in her father's house. But that night, the night after she found that young girl's body, that was the last night we shared a drink together. Edith wasn't a drinker. There again, I drank enough for both of us and the rest of my unit as well.

Chapter 43

Brian

Thursday 24th September 2020

I closed Arthur's journal. It was late and we had processed enough. Jean agreed. Two cups of cocoa later we headed to bed. Jean fell asleep as soon as her head hit the pillow. I envied her that. Normally I was the one who fell asleep quickly but woke often. Years of duties and military exercises meant I could nap practically anywhere but after reading those journals, sleep eluded me.

I couldn't quite shake the image out of my head of that poor girl, Gráinne Delmer. My dreams that night were haunted by my former comrade Luke's blood mingling with the blood of young women.

When I eventually woke, the bed was empty beside me. The sound of activity in the kitchen carried up the stairs. By the time I made my way downstairs, Jean had breakfast ready.

"You didn't sleep too well last night, did you?"

"No, no, bloody awful nightmares."

"It's those damned journals. Maybe we should just quit reading them."

"I can't, Jean." I shook my head. "See this?" I lifted the flowery journal. "Edith Torrington. She lived here, in this house, and the bit we read last night was all about her finding a young girl's body."

Jean nodded.

"And this one; Sergeant Arthur Torrington, Edith's husband. A Connaught Ranger. He stood in this very kitchen over a hundred years ago. He wrote about the murder as well."

"It has to be the same murder as in Henry's journal."

"I think so. The details are the same. So, in this journal, we have Henry confessing to a murder. In this one," I pointed to Edith's journal, "we have Edith finding the body, and in this one," I lifted Arthur's journal, "Arthur tells us about his wife finding the body and the talk around the camp about the murder."

I placed all three journals on the table and sat down heavily. Jean put a mug of coffee in front of me and sat beside me.

"I rang my mother this morning, couldn't wait until lunch to find out if she knew anything. She remembers her mother talking about it. The family lived out near Maddenstown; her father worked with the horses. The golden years, that's what they called that time on the Curragh. Sure, it was the best barracks in the empire. The Boer War was over, and there was no sign of the carnage that would eventually become the First World War."

"What did she tell you about the murder?"

"Not a lot. It was never solved. She knew that much. That girl's body was found out past the prison. It was the talk of the camp. Terrible sight. She had been cut open in the same way that the Zulus did to the bodies of the British during the Boer War. They reckoned it had to have been a soldier, but no one was ever caught."

Jean blessed herself. "God rest her soul. Mam said that her family never got over it. They lived just down the road from the grandparents, supposed to have been lovely people. Gráinne was the youngest, and her poor mother was never right after that. The son was in the Hussar's, based here in the Curragh. He was killed in the war, somewhere in France. There was another son, but he left for America. They said the mother died of a broken heart after he went. Sure, they're all dead and buried now."

"Were there any other murders, do you know?" I asked watching Jean stir two large spoons of sugar into her mug of coffee.

"Mam said there was a girl murdered around the time of the civil war, but let's face it, there was a lot of death and destruction going on at that time."

Jean took a sip from her coffee and added more sugar.

"Do you think it could have been a serving soldier who murdered her?" I asked.

"Looks like it. The killer was never caught, but back then, there was something like six thousand men stationed in the Curragh. There were battalions from all over the empire; sure, it was the main training ground for the British. Mark my words though, if he murdered a girl in the Curragh, there must have been others. What he did to that poor girl was sadistic. She wasn't his first. I'd lay money on it."

"There *were* others, Jean."

I looked at the journals sitting in the middle of the table in front of us and felt the burden of the secrets they contained. My hand shook as I picked out the dark green cover and handed it to Jean.

"Should we give these to the military police?" Jean asked, flicking through the pages.

I said nothing. Sitting there, I watched Jean's expression change from jovial to horror. She looked up at me, her mouth open, a question on her lips that she couldn't seem to ask.

She put the journal on the table and backed away from it,

staring as if expecting Henry to jump out from its pages and grab her throat.

"There's pure evil in those pages. Who the fuck is Henry?"

"That's what we need to find out. There are confessions in here to four murders. All young women, one in Egypt, two in India and Gráinne Delmer here in the Curragh."

What Jean had to say got me thinking, and I swore to get to the bottom of it and solve the mystery of who murdered Gráinne Delmer. My internet searches had yielded few results, so I knew I had to finish reading the journals, even Henry's. Hopefully, one of them would have the answers.

I picked up Henry's journal, opened it at the next page and started reading.

Chapter 44

Henry's Journal

Curragh Camp: 22nd September 1911

That was a lazy salute, but I will let it go, for today anyway. Normally I would eat the face of a private that gave a salute like that but I am in a good mood today. Sated, content. I can still smell her. It is like she is in my blood, like the garlic and herbs they use in India that seeps out through your skin and invades the air around you.

I inhale. Great breaths of sharp damp air that summon up images of shiny black parade grounds and lush grasses that shimmy in the breeze. I close my eyes and I can see her. I can see that light in her eyes slowly flicker and extinguish. I open my eyes and exhale. It is good to be alive.

The troops are waiting on the parade ground, the daily roll call and inspection due to start in two minutes. I can taste the anticipation, the fear of being called out over boots not polished to my satisfaction or berets too low on the forehead. The clip of my heels on the tarmacadam surface echoes around the parade ground.

I pace down each row, my eyes darting from one soldier to the next, examining their boots, their belts, their buttons, their stance. It is imperative that each soldier's appearance should be exemplary. I will not tolerate shoddy appearance in any of my men. I flick my finger at the chin of Private Smith.

"Lose your razor, Smith?" I bark and he trembles, and I smirk.

I enjoy pulling them up on minor details. Seeing the fear in their eyes, the shake in their chin. Of course, not all of them show their fear. Some of them stare back at me but they can never hold my stare. Never. I am in charge. I need to show them I am in charge. And that is what I do. I rule with an iron fist. I have earned my rank.

My office door is held open as I approach, exactly as I had instructed. I place my baton in the rack in the corner along with my topcoat and gloves and dismiss the orderly with my usual instruction to close the door behind him. I have paperwork to get through today. This army needs discipline. I shout to my orderly for the training records. My responsibility may be for only a tiny corner of the British Empire, but I will ensure that my men will not be found wanting. They will be the best trained, the most prepared, the jewel in the crown.

My thoughts are interrupted by the men gossiping in the outer office.

"Lovely girl she was too. Her brother Mick is in Ponsonby Barracks, grand chap."

"It had to be someone in the camp."

"Jesus, don't say that. How could anyone do that to a poor innocent girl."

"Silence." I step into the outer office. "You're like a bunch of old women, standing there gossiping. You have your orders, now get on with it."

The men stand with their mouths gaping at me. "But..."

"I said now." The shout silences all objectors and I step back into my office and slam the door behind me. I can hear *the murmurs of dissent, but I do not care. This is the army, for God's sake, not some mothers' meeting.*

Curragh, October 1911

I did not do so well in the shooting competition. There is a shake in my hands I cannot control. Either that or the target was moving for I could not seem to hit it. I blamed competition nerves, but Arthur said it was the porter. He can talk. He was not much better and the two of us were the best shots in the unit not so long ago. It was disappointing but the night in the mess more than made up for it. Arthur was in rare form, telling yarns to beat the band. It has been great having the old Arthur back. That Sandes home had him under their thumb for long enough. Or rather, the Sandes home and that wife of his.

We have had some great times in the mess, me and Arthur, like long lost brothers we are. I understand him, you see, not like that wife of his. No, she tries to tell him what to do. Do not drink, Arthur. Stay home with me, Arthur. Ha! Women do not understand. Us men need the company of men. What harm is there in a few bevies with the lads? Standing in the mess, pint in hand, Arthur can tell stories like the best of them. He is well able to hold his drink. Okay, sometimes he drinks a bit too much, but sure, don't we all!

Arthur is my best friend. A man's man he is. Kindred spirits we are. Two of a kind, two sides of the same coin. It is just a pity he married that woman. Besotted he was and he would not listen to me. A colonel's daughter, no less. I knew he was asking for trouble. I tried to stop him, make him see sense when I dragged him to the wet canteen. He was mine in India, before the mother in the Sandes home got him. Women! Those women in the Sandes homes have a lot to answer for.

197

Maria McDonald

Interfering God worshipping women with their homes for Soldiers across the empire. Enticing men like Arthur with their tea and their prayers, keeping them away from loose women and porter. I do not want to lose Arthur again. He's mine. I will not lose him to the Sandes home and that wife of his.

Chapter 45

Brian

Thursday 24th September 2020

There is a camaraderie between soldiers that doesn't exist in any other walk of life. I know that indisputable fact. But what was the relationship between Arthur and Henry? Arthur had a drinking problem, that much is evident, but at least he was trying to deal with it. Whereas Henry seemed to encourage him to drink. The relationship was toxic, as far as I could see.

From what I had read so far, Edith was Arthur's saving grace. The more I read of Henry's journal, the more I hated the man. Not only was there a badness in him, but he tried to bring Arthur down to his level.

I wonder how Edith felt about Henry. Did she recognise the badness in him, the propensity for violence? She's bound to have known it was Henry who dragged Arthur to the mess and encouraged him to stay, one of the lads. The thought made me sit up and wonder about my own behaviour at times.

After military exercises or competitions, there were nights when I forgot to come home from the mess. The craic would be ninety after something like that. Packed with testosterone and beer, stories, and raucous laughter. I had some tremendous all-male nights in the mess. Jean and I had some arguments over those nights as well. Nights when I had promised Jean, I'd be home by five and didn't arrive home until after midnight, the worse for wear.

Jean understood though. Born into a military family, she understood the need to kick off sometimes. The debrief, we called it. Having said that, I didn't overindulge, but I've known many a soldier who did and who eventually paid the price with a broken marriage. Thank God, or rather thank Jean, I'm not one of them. I picked up Edith's journal to find out more.

Chapter 46

Edith's Journal

September 1913

I could tell there was something on Arthur's mind the minute he walked in the door that evening. He was absent, or should I say, distracted, and I knew there was something important brewing. It was a wet and miserable evening – the Curragh Plains' greenery hidden under a grey mist that soaked every object. The sheep huddled under trees, their coats sodden as the soldiers hurried to their quarters, glad to be out of the weather.

Arthur shook the excess moisture from his raincoat and hung it on the hook in the front hallway. The children clambered all over him, their energy levels high after an afternoon of sitting by the fire. Arthur was having none of it. He barked at them, and they slid away and cowered around the table, throwing anxious looks at their father and at me. Our evening meal was quiet, not a word spoken as the children ate in silence, and Arthur brooded at the head of the table. When our food was eaten, he barked at them again.

"Bedtime, all of you."

My children have never gone to bed as quickly and easily

as they did that night. I followed them up and tucked them in, giving each of them a reassuring hug and a goodnight kiss. When the children were settled, I made a pot of tea for us. I stirred three large spoons of sugar into his favourite cup and brought it to him. He was sitting in his armchair at the side of the fire, staring into the flames, deep in thought.

"Sit, Edith," he said, and I did as I was bid.

"We are shipping to Aldershot."

My heart sank, and I am sure my mouth must have fallen open, like a fish on a riverbank, for that is how I felt. Recovering my voice, I asked, "Where? Why?"

Arthur looked up at me, and I could see the soldier in his eyes, all trace of my husband buried under discipline and training.

"England, Edith. You know that. And as for why, I am a soldier. My duty is to go where I am posted. My allegiance is to my unit first."

His words stung me. We had settled into a way of life here in Ireland. Once he had stopped drinking, he had mellowed, become a good husband and father. We were a close family unit. Or so I thought. His closed expression and his clipped words were like a slap in the face. It was like a denial of my part in his life or his part in our children's lives, and I was hurt.

"What about us? Me, the children?"

"Family quarters in Aldershot is on a par with the Curragh. You and the children will be fine. They will settle in quick enough. We leave in four weeks."

Arthur rose and put his empty cup down on the scrubbed table. "I am expected at Sandes home. Good night."

Arthur lifted his coat and was gone, leaving me sitting there, in the light of the fire, any questions I had unanswered and my life in turmoil. The idea of packing up my home, our home, and moving to another barracks filled me with dread. But what could I do? Arthur is my husband. His life is my life. I could nearly hear my father's voice, reminding me that I could end up living anywhere in the empire as the wife of a soldier. At the time, I thought that was exciting, but that was before I had my children.

Over the previous five years, I had grown to love our life in Ireland. The Curragh Plains were my children's playground and my solace on a summer evening. But even I had heard the rumours of civil war in Ireland. The papers were full of the Home Rule campaign, although Arthur held no opinion, one way or the other. He was more concerned about unrest in the Balkans, a place I was only vaguely aware of. That night, it dawned on me that my world was about to change forever, no matter what was happening in this world.

I rose from my chair and moved the cups to the sink. My legs felt as heavy as my heart, and I could feel the tears welling. My mending basket sat beside my chair, its contents spilling over. Arthur's socks, the heavy woollen ones that kept his feet warm in the Wicklow Hills. Imogen's smock, torn on a gorse bush, when she tried to catch her older sister in a game of tag. George's shirt, its collar in need of turning, although, at the rate he was growing, it wouldn't fit him for much longer. I glanced at the wall in the back hall where I had marked their heights each summer and Christmas and noticed how much they had grown since we came to this house. My life is tied up in these walls.

When I think of India, I remember a life of privilege and a life of pain. My precious firstborn baby is buried in India, and I will never forget him. George and Rose were born in India too, but they have grown up here in Ireland, blossomed in its fresh windswept days spent in the majesty of the Curragh Plains. How could I leave this home we all have been so happy in? But at the end of the day, what choice did I have?

Over the next few weeks, I packed up our belongings. We did not have much. Any clothing the children had grown out of, and I could not remake with my needle and thread, I gave to Betty. I would miss Betty. She was a great friend to my family and me. My privileged upbringing had not prepared me for cooking and mending, and Betty had taught me everything she knew, and for that, I would be eternally grateful.

On my last day, we sat in Betty's kitchen, over cups of tea and apple tart and toasted our new beginnings, for Betty was a born optimist. She believed that change happened for a reason and that life could only get better for us. I hoped she was right.

Chapter 47

Edith's Journal

Aldershot and the War, 1914

We were barely settled in Aldershot when news came of the war. I had written to Betty telling her all about the married quarters. To be fair, the whole camp was better than I had expected it to be, and the children settled in quite quickly. Children are resilient. They take whatever life throws at them and adapt to it, more so than adults. Are we just too set in our ways to embrace change, too afraid of the things that can go wrong instead of embracing the idea that change might make life better? Or does experience ground that hope out of us as we age? All I knew was that life was good, and I wrote to Betty to thank her and tell her she was right. Even Arthur was more relaxed in Aldershot, back to the husband and father I adored. Then Britain declared war on Germany.

Arthur's unit was one of the first to go to France. Before they shipped out to Europe, he was given a full three days' leave, and we had a lovely time. The excellent weather lent itself to picnics and long walks, and we had fun with the children. At night we retired and became reacquainted, like the newlyweds we once were but with the added experience of knowing each other intimately. It was the best we have ever been together. The only shadow hanging over us was his imminent posting to France, but Arthur assured me it would all be over within months. He promised to bring me home French perfume for Christmas and bonbons for the children. But it was not to be.

Arthur kept his letters home brief and cheerful, but he would write something intimate every so often, and my heart would miss a beat. There was a list in the main square in the barracks, refreshed every day, of the dead and the injured. Every morning, after I had dropped the children at school, I walked up to the main square, my heart beating in my ears, anxiety clawing at my chest until I checked the list for Arthur's name.

The relief that washed over me was indescribable, mixed with guilt at the outburst of grief I witnessed from others. Women less fortunate than I, who saw the name of their loved one on that fateful list. I started to hate that morning ritual yet could not stop it. I figured I would rather know than go through the day in ignorance only to face the dreaded telegraph when least expecting it.

There were heavy casualties on the Western Front, and I prayed for Arthur's safety. There were no letters for weeks, and I became increasingly worried. Arthur's letter arrived in the run-up to Christmas, and I broke down and cried before I had even opened it.

My dearest Edith,

I hope you and the children are well. Just a short note to let you know that I am fine.

You may have heard that the 1st and 2nd

battalions have merged. We have had new recruits from Ireland and are ready for the next stage. They said it would be over by Christmas, but I do not think so. We have lost a lot of men. The war is going very badly for the allies.

I miss you, Edith, you, and the children. It is lonely here, surrounded by men like me, away from home and family. I look forward to your letters. Thank you for the photograph. I carry it with me in my shirt pocket, close to my heart and treasure it. Kiss the children for me.

Your loving Arthur.

Needless to say, I cried all day after reading that letter. My poor Arthur. He is very much a man's man. Born to be a soldier, you might say, but underneath that, he has a heart of gold. He loves the children and me. Of that, I have no doubt. I worry for him, worry that away from the healing influence of the children and me, he will succumb to the darkness that haunts him.

It was almost a year later that I next saw Arthur in person. He had changed. While he smiled at the children and at me, it never quite reached his eyes. The crystal-clear blue was clouded, and I could sense the distraction in him, the feeling that while he was physically here with us, his mind was elsewhere.

But he tried. I know he did. He even brought me the French perfume a year later than expected, but at least he thought of it, and I was touched. I still treasure that bottle, it sits on my dressing table, and I use it sparingly, its scent bringing me back into my Arthur's arms, if only in my mind.

He promised to bring me to France sometime when the war is over and life goes back to normal. We made such plans, had so much fun and then it was time for Arthur to go back to war, not to France this time but to Mesopotamia.

"The cradle of civilisation. Under different circumstances, it is a place I would love to visit, Arthur."

"Someday, Edith. When all this nonsense is over, I will take you there. For now, I go to fight the Turks."

Arthur left, and normal life resumed for the children and me. Or what could be classed as normal during such times. Food shortages meant careful planning to keep my children fed, yet I knew we were the lucky ones. Betty had taught me invaluable household skills that kept us fed and watered.

Arthur's letters gave me snippets of information about the war. The rest I gleaned from newspapers. He was not allowed to hint at any clue to his whereabouts in his letters, just in case: security reasons they were told, and the little he did tell me was often scored out by heavy-handed censors. Yet the newspapers printed reports day after day of battles and loss of life that terrified me.

When I read that the Connaught Rangers lost 285 men in Umm al Hanna, I could not eat until all the names of the dead were listed. Arthur wrote about long marches, over hundreds of miles, of heat and disease and hard-fought battles, but he always tried to keep the tone light, and I prayed for him. We all prayed for all those men and boys, and as the years passed, we debated about the point of it all. I saw young men arriving back from war, mere shadows of their former selves and I worried for my Arthur.

In the desert of Mesopotamia, Arthur and the Connaught Rangers dealt with the torrid summers, fighting heat and malaria, which gave way to the freezing winter nights, all the while fighting the enemy. I read the place names in the newspapers. Strange sounding towns where the men of the allied forces were fighting men from the Turkish troops. Places like Dubailah, Beit Aeissa and Mespot and I dreamed of my Arthur in the midst of it. When I received a letter, I treasured it, reading and rereading until I knew every word by heart. I keep the latest letter flattened between the pages of my journal.

My dearest Edith

I hope this letter finds you and the children well. I am fine. We landed in -- in January and spent 8 days travelling up the -- on paddle boats to get to the battle lines at --. The winter is hard in --, freezing rain and little shelter. It does not feel like the cradle of civilisation to me, more like the end of civilisation, if I am honest.

I am sure you have read the newspaper reports about the battles. It has been bad, but I am still standing, thank God. There has been a cholera outbreak in the camp, but I am a hardy fella, as you know. It must be your prayers and the supplies of chocolate and tea you send me. I ran out of tobacco, but Henry gave me some Lambkin Tipperary tobacco to keep me going, and it is quite pleasant.

I am glad to see the back of winter and welcome the heat of the sun. It brings memories of India and our first meeting on the veranda of the colonel's bungalow. Such a magical time and place.

Last night we had a bonfire outside the camp. We are far enough away from the enemy lines, or what is left of them, to have some time for R&R, and it is very welcome. The lads are primarily new recruits, fair-skinned and red-necked, from the west of Ireland. I swear, Edith, some of them can barely speak English, yet here they are, fighting for king and country. Kitchener has a lot to answer for. They have fine voices though. One young private sang a ballad last night that sent shivers down my spine and thoughts of you into my head. Not that you are ever far from my thoughts.

We ended the night with a rendition of 'Long Way to Tipperary,' of course. We sang with gusto and a longing in our hearts. Funny to think not one of our number has ever been to Tipperary. Those that had died in the mud in France.

It got me thinking, I tell ya. Being away from you is the hardest part of this war. I miss your smile, your gentle touch. I miss the scent of ya. I love the bones of ya.

There is no home leave – no way of getting us there – but as soon as that changes, I will be home. I promise you.

Your loving husband
Arthur.

As part of the war effort, I got myself a job. Seamstresses were in demand. While I could never be classed as skilled, I was good enough to get a position working within the camp, repairing uniforms, usually for the officer classes. My working day started after the children started school, and I finished in time to reach home at the same time they did. The money was small, but it was adequate. The work was undemanding, mind-crushingly so, but it filled my day, chasing fear for Arthur and the war in Mesopotamia out of my head and filling it with the hopes and fears of other women just like me. Women who became my friends.

Helen was a sergeant's wife, just like me, but that is where the similarity ended. She was English born and had never been outside England. I told her what little I knew of Arthur's childhood in Manchester, and she told me about growing up in London. Her working-class background was quite different from my life in India. Like me, she had children who needed to be fed and nurtured, so our lives revolved around them, but we were fascinated by the younger women who joined the war effort.

Our postman went off to war, and his position was filled by Laura, a vibrant young woman from a large country house further along the coast. She was efficient and full of cheer, delivering our letters as if they were precious cargo, which to us they were. It was the days she brought the telegrams we avoided her. Each and every one of us army wives dreaded the arrival of the telegram.

We watched with beating hearts and bated breath and breathed a sigh of relief when that knock went to someone else's door, then cringed with guilt, guilt at the relief we felt and compassion for the grieving family. We swung into action then to help the new widow and orphans with bread and stews and a shoulder to cry on. They were terrible times. Our world was a dark place, inhabited by death and destruction, with little to lift our spirits.

My children were my saviour during those dark years. When George turned thirteen, he was as tall as me, with the look of his father, who we had not seen in three years. They barely remembered him. Sometimes I struggled to picture Arthur's face, but I held it in my heart, and I yearned for the end of the war and his safe return to me.

I treasured Arthur's letters. When he first went off to war, his letters home were brief and to the point, more like a travel writer's journal than a letter to his wife. But as the years passed, his letters became more poignant, sometimes reducing me to tears. Towards the end of the war, his unit went to Palestine. He did not write much about the battles. Well, they were forbidden to write about their location or how the war was going. An army of censors opened every letter, which at times broke my heart as I tried to decipher what Arthur was trying to tell me in his tidy handwriting between the blacked-out lines.

Then it was over. The eleventh hour, of the eleventh day, of the eleventh month, and the bells rang out all over England. We danced in the street: Helen and I and the other wives and our children. Finally, our men would be coming home.

Chapter 48

Brian

Thursday 24th September 2020

Reading Edith's account of waiting for Arthur to come home got me thinking about Jean. Okay, it was vastly different in that Arthur was off fighting in the First World War. I've seen the films, read the stories. It was a horrific time, a terrible loss of life, and all for nothing as far as I could see. Men, soldiers like me, were used as cannon fodder. While at home, the women raised the kids with little or no support and kept the home fires burning, so to speak.

I have served overseas as a peacekeeper with the UN five times. Each time I went to further my career. I went because I volunteered, partly for the extra money but also for the soldiering experience. During all those trips, I had never considered what it was like for Jean. She was the one left at home to look after our kids. We always discussed it in advance. Let's face it, me and Jean, we're partners first and foremost.

Decisions in our house are made jointly. But...if I wanted to go overseas, I went. I might have discussed it with her, but I always got to go; she never stopped me. She never said, no, you're not going, it's too dangerous, or it's not worth it. For it was worth it. It was the only way for the likes of me to earn some extra money, and with three kids, we always needed extra money for something. We would never have been able to put them through college without the overseas trips.

If I'm honest with myself, those trips shaped me, made me the person I am. We are all shaped by the life we lead, and the people we meet along the way. Sometimes for the better, sometimes worse. That trip in '89 was rough. I lost my way on that one, to the extent that I nearly didn't come home to Jean. She knows very little about it, for I only told her as much as she needed to know. I was overly fond of the jar at that stage of my life. Why, I don't know, although, with hindsight, I can see that it was probably something to do with the death of my son.

These days men are expected to talk about their feelings, and express their sorrow, but not back then. My job then was to be strong, to support my wife, and help her grieve. I shook hands and accepted the "sorry for your loss" mumbled hundreds of times. I went into autopilot and buried my grief somewhere deep inside me. When I realised that Jean was drinking too much, I lectured her. I got her help and counselling, and I helped bring her back to herself.

Me, I ignored. I was the man of the house. All I needed was for my wife to be okay and my work would sustain me. So, once I was happy that Jean was coping, I volunteered for overseas duty. In April of 1989, I went to Lebanon with the 65th Battalion.

It was a tense time in Lebanon. Three soldiers serving with the 64th Battalion lost their lives in a targeted landmine attack just weeks before finishing their tour of duty. The attack happened near Bra'shit, on what was more of a dirt track than a road. The Irish Battalion was under serious pressure, and we were all on high alert.

I work well under pressure. It's part of being a soldier, that ability to compartmentalise. It came naturally to me, and I

excelled. But every night, I made my way to the mess. At the
time, it was just a beer or two to unwind. The mess only sold
beer and opened for two hours in the evenings. We all got into
the habit of a few beers before bed at ten pm.

Within weeks, my "few" beers had progressed into as many
cans of Almaza as I could get down my neck in two hours. Frank
Egan called me out on it.

"Slow down, for fuck's sake. It's not a race, Brian."

"Ah, shut up and drink. What harm?"

"You're drinking too fast. Take it easy."

I squared up to him. "What's it got to do with you?"

Frank said no more that night, but the next day he
tackled me.

"You're drinking beer like your life depends on it. And
you're getting aggressive. If I was you, I'd think about slowing it
down a bit."

Frank was my best friend, and he saved my skin more than
once. I pushed that friendship to the limit on that trip and in the
months afterwards. We had met in recruit training. Born and
bred in the Curragh, he knew everyone and took me under his
wing, introducing me to his family and his circle of friends.

I knew him longer than I knew Jean. We double-dated for
years. Married within months of each other. I trusted Frank
with my life, so when he told me I was drinking too much, I
listened. But that night, I forgot everything he said and ignored
the looks he gave me as I drained the last of my fourth can in
twenty minutes.

I was on a roll, playing the Seanchaí embellishing stories.
Until someone pulled me up on some outlandish statement I
made. I got aggressive then. Downright nasty. When I started to
insult him, he laughed, but when I began insulting his wife, he
got up off his stool and threw it at me. I would have retaliated,
but Frank got in the way. He pulled me back and hauled me

outside to my billet. All he was short of was giving me a clip across the ear like my mother would have done.

There was no more said, but the following week a few of us had four days' leave, and we ventured as far as Naqoura. I was looking forward to it. It's a grand spot – a bit of civilisation after the hills. There were hotels and bars, regular social activity and we couldn't wait. We dropped our bags at the hotel and went straight to a recommended restaurant for a slap-up feed. The food was good, the wine was flowing, and the bar beckoned.

I was the only married man of the four, and I was quite content to sit at the bar, but the others wanted to go to a nightclub. In hindsight, I should have just stayed where I was or gone back to the hotel, but I didn't; I went with the crowd and kept drinking. I was having fun, laughing, and talking until I woke up in my hotel room with a strange woman in my bed and no memory of how I got there or who she was.

When I woke first, I thought I was at home, and Jean was beside me, curled under the crook of my arm. Her dark head of hair and flowery perfume lulled me into a false sense of home, but then she moved. Suddenly, I was awake and painfully aware that I was lying beside a stranger.

I leapt out of bed; my heart pounded in my chest nearly as loudly as the hammers in my head. An anxious glance around me showed clothes strewn from the door to the bed, mine, and hers, mixed up, silent witnesses to our coupling hours earlier.

I felt sick. My stomach churned as flashes of me and that woman jumped unbidden into my brain, and I realised what I had done. I ran to the bathroom and threw up. A knock on the door sometime later alerted me that she was still in the bedroom. I threw cold water on my face and took several deep breaths.

"I go now, Irish," she smiled, "hangover pill," and she handed me paracetamol.

She was fully dressed and ready to leave. Confusion must have shown on my face, for she laughed.

"You pay me one night only, Irish. I go now."

She left, and I sank back into bed, exhausted, sickened, racked with guilt. While I had flashbacks of dancing with her, I had no recollection of returning to the hotel or what had happened to the lads I was with. I groaned as my face flushed with shame at the thought that they probably knew I had brought her back here. I was sharing a room with one of the lads, and he wasn't there, which meant he knew I was here with a prostitute. I hauled myself out of bed and into the shower.

Showered, dressed, and looking presentable, I made my way to the breakfast room even though I was feeling decidedly rough. My insides shuddered as I waited on the slagging, but it wasn't forthcoming. Sammy, a sergeant from Drimnagh that I was meant to be sharing the room with, sat down beside me.

"Thanks, Brian. You locked me out of the room last night. I had to bunk down with Ger and Mick."

I didn't hesitate for a second.

"Jesus, sorry, Sammy. I didn't realise. I was wondering where you got to."

We ate, and they talked, the previous night's events were laughed about, and not one word was said about that woman and me. I was wondering if I had gotten away with it, but something was niggling at me. There were odd snide remarks and half-formed smirks from Sammy that I didn't quite get, and he didn't elaborate on. I didn't want to call him out in case he didn't know anything, and I only drew attention to myself, so I shut up, ate my food, and ignored him.

I was sorry afterwards. Turns out Sammy had seen me leaving the nightclub with that woman and had heard us through the door when he went back to the hotel. He didn't say anything at first, but he told Frank of all people when we got back to camp. It seems I had rubbed him the wrong way once too often.

He was a lazy fucker. I had pulled him up on numerous occasions during our time there for not doing his job, basically. It's not as if I embarrassed him publicly. I had always pulled him aside and told him what he needed to do. He took offence to that. It seems I had also insulted him in the mess at night, although that I don't remember. So, when I presented him with the perfect opportunity to take me down a peg or two, he ran straight to Frank.

"Jesus, Brian."

I hung my head as waves of shame washed over me.

"What if you caught something, for Christ's sake. What the fuck were you thinking? No, don't fucking answer that. Jesus."

Frank paced up and down in front of me; the veins in his forehead were popping.

"I don't know, Frank, I don't know. I'm sorry."

"Sorry, sorry doesn't cut it. Did you use a condom?"

"No. I don't think so..."

"Jesus, Brian. Well, you're going to have to go to the hospital. You may get tested. You can't go home to Jean after sleeping with a prossie and not get checked out. Fuck's sake."

I started to laugh, a nervous laugh borne out of frustration, fear, and embarrassment. For some reason, something I had read a few months back came into my head.

"Do you know the origin of fuck?"

"What? What the fuck are you on about?"

"In India, the British soldiers who had sex with the Indian natives were charged 'for unlawful carnal knowledge' shortened in the records books to FUCK."

"What?"

"Yea, it's true. And what they did was, the ones that came down with venereal disease, they shipped them to Tipperary, for cleansing, rest and relaxation, but more importantly cleansing, before they let them back to their families in England or Scotland or whatever part of the empire they came from."

"Jesus, Brian. You've lost the plot, my man. You're in deep shit, and you come out with that pile of crap."

Frank was right, of course. I was talking for the sake of it, regurgitating stuff I had read, saying anything, rather than face up to what I had done. My wife was the love of my life. We had lost our son. I had lost my mind. At that time, I thought I *was* losing my mind. I did not know what to do or where to turn, and for the first and only time in my life, I thought of taking my gun and going off to a quiet corner and blowing my brains out. But I didn't. I got through it with the help of Frank and one dedicated Swedish medic. Looking back on it now, I realise how lucky I was.

Remembering how I felt made me think about Henry. I wondered if someone had intervened with Henry at a time when he needed it, would his life have been different. Could someone have prevented the deaths of those women? Did someone know about Henry's compulsion but didn't stop him. I needed to know more so I lifted Henry's journal and opened the next page.

Chapter 49

Henry's Journal

Nazareth: October 1918

We were billeted in Nazareth for several weeks before I saw her. We were hailed as conquering heroes when we entered the town. Nazareth had been the general headquarters of the Turkish/German command in Palestine but now we were in control. And the locals loved us. The moment I saw her I knew I wanted her. She was spirited. I could see that in her, in the toss of her head as she flicked her hair off her face, in the hold of her head as she returned my stare.

It was easy to find out where she lived. The war was nearly at an end and we were no longer under constant bombardment. The flirtation was easier than I thought it would be which got me thinking that maybe she was not who she said she was. When she arranged to meet me, I got suspicious but went along with it.

I slipped out under cover of darkness and made my way to her shell of a flat. She opened the door with a false smile, and I knew it was a trap. My senses on alert, I walked into the room and there he was, hiding behind the door, but I was ready for him. He did not even see the knife until it was embedded in his stomach. The surprised look on his face made me laugh out loud, and her scream made me laugh harder. What class of an idiot did they take me for?

When I grabbed her wrist, she slapped my face. I loved that. Grabbing her by her shoulders, I flung her across the room. She hit the wall and would have collapsed onto the floor if I had not caught her. Ripping her clothes off took seconds as she begged for mercy. Her partner, brother, husband, friend, I do not know what he was to her, but he was watching, his voice gurgling as he choked on his own blood.

That made me harder. I had never had an audience before, especially one so invested in what was going on. I took her up against the wall, muffling her screams with my hand over her mouth. At the appropriate time, I raised both hands to her throat. I watched the fear in her eyes as my impending climax brought my hands tighter and tighter until her spirit dimmed and extinguished in front of me. I allowed her used body to slither to the floor, and exploding with exhilaration, I kicked her out of my way and on top of her partner.

Chapter 50

Brian

Thursday 24th September 2020

"Christ. I can't read this." I fired Henry's journal across the table. The evil contained within those pages sickened me, and I swore that I would get justice for Henry's victims. There had to be some clue as to who he was somewhere in those journals. His first name wasn't enough. I needed a rank, a second name, a serial number – something, anything that would identify him. My laptop beckoned, and once again, I called on my friend Google.

My initial search returned thousands of hits. Fired up by my supposed success, I clicked on the first link. I learned that the records of all Irishmen serving in British regiments were transferred to the UK after the Irish free state was set up. Those records were held in the Ministry of Defence, bombed during the London blitz in World War II, and only a few records survived. The surviving records are kept in the National Archives in Kew, London.

No matter how many different searches I tried, nothing showed up online to take me any closer to finding Henry's identity. One website looked promising, but it was a subscription site. I weighed up my options and reckoned I could unsubscribe after the first month. £8.95 and a few clicks, and I might find out something worthwhile. I didn't; it was a complete waste of time.

With only a first name and a guess at a rank, there were just too many variables. I wondered how Jean would feel about a trip to London, taking in the National Archives. But before I ran that past her, I needed more information. Arthur's journal beckoned.

Chapter 51

Arthur's Journal

Sandes home, Curragh Camp: 21st June 1924

I have stared at this blank page for an age. Mrs Magill said not to think about it, just write it down, but it is so difficult when it comes to the war. What do I know? I was just a lowly Sergeant, following orders, not privy to the planning. Although I do not believe there was any planning. How could any person in their right mind plan that carnage? For that is what it was, carnage and bloodshed on an unimaginable scale.

The War

We went off to war in high spirits, expecting to give the Germans a beating and be back home by Christmas. We were soldiers of the empire, well trained, disciplined, fearless, shipping to France to do what we were trained to do. The atmosphere in France was electric as we marched in formation. The fearsome Connaught Rangers, "The Devil's Own" singing "It's a long way to Tipperary". We were admired and feared in equal measure. But then we got to the trenches, and the carnage began.

Our numbers were decimated within weeks. Words cannot adequately express the horror of the trenches, the rats, the smell of human excrement and decaying flesh – the fear as we waited our turn to go up and over. I have never been so cold and wet and utterly miserable. We stayed in the trenches on shifts with other units. A few days on the front, then pulled back to regroup while another unit faced the horrors until they too were pulled back, their numbers reorganised and reinforced before they took their turn once again.

It was a few weeks before Christmas, and we were greeting our desperately needed reinforcements. They were mostly young Irish men. Those young Irish lads taught me how they believed that they were fighting for the freedom of small nations: that by joining the fight, their small nation would be granted the right to govern themselves. Admirable stuff, but as a professional soldier, I wondered had they been adequately trained in the short space of time they were in the army. Mind you, I also wondered if it was possible to prepare for the type of battle we were facing, for none of us, experienced or not, had ever witnessed anything like the trench warfare we were engaged in.

In early December, I wrote to my Edith. I had hoped to be home with her and the children for Christmas, but that would not happen now. I had not told her that we had lost so many men. I did not want her to worry. There were not enough of us left to fill two Battalions, and they merged the 1st and 2nd Battalions of the Connaught Rangers into one. Those soldiers of the 2nd Battalion left alive just put down their weapons as 2nd Battalion and lifted them again as serving in the 1st Battalion, simple. It changed nothing for me. We remained as 1st Battalion with the Lahore Division.

I do not know how I survived the trenches, but I did. A trip home to see Edith and my children at the end of 1915 helped ground me, and I felt almost human again. But then I returned, this time to Mesopotamia. I had thought the cold and dampness in France unbearable, but the heat and disease in the Middle East was worse. Over the trenches, we fought the Turks. German, Turks, it did not matter. We could not understand their language, and even if we did, our orders were to kill, our minds programmed to survive, and we did that to each other in equal numbers. We all fought the torrid heat, the winter freeze, the malaria, for mosquitos do not care what side you fight for.

Early in 1918, we left Basra for Palestine, disembarking at Suez in mid-April. We camped at Moascar for about three weeks. It was a welcome release after Mesopotamia. But it was not to last too long, for once rested, we were moved on to El Kantara, where we were re-trained and re-equipped to face the Turkish 8th army on the Plain of Sharon. We fought and won battles and skirmishes. We rounded up prisoners as we made our way towards the General Headquarters of the Turkish/German command in Palestine.

At noon on the 25th of September, we entered Nazareth victorious. Lieutenant Colonel Hamilton took over the government of the town ending our crusade. There were not that many of us left. Our numbers had dwindled as much from malaria as from battle. How Henry and I got through those years, I do not know. What I do know is, when the bells of the armistice rang out, we celebrated with whiskey and relief such as I had never felt before.

Fear haunted me in those last few days. I was convinced that I had got this far only to die, needlessly, stupidly in the final hours of the war. My dreams were of my beloved Edith, and I longed for her. My memory of that time is patchy. All I know is that Henry and I held each other up until we got word that we were shipping home in time for Christmas.

I do not remember much about the journey home, but I do remember arriving. Word had spread throughout the ship that land had been spotted. We raced to the deck to get that first glimpse of England. It was more of a shadow on the horizon at first, until hour by hour, we grew closer, and that dark mass in the distance started to take shape and colour.

We docked at noon, ready to disembark from early morning, our kitbags packed and slung over our shoulders just waiting. Some were tempted to jump overboard and swim the last hundred yards or so, so anxious we were to touch dry land, to finally plant our feet on English soil. The docks were packed with families waiting to greet us, and I scanned the crowds for sight of my Edith.

When I could not see her, I panicked at the thought that I did not even recognise her, it had been so long since I had set eyes on her. My stomach clenched at the thought of my children. Would they know me? Would they recognise me, for I surely had changed? I know I had. My once pale skin is tanned, my head bald and shiny under my cap, my eyes bloodshot from the constant drinking.

It was then, lost in my world of crippling anxiety, that I heard her call my name. In the midst of the crowd, I saw her waving her hat at me, and I nearly jumped off the ship and into her arms.

When we finally were permitted to disembark, I hurried down the gangplank and straight over to where I had seen her. She was standing in the same place, with a child holding each hand and a tall boy I barely recognised beside them. I was a stranger to my children. Imogen hung back, clinging to her mother, just as she had as a toddler. She was nine and looked at me with wary eyes from behind her mother's shoulder.

Rose shook herself free of her mother's grip and hugged me. Suddenly we were all laughing and crying. George held out his hand to shake mine, and I took it, conscious that my son had grown into a young man while I was away at war. I took Edith's soft white hand and pulled her to me; unable to speak, I embraced her. Her scent overwhelmed me, her softness, her love, and I was overcome with emotion. I cleared my throat and pulled back my shoulders. It would not do to show emotion in public. What would the men think? I squeezed her hand, and she smiled at me, a radiant smile, and I choked with love for this woman.

"Let's go home," I said.

We left the port and made our way back to married quarters. There was a convoy of us. Soldiers and their families reunited after the years of war. Glad to be reunited. All anxieties banished, at least for that one day, that honeymoon period when the joy of greeting loved ones drowned out the agonies endured over the four years and four months of war and devastation.

Our home life was awkward at first. It was as if Edith had become accustomed to life without me and now had to readjust to life as a married woman. I was a bit put out. She did her best, I suppose, but it was as if she had forgotten who the head of the household was.

The children needed taking in hand. They were boisterous and noisy and, in my opinion, had missed the firm hand of a father. I made it clear straight away that I would only tolerate complete obedience. After all, children should be seen, not heard. And as for George, at thirteen, he should have been working, but Edith had indulged him. I know education is important, but he knew his letters; he could read and write and even do arithmetic, so I told Edith it was time to find work for him.

But then he got sick. Spanish flu, the doctor said. He was as right as rain one day and coughing up his lungs the next. Dead within forty-eight hours. I could not look at him. Could not look at Edith. Her grief frightened me. The other women, the army wives, rallied around, brought us food, and comforted Edith and the girls. Me, I had Henry.

The night after we buried George, me and Henry drowned my sorrows in Irish whiskey and pints of porter. I did not stop to think about Edith. She had the support of the other women: the wives and sweethearts. They were a clique, connected with a bond as strong as the one that joined us soldiers to each other. Stronger even, for I believed then and still believe to this day that women are the stronger sex.

My Edith is made of sterner stuff than me. She can take whatever life throws at her and deal with it. Sometimes the thought struck me that if our roles had been reversed, and she was the soldier, and I was the wife, would she have been better suited to war and destruction?

But I dismissed those thoughts and laughed at the nonsense of it. Women do not fight wars. Women should never see the stuff that we men witnessed during those dark years. My Edith should not. She had enough to cope with. Burying our firstborn in India was hard enough, but now to bury George as well.

Almost a man, he was. Just at the cusp of manhood, his future, our future, wiped out in forty-eight hours. I never got to know him. Fighting for king and country kept me away from him, away from my wife, my daughters. I did not set foot in the country for over three years, did not get to look after my family. That was left to my wife. Do not get me wrong. I am sure she did a fine job of it, but every family needs a man at the head and a woman at its heart.

Up and down the country, there were families like ours, trying desperately to readjust to life in peacetime. We were luckier than some I could mention, but it did not feel like it when we were standing over George's grave. If I believed in a god, I would have been shaking my fist at him that day. Why spare me from war and then take our son away from us when he already had our firstborn.

I could not talk to Edith about George. She had her friends. I had Henry. Every evening after work, me and Henry walked over to the wet canteen for a few. We never stayed late. I always arrived home before Edith retired for the night, but she continually berated me. I could not listen to Edith, did not want to hear what she had to say. To my mind, Edith had her friends to support her; I had Henry. So, what if I had a few drinks with him as long as I came home. Edith did not see it that way. Words were exchanged, and I am ashamed to say that I used my fist to finish the argument more than once.

Sandes home, Curragh Camp: 21st June 1924

I am so ashamed writing these words. I do not know why my Edith stayed with me. Not then and certainly not now.

Chapter 52

Brian

Thursday 24th September 2020

I put Arthur's journal down, memories of what happened after that Lebanon trip in eighty-nine running around my head. When I got home from that trip, things did not go well between Jean and me. When I was still over there, I decided to say nothing about what happened, but guilt ate me alive.

Frank and my Swedish medic had convinced me of the benefits of staying teetotal, and that is what I became. I did not touch a drink for months afterwards. Jean believed me when I said it was for health reasons. She did not drink at that stage either, so it suited both of us simply fine. Our problems ran deeper than that though.

It was as if she had become accustomed to life without me and was enjoying it a little too much. Before I went to Lebanon, I always drove when we were going somewhere. While I was away, she discovered she liked to drive. So, when I automatically resumed my driving duties, she didn't like handing the car keys back to me as I saw it. It was the same when it came to paying the bills and cleaning the flat.

The first few weeks were a minefield. I had four weeks' leave and wanted to spend as much of that time as possible with her. Every morning I got up and drove her to work, which irritated her. At the weekends, I annoyed her if I slept late. She complained about me leaving my washing out, cribbed if I left my cup on the draining board or my shaving gear beside the bathroom sink. If I left the toilet seat up or forgot to refill the toilet roll holder, she sighed. You name it, she complained about it. By the time I went back on duty, we were sniping at each other every day.

My guilt didn't help. I couldn't look at Jean without seeing that woman's face. Sometimes when I lay in bed at night and listened to Jean's deep breathing beside me, I wondered if I should come clean. Tell her everything. Frank reasoned with me that Jean had been through enough. He said that if I confessed to Jean, I would be easing my own conscience, but I would be hurting her, and there was nothing to be gained from that. I agreed with him up to a point. But I didn't realise that she had her own confession to make.

I was back at work at that stage. Twenty-four-hour duties along with normal day to day. After an all-nighter, I had been at home that day sleeping it off and had got up in time to start preparing dinner. Not that I was much of a cook, but I could fry a pork chop and shove frozen chips in the oven. I had made a bit of an effort with the dinner table, setting it nicely the way she liked it, and I put her plate in front of her with a flourish.

"Voila, not quite to the Shelbourne's standards, but it tastes all right."

She smiled at me, a budget version of her usual radiance that didn't quite chase the sadness from her eyes. "I think we're in trouble."

"What do you mean?"

"Things haven't been right between us since you got back from the Leb. We haven't reconnected."

I knew she was right and felt my face flame as guilt

threatened to overwhelm me. It was my fault, of course, it was my fault, or so I thought.

"It's me, Brian. I'm finding it hard to adjust to having you back in my life. These past few months, I've felt a sense of independence I've never had before."

She covered her forehead with her hands, her elbows on the table so that all I could see was the top of her head. A sob escaped her, and my heart broke. By carrying this guilt around, was it chewing me up inside and destroying what we had together anyway? I was conflicted. That was until she dropped her own bombshell, and God forgive me, I let her take the blame for everything that was wrong between us.

"I've been so tempted. Nothing happened, I swear, but I came so close."

Jean choked with tears, slumped over the table. I froze as if I had been slapped. Her words repeated in my ears. Tempted! I watched her as if in slow motion as she raised her head and spoke.

"It was a guy at work. You don't know him. He just started, but there was a moment, well, more than one, if I'm honest, when I was sorely tempted. Nothing happened, Brian, I swear, but it got me thinking. I shouldn't be tempted, not if things were good between you and me. And now I'm left wondering if I still love you. Is everything we had between us gone?"

Anger bubbled up from somewhere deep in my stomach. I could feel it rumbling and pushing its way up until it erupted with a roar, and I flung the cup I was holding at the wall. It shattered, spraying hot strong coffee in great dancing blobs that hit the wall and the floor and the ceiling.

Jean yelped and covered her head with her arms. I stood there, staring at her, feeling like some cartoon character, my eyes bulging, my body quivering. And then I left. I just turned, walked out the door and didn't go back for three months.

For three months, I told myself that Jean had cheated on me. That everything that had gone wrong between us was her fault, not mine. I slept in the barracks and ignored the gossip. And then Frank pulled me aside.

"What are you at?"

I was leaving the dining hall on a wet and windy night and heading for the mess. It had become my usual routine. Frank had joined me there the odd night, but he had his wife and kids to go home to. Even though I hadn't said anything to any of the lads, I knew they were talking, and I also knew that the rumour was that Jean had played away. Frank heard the rumours too, and he wasn't standing for it.

"This is crap. How can you do that to Jean? You know what you did."

"Jean told me that she might as well have had an affair. Emotionally she was having an affair; she just didn't have the sex, that's all."

"Oh, that's all, is it? That's crap, and you know it. Your wife stayed faithful to you. She might have been tempted. She might have flirted with someone, but God almighty, Jean didn't take it to the next step. No, instead, she was completely honest with you."

"That doesn't make it all right. She said herself that if she was that tempted, then maybe the problem is with us. If she loved me, she wouldn't have those feelings for someone else."

"Crap, Brian. You're talking complete bullshit, and you know it. We both know you slept with another woman. Does that mean you don't love Jean?"

"Yea...yea I do, you know I do."

"Your wife loves you, and you're throwing that all away and for what? Because you feel guilty. You're punishing her for your guilt, and it's not on. Not on at all."

Once again, Frank saved me from myself. I could see sense

in what he had to say, but I just didn't know what to do about it. He was right, of course. Me and Jean, we were both miserable, even though I didn't know that at the time. I knew I was miserable without her, but I presumed she was doing okay. How wrong I was.

It took another day or so before I gathered up the courage to go and see Jean. No mobile phones or social media then to break the ice. I had to use the payphone in the mess to ring her at work. There was no privacy in the mess hallway, with the lads going in and out for tea breaks and meetings and whatnot. She was the same at work. No privacy for an intense conversation like we needed to have. But we arranged a date for the following night: dinner and a talk.

The following night I was showered, dressed, and drowning in the knock-off Boss cologne I had brought back from Lebanon. My stomach was churning with nerves. I rehearsed in front of the mirror what I was going to say.

Everything I planned went out the window the second I set eyes on her. My heart melted when she smiled at me, and I knew in that instant that we were going to be okay, for my Jean loved me. I could see it in her eyes, in the way she smiled at me, felt it in her kiss as she leaned over to kiss me on the cheek. I wrapped my arms around her and told her I would never let her go, and I meant it.

Relief flooded through my veins when she hugged me tighter and told me she loved me. It was the happiest I had ever been, well, up to that point in my life. Since then, there have been babies and birthdays and so many times when I have felt love and been loved. Thinking back on those few months when I pushed her away, I could kick myself.

I have been so lucky to have Jean in my life. I just hope she feels the same way. My eyes strayed to Edith's journal, and I wondered what she had to say about Arthur's fists.

Chapter 53

Edith's Journal

India, 1919

We got word that Arthur's unit was to be posted back to India, and I told myself that it was a blessing. That posting saved us, saved Arthur, for his drinking was out of control. It broke my heart to leave my friends. These women were true friends. Without them, I would never have survived George's death. It was so unexpected.

After years of worrying about my husband dying in battle, years of struggling with food shortages, fighting to keep my children fed and healthy, influenza took my son, my young and healthy son. His life, his vitality wiped out in an instant. He was thirteen years of age with so much potential, so much love to give, and for a while, I wanted to die with him. It was only the thought of my girls that kept me going.

My husband's name may have died with my son, but my girls needed their mother. My friends convinced me of this. They let me grieve, then pulled me back from the abyss and reminded me that I was still a mother to two girls who needed me. I thank God for those women, for Arthur abandoned us. He chose alcohol.

Late at night, when I was alone with my thoughts, I sometimes pondered if my life would have been better if Arthur hadn't returned from war. The guilt ate me up. He was my husband, the father of my children. I had promised to love, honour and obey him, and I did until he arrived home drunk and abusive. That man, that drunkard, was not the Arthur I made those promises to. It was as if he took on a different persona. Once alcohol crossed his lips, my Arthur was extinguished, and this arrogant pig of a drunkard took him over.

I prayed, night after night, for someone to take him and give me back my Arthur. My gentle blue-eyed man who loves to grow vegetables in our allotment, who reads fairy tales to our children, and beavers away in our shed, making furniture for our home.

He did come back to me. My Arthur came back to me in India. Our ship docked in Bombay on 24th November 1919. We took the train to Wellington Barracks, Jullundur in Punjab, the most northerly province in British India. The lower slopes of the Himalayas dominated the background, and the town of Amritsar was eighty kilometres away. It had been a whole year since the end of the war, but it was troubled times in India.

In April of that year, at least four hundred Sikhs had been killed by troops of the British Indian Army in the town of Amritsar. They were under the command of Acting Brigadier-General Reginald Dyer, a man I had met in my father's house as a young captain. His actions were lauded by most of the serving soldiers in Jullundur, but I had my reservations. Many of the dead and injured were children. While the British military's line was that the meeting that day had been banned, it seems the Sikhs who attended did not know that and were gathered in good faith and, most notably, were unarmed. I could not fathom why our forces had to open fire on these people. The loss of life was appalling.

"Don't fret over it, Edith. We are here to protect the interests of the empire. There must have been a reason. We are not savages."

"I know that, Arthur, but this...this was horrific. So many people, dead, so many injured, and what about the children."

Arthur hugged me. Not a quick "everything will be fine" type of hug, no, this was a proper embrace. He wrapped his arms around me and held me for several minutes, his head buried in my hair, my head against his heart. Held in his arms like that, I believed that all would be fine with our world. Together, we could deal with any hand life dealt us and that India was where we were meant to be.

Arthur worked hard, and I took pleasure in seeing him off every morning from our bungalow. His uniform was immaculate. He carried it with such composure, such confidence in his role, for the army was everything to Arthur. I knew that, and I loved him for it.

Even though I missed the chat around my kitchen table in England with Helen and the other army wives as we mended britches, I took up my old life in India with enthusiasm. I became convinced that after everything Arthur and I had been through, life could only get better. And it was better for a while.

George occupied my thoughts on a daily basis, but my girls kept me busy. We all spent time with my mother, who appeared to have aged rapidly since we last saw her. When I had spare time, I volunteered to help at the local hospital and became friendly with Mrs Carney, the doctor's wife. She was Irish born and had a strong character. I learned a lot from her.

As the following summer approached, the days got hotter and hotter. When it was our turn to move to the cooler camp in the lower Himalayan hills, I was thankful, even though Arthur could not join us. In the days before we left for the hills, I had the niggling thought that without the girls and me to keep him grounded, Arthur might fall off the wagon. I tentatively broached it to him over supper.

"Arthur, if I ask you something, will you listen and give me an honest answer."

"Of course, what is it?"

"When the girls and I are away, you must promise me that you will keep up your evenings in the Sandes home."

He stopped eating and placed his fork on the table before reaching over and taking my hand.

"I promise you, my darling, I will not go near the wet canteen. It is the Sandes home every night or my chair here on our veranda."

He raised my hand to his lips and kissed it, and I knew at that moment that Arthur loved me and wanted to be the husband I needed him to be. But experience had taught me that Arthur couldn't always keep his promises. I returned his smile with a silent prayer that this time he would stay sober. I was so proud of him. My Arthur.

Chapter 54

Brian

Thursday 24th September 2020

I closed Edith's journal and sat back in my chair. After everything Edith had been through, she was still proud of Arthur. What a woman. But that's what you do when you love someone. As if she sensed my thoughts, Jean appeared in the kitchen. She is a fine-looking woman, my Jean. I am as attracted to her now as I was over forty years ago.

We are lucky, me and Jean. So many of our friends have failed marriages behind them. Some went on to better relationships the second time around. Others floundered, unsure of their place in the world without their partner by their side. I don't think I would have coped if Jean and I had broken up that time all those years ago.

If I'm totally honest with myself, I think I would have been tempted to frequent the pub. Any ambition I have ever had has always been directed towards my army career, and I had excelled in that. But looking back now with the benefit of hindsight, I wonder how well I would have done in the army if Jean had not been at my back, supporting me and looking after our children.

When Jean became pregnant with Jenny, we were delighted

and scared all rolled into one. I don't think either of us slept during her first year. We had monitors, but we didn't trust them, both of us hanging over her cot, checking her breathing every other minute. Jean's mother took her to one side and told her, in no uncertain terms, that she needed to stop fussing over Jenny, but she couldn't.

The net result was a baby that didn't sleep very well, mainly because we didn't let her. When Sinéad was born two years later, we were both accustomed to existing on broken sleep, but we were a little more relaxed. By the time Conor came along, our sleep patterns were normal, or rather, as normal as they can be with three children under the age of six.

Jean took a leave of absence from work. She planned to go back when Conor started school, but in the meantime, funds were tight. It was the year of all the fuss over the new millennium. I mentioned going overseas. It was a definite no.

"You think you can just sail off into the sunset and leave me with three small kids. No way, Brian. It's not on. Forget about it," Jean said. "And anyway, if the papers are right, the world is going to fall apart over the New Year. There's talk of computers crashing, unable to cope with the year 2000. God knows what we're facing."

She made a fair point, and I let it go. We celebrated the demise of 1999 with champagne and friends in our house, with the kids safely tucked in upstairs and an optimistic outlook for the new century. By the following summer, Conor turned four, and we enrolled him in preschool. Jean started a back to work course, and I signed up for Bosnia. It was a short six months, and I was sorry I went. I missed my family so much. Six months is a very long time for a four-year-old.

I had applied for larger accommodation when Conor was born, but nothing suitable was available at the time. Then shortly after I got back, the house in Warrant Officers came vacant. I jumped at it. It had three bedrooms, larger rooms, and views over the plains. We were delighted with it. Still are. I will be sorry to leave it. Such happy memories in these walls were made all the more special by Jean.

I am acutely aware that my Jean is the backbone of our family. She is the planner, the saver, the organiser and without her, I would be nothing, have nothing. I would never have gained the rank of company sergeant without her support. I certainly wouldn't be getting ready to retire with a newly built home in Waterford waiting for me.

"Penny for them," Jean said as she filled the kettle.

"Cost you more than a penny."

Jean's laugh tinkled around the kitchen. I had always loved her laugh. It was hearty and joyous, like her, I suppose – all or nothing.

"Are you proud of me, Jean?"

Jean stopped the teapot in mid-air and looked at me.

"What's brought this on?"

"Ah, nothing really. I was just reading Edith's journal, and she mentioned that she was proud of Arthur, and it struck a chord."

"I see." She smiled. "Well, yes, I am proud of you. Always have been. You are my knight in shining armour, my officer and a gentleman."

"Ah, jeez, that's pushing it," I said but couldn't stop my chest puffing out with pride at her words, even though they were accompanied by laughter.

"Brian McElroy, I love you."

Jean sat on my lap and kissed me. Her warm earthy scent sent waves of longing through me as I returned her kiss. Jean laughed as she jumped to her feet.

"Hold those thoughts for later, my love. Let's find out if Arthur kept his word."

Chapter 55

Arthur's Journal

Sandes home, Curragh Camp: 21st July 1924

My wife is never happy. She insisted that I give up drinking. I did what she asked. We moved to this priest-ridden country to make a new start, but she sulks every day. Sulks when she hands me breakfast, sulks when I go home for dinner, sulks when I go to the Sandes home. I have forgotten what her smile looks like.

The girls are just as bad if not worse. Lazy, ungrateful, constantly whining. They all hate Ireland. Most of the time I'm in agreement with them but at the end of the day, it puts food on the table and a roof over our heads. They miss India. I don't. India destroyed my regiment. Edith needs to remember that. In truth, the memory of the mutiny breaks my heart.

India, June 1920

Thankfully, Edith and the children were in the hills. At least they had some relief from the unbearable heat. We usually finished daily training by ten o'clock because of the heat in the middle of the day. Not that it was much cooler in the bungalow. The punkah wallah did his best, but those large cloth fans just pushed the hot air around, and we sweltered in our bunks until the wet canteen opened at eight, and we could down pints of beer. I did not keep my promise to Edith. Within days of the families resettling in the relative coolness of the hills, the intense heat, the boredom, and Henry's insistence wore me down.

Every evening I sat in the corner of the wet canteen and listened to the men talking about their homeland. The activities of the Black and Tans were the sole subject night after night. As more soldiers came back from leave, stories abounded. Letters from their homes confirmed the rumours we had heard, and there was disbelief, followed by anger. I could see their point; here we were, after fighting for king and country for years, shipped now to India, as far away from Ireland as they could post us.

I listened to the men mutter about broken promises, about how they signed up to fight for small nations in the belief that their reward would be Home Rule for Ireland, and then the British government reneged on their promise. In muttered conversations, the men debated that if Irishmen can fight for the freedom of small nations, why can't Ireland have hers?

It was different for me. I did not have the memories they had, the ideals of a country post-war, ruled by Irish, for the Irish. My parents might have been born there, but they never spoke one kind word about the place between them. They never mentioned it at all, other than to call it "that godforsaken country". What do I know?

I liked it well enough when we were stationed there. Could even go as far as saying I missed the Curragh. The years spent there were some of the happiest, despite everything that happened, and maybe when this posting was finished, we would end up in the Curragh or even Galway. The army would get no complaints from me.

The night of the twenty-seventh of June, I was outside the wet canteen at precisely eight, waiting for it to open along with most of the men in my bungalow. That day was the hottest on record. We were wrung out with sweat, our uniforms stuck to us in patches, and our tongues hanging for a pint. The earth was parched, and the red dust rose and covered our boots and legs.

Insects buzzed around, attracted to the sweat and the body odour of the men. We swatted them with weary, ineffective swipes of damp palms. I pushed my way inside the second the door opened and settled myself in my favourite corner. My chair backed into the wall beside an open window on one side and the bar on the other. From my vantage point, I had a full view of the canteen and the advantage of having the bar, and more importantly, the barman, at my elbow. The punkah wallah helped circulate the hot air, but it did not help that much.

That night I noticed Private Hawes and his pals, their stance, and their body language, more than anything else. They were in a different bungalow to mine, a different platoon. I heard the odd word. Amritsar was mentioned more than once. I was intrigued until the fifth beer, but then I stopped caring, losing myself in quenching my thirst while chasing my demons.

The next morning my platoon fell in as usual, and we set off to the rifle range. On our way back, we could hear singing, men's voices singing Irish songs, lots of them. The guardroom of Wellington Barracks was open on all sides, like a large cage, with shutters that could be closed over in case of storms, but today, in the sweltering summer heat, all the shutters were open and inside the bars stood thirty-five men singing like they were an all-male choir.

Astounded, we stopped. The men sat on the ground, holding their rifles across their knees, some joining in the sing-song, others chatting like it was a tea party. At the corner of the guardroom, I could see Colonel Deacon arriving, causing a flurry of activity. The men inside the guardroom stopped singing and lined up outside in the heat while we watched. Private Hawes stood to attention in front of those lines of men and spoke so clearly that we all could hear.

"In protest against British atrocities in Ireland, we refuse to soldier any longer in the service of the king."

A murmur went around the watching men, like the hum of bees gathering nectar. The colonel looked momentarily flustered, but then he started to talk, not only to the men standing to attention in front of him but to all of us, sitting around the guardroom.

"This is a serious matter...mutiny, no less, and it cannot continue. Let us not forget that we are in India for a purpose, to defend the empire. Just over sixty years ago, the locals rebelled against the crown and lives were lost. Do you want a repeat of that? The locals will take advantage of this...this mutinous behaviour.

"Your wives and children are in danger. Every second that you refuse to soldier, you are putting their lives in danger. You are putting your own life in danger. Men, remember our motto, remember our proud tradition of serving the crown fearlessly. Think of the honours we have won, the respect we have gained. We are the Connaught Rangers, a force to be reckoned with, a regiment respected throughout the empire."

Pride in my regiment welled up in me and in the men around me. I could see it in their faces, in the manner they puffed out their chests and nodded their agreement to everything the colonel was saying.

"We cannot have men refusing to soldier. The political situation in Ireland has nothing to do with us. When I file my report this week, I will pass on your concerns about Ireland and am happy to do so, but you must return to normal duties at once."

Private Hawes again reiterated their refusal to soldier in service to the king because of what was happening in Ireland. The expressions on the faces of most of the men changed from pride to anger. The dull rumble of disgruntled voices rose as they remembered their homes in the west of Ireland and the families they had left behind.

Never before had we witnessed anything like this. The men ignored the colonel's commands. They held a meeting and decided that their aim should be to protest against the British government's policies in Ireland and demand that Ireland be given its freedom.

I left the meeting to report back to the Adjutant and passed by the bungalows they were occupying. It was shocking. They had removed the Union Jack and had hoisted a Tricolour. Looking across the grounds, I saw the Tricolour flying over the guardroom as well. What surprised me even more, was the colonel and his entourage accepting what was said to them and withdrawing from the bungalow without further argument.

It was hard to know what to do. While I had sympathy with many of the mutineers, my first duty was to king and country. Most of my fellow rangers were new recruits, born and bred in Ireland. To my mind, the army should never have recruited them, but there again, what did I know? If the officer classes were standing back and letting this happen, what was I to do?

Within a few days the mutineers were rounded up and sent to Dagshai Prison. Seventy-six men in total were court-martialled. Life returned to something like normality in Jullundur. The Connaught Rangers were seriously understrength. How could they be otherwise with seventy-six of their number interred? Relations between the Rangers and the other regiments were tense. For the first time, I had doubts about my future military career. Six weeks after the mutiny, the court-martials began with a few acquitted, some sentenced to prison for terms of between three years and fifteen years.

Then came the news that fourteen men were under the death sentence. They were segregated into separate wings. Around mid-October, most of them were told their death sentences had been commuted to life imprisonment. The exception was Private Jim Daly. On 2nd November, he was shot by a firing squad, made up of the ranks of the Royal Fusiliers.

Edith and the children were back from the mountains by then. I could not talk about it. She was friendly with Mrs Carney, the doctor's wife, who had remained in Jullundur and had helped tend some of the mutineers. Maybe Mrs Carney filled her in on the details, but I believed it was not a woman's place to discuss such matters, so when Edith tried to talk to me about it, I would have none of it.

On several occasions, she tried to talk about the families of those mutineers in Dagshai Prison, but I forbade her to mention their names. She surprised me, being the daughter of a British Colonel, brought up in a military family in British India. Criticism of the ways of the empire would not have been tolerated in her childhood home, and I certainly would not allow it in mine.

Sandes home, Curragh Camp: 21st July 1924

The end of the Connaught Rangers was so difficult to put down on paper. The torn loyalties destroyed us all. I thought Edith would have understood my feelings on what happened, given her upbringing. Once again, I was wrong.

Chapter 56

Brian

Thursday 24th September 2020

I lifted a well-thumbed copy of *An Cosantóir* and used it to mark my page in Arthur's journal, while Jean made tea. I was struck by how regimental Arthur had been, and I wondered if I had been the same with my family. If so, it was my father's influence, of that I had no doubt. He had never been in the military, but he was patriarchal like most men of his generation. He ruled his home until the day he died with an iron fist, and I had often felt the force of his hand across the back of my head for simple childhood misdemeanours.

When my children were born, I swore I would never lift a hand to them. It was different times, I know that, but some men were harder than others, and my father was harder than Tuskar Rock. My mother was a timid woman, who loved us dearly, but she too was kept in line by my father with the odd slap and a look that could cut steel.

Jean and I reared our children to treat others with respect. At least, I hope we did, but I do acknowledge that it was mainly Jean. I was away on duties, either in the camp or border duties, or prison duties, cash escorts, and then there were the overseas trips – five of them in total, all six months long. Six months away from family, totally immersed in military life.

The homecomings were always great, for I missed my family and longed to be with them. But after the initial euphoria, there were difficult days when me and Jean learned to live together again as man and wife. I struggled with family life, and Jean struggled with handing back some of the total control she had when I was away, and she had to shoulder all the responsibility.

In 2010 I went overseas straight after Christmas. It was freezing when I left Ireland to serve with the United Nations in Africa. Ireland was covered under a blanket of snow when we left Dublin airport, and we were shivering while boarding our flight. Different story when we finally disembarked in Africa. The temperatures were in the high thirties, and the semi-desert earth was baked a dark red. I was part of the staff at Camp Ciara, and despite the heat, I enjoyed the trip. It was a different mission from anything I had been on before, and I found it fascinating. Africa was hot and dusty but uneventful from a military perspective.

The money I earned was earmarked for college fees for Jenny and Sinéad. I got home towards the end of June to good weather and a happy family. At that stage, exams were over. Jenny had sat her leaving cert and Sinéad the junior cert. They were waiting at the house, and there were excited giggles and hugs all around as I handed out the customary presents.

It was Conor I saw the biggest change in. He seemed to have grown into a man in my absence. As tall as me, with broad shoulders, he had lost that gangly calf look. He was interested in hurling and girls and spent all of his time and energy out of the house. It was towards the end of my second week home that his absence started to irk me.

I stopped Conor in the hall. "Where are you going?"

"I'm meeting the lads for a puck about," Conor replied over his shoulder.

"As far as I can see, your mother lets you away with murder. You don't do anything around the house; you're constantly out and about with your friends."

Conor stood still, his head bent and mumbled something as Jean appeared in the doorway behind me.

"Conor, off you go. The lads are waiting for you," Jean said, waving Conor back out the door.

"Now hold on a minute," I said. "That lad needs taking in hand."

Jean hustled him along the hallway and out the front door before turning back to me with her hands on her hips.

"What do you think you are doing, Brian?"

"That lad just sails in and out of this house. Treats it like a hotel. It's not on."

"Conor has already done his chores for today. The kids take their turns in doing jobs around this house and have done for the last six months. And for the record, I do not let anyone away with murder, as you put it. They all pull their weight around here."

"You can't see it, Jean. That lad can do no wrong in your eyes."

"That lad...is fine. You can't walk back in here after being away for six months and start laying down the law. There's no need for..."

"Go on, say it. No need for me to be here, is that what you mean?"

Jean gave a long slow shake of her head, her hands outstretched to me as if to plead her case.

"No...Jesus, no. That's not what I meant, and you know it. I just mean we had to manage by ourselves while you were away...and we got on grand. Now that you are back, it's different, and we all need to adjust to a different family dynamic. But if you go shouting the odds and enforcing your authority, you're only going to push Conor away."

"Rubbish. You have that lad ruined, he does what he likes, when he likes, and you let him away with it. Well, I won't stand for it."

Jean saluted me. A half-hearted Benny Hill type salute with a smile on her face and a sparkle in her eye. I snorted my derision which heralded a look from her that could have cut steel.

"Have it your way," she said as she marched past me to the kitchen.

I followed her, but my annoyance was picking away at my insides. Jean put on the kettle, then picked up a recipe book and flicked through it, with her normally full soft lips firmly set in a straight line and two pink spots on her cheeks. The kettle came to the boil and clicked off. Jean ignored it.

Anger started to bubble up from my stomach into my chest. I stood in front of her, and she ignored me as if I did not exist and I felt cut off, surplus to requirements, a blimp in the otherwise happy lives of my wife and children.

"To hell with this."

I walked out of the kitchen and out of the house and strode out across the Curragh Plains. It was a beautiful day. The summer sun beamed out of a cobalt-blue sky with not a hint of a cloud. Groups of people were dotted all over the plains, some enjoying picnics, flying kites, playing rounders, and some strolling enjoying the sun. My anger dissipated with every step, and I started to feel guilty as well as angry. Jean was right, or was she? The argument raged inside my head.

Who was I to lay down the law in my own house?

But if I didn't lay down the law, who would?

I was so conflicted and every pace I took got me more and

more confused. Without even realising it, I reached the outskirts of Newbridge. It was busy with Saturday shoppers, the roads clogged with traffic. My throat was dry, and I realised I was parched. Neeson's pub beckoned, and I stepped in through the side door to the oaky semi-darkness and the discreet mumble of several old men talking around the bar.

Most were strangers to me, so I took my pint and retired to the beer garden, where I could sit in solitude. For I didn't want to talk to anyone. I wanted to be alone with my thoughts. Figure out what was going on with Jean and with me. Two pints later, I knew I should go home, but I didn't.

The house was in darkness when the taxi dropped me off. It was well after midnight. Jean had left the front door unlocked for me, and I stumbled in, closing it gently behind me. I weaved in the hallway, trying to decide whether I should attempt the stairs or stumble to the couch in the front room. The couch won, and I was asleep the second my head hit the cushion.

The early morning sun woke me, its rays piercing my brain and setting off hammers that pounded the backs of my eyes. I didn't hear Jean enter the room, just saw the outstretched hands in front of me holding a glass of water and two paracetamols. She turned and left as silently as she had entered, and I groaned. Fuck...

The mantel clock chimed six as I downed the water and pills. I could hear Jean moving around the kitchen, so I stood, swaying slightly, and made my way upstairs. A quick shower sorted me out, and I went downstairs ten minutes later, feeling less like a walking corpse.

"Tea?" I asked.

"Yes," she replied and sat at the table as far away from me as the small kitchen would allow with a magazine spread out in front of her.

I made her tea the way she liked it. Strong, a small drop of milk, no sugar, in a china mug and placed it in front of her. She barely lifted her head, just took a sip and continued to read.

"Are you not talking to me?"

Jean sighed and closed the magazine. I sat beside her and took her hand.

"You can't walk back into our lives and take over, Brian. We're not the army. We're your family, and you can't talk to us the way you talk to the lads in the barracks."

"I didn't mean to do that, love. I don't...When I put on my uniform, I am a different person from the man I am at home with you and the kids. And I'm not trying to take over; I'm trying to fit back in. It's not easy, you know."

"It's not easy for any of us. Walking out on us doesn't help matters either. Where did you go yesterday? You left here in a temper and not a word from you."

"I went for a walk across the Curragh, ended up in Neeson's. I was just leaving when some of the lads arrived, and I ended up having a few pints with them."

"More than a bloody few, I'd say."

"Yea, yea. I shouldn't have. I'm sorry, okay?"

"No, it's not okay. I bet you those lads you met were single, or if they were married, they're not anymore...You're a married man, for God's sake, with responsibilities. You can't just feck off to the pub whenever you feel like it. It's not fair. Not fair on me, not fair on the kids."

"What difference does it make to ye? Sure, you told me yourself you can manage without me. The only reason you need me is to go overseas to earn extra money."

I slammed my cup down on the table, spilling some of the contents over the patterned vinyl cloth. Jean tutted her disapproval, sending my anger spiralling up into my chest again. Without thinking, I lifted the cup and fired it against the wall. Jean jumped to her feet. Blinded by tears, she started to pick up the pieces of red and white crockery. My anger slithered away as if ashamed by my outburst, and guilt gnawed at me. I tried to touch her shoulder, but she shrugged my hand off. I lifted a cloth and wiped the tea stains and picked up the rest of the broken crockery.

"I'm sorry, so sorry."

Jean just sat there, looking at me. She started to speak several times, then stopped as if rehearsing in her head what she wanted to say, then stopping each time trying to word it better.

"We do need you. I need you. I love you; don't you know that? I have always loved you, probably always will..."

"Yea, but you don't need me. You can manage very well without me."

"It's true...when you're away, we do manage without you, but wouldn't it be worse if we couldn't? And then when you come back, it takes a little bit of adjustment to get used to you living with us again. That's only natural. It doesn't mean we don't need you."

"I suppose you're right. I find it hard too. Living life in a camp for six months then stepping back into family life. It's odd at first. But it's been harder this trip. Is it because the kids are older, we're older?"

"I don't know, love. I suppose every trip will be different. We will have to try harder. You're coming home at a different time of year this time, as well as everything else. You just need to remember that it's summer. The girls had exams, and they worked hard. They're entitled to have some downtime before September, and as for Conor, he's a normal fourteen-year-old, no different from any of his friends. Don't be so hard on him."

I took her in my arms, trying to hide the tears that had welled up in me. Men don't cry. My father had taught me that. Jean wiped my eyes and held me close. She made me realise that everyone needs to cry now and again. Even tough men like me.

There are not many women like my wife. I am blessed to have her by my side, for she has saved me from myself so many times. She is the love of my life. Reading Arthur's journal, I knew Edith was the love of his life, and I wondered if that love had survived their separations. With thoughts of Jean in my head I lifted Edith's journal to read more.

Chapter 57

Edith's Journal

Jullundur, 1920

"A woman's place is with her husband."

I knew before I even broached the subject that that would be my mother's answer. Arthur was drinking again. For nights on end, I was left alone with the children while he frequented the wet canteen. The whole debacle of the mutiny had its toll on him. He struggled with his identity and his allegiance to his battalion. I understood that, of course, I did.

When Private Daly was executed for his part in the mutiny, it sent shock waves through the entire empire. Although I was not surprised. That is how the military dealt with its enlisted men who dared to raise their voices against the establishment. A soldier's role is to serve king and country. That ideal had been instilled in me, a mere woman, from infanthood. But these men of the Connaught Rangers were different, I suppose.

They were Irish in a way that my father, as an officer of the empire, will never understand. Ireland was now fighting the British for their independence. The army had recruited these men to fight for the freedom of small nations, and they had answered that call. But now, the men they had soldiered with had turned on them. The stories coming out of Ireland told terrible tales of brutality against the Irish by the forces of the crown. It was no surprise to me that the men of the Connaught Rangers felt they had to do something.

It was a terrible time, yes, but that was no excuse for Arthur to abandon us for the questionable pleasures of whiskey and beer and God knows what else. Until that evening, my mother had been unaware of Arthur's drinking. I had hidden it from her. Even the children were unaware of how bad things were. I had some money squirrelled away.

That was a lesson I learned early on in my marriage. My children and I would not starve, but my meagre savings would not last long if Arthur continued to squander our money on alcohol. Now that I had heard that the unit was being posted back to England, I was worried. Money went much further in India than in England, and I did not want to go.

"What will I do if Arthur continues to drink all our money? How will I feed my children? How will I keep them warm through the English winter?"

"You cannot stay here, Edith. You have made your bed..."

We were scheduled to leave in seven days. I was tasked with packing up our belongings once again and bringing my children aboard a ship to England. It hardly seemed worthwhile shipping us to India in the first place, only to ship us back again. At least in India, I had my mother, but in England, I had no one.

"Your father would never hear of it, Edith. I know this is hard for you, but that is the way of the world. You are a married woman, and your place is with your husband. You need to speak to Arthur, show him the error of his ways. That is your position in life. That is what you should be doing, not coming here expecting myself and your father to take you in like some wayward strays. Why, that would be unheard of."

The drawing room was dimly lit, the shutters closed to try and diminish the fierce midday sun. Sitting in the corner on her straight back chair, my mother's face had turned quite pink, whether from heat or exasperation, I could not tell.

"Your father has a standing in the community. What would people think? It was bad enough when you married beneath you but to come running back now, after all these years. Really, Edith. It's just not good enough."

I could not suppress the sigh that escaped my lips. Even though my mother's reaction to my request was exactly what I had expected it to be, part of me was disappointed, no, saddened, that she could not put the welfare of her only daughter and her grandchildren above her petty prejudices. To be fair to her, I was asking a lot. To move back into my childhood home with my children in tow but without my husband or any means of financial support. When I blurted out my predicament, I realised that I could never have gone through with it even if she had said yes.

Maybe I needed to realise how desperate I was, how dire my situation was. I made up my mind, there and then, as I watched my mother shake her head, her lips set in a tight line of disapproval, that I needed to get Arthur sober again. The Sandes Soldiers' Home had worked for him before, and I was sure it would again. Returning to England might be the change of scene he needed.

That night I told myself that it was a good thing, that it would save us, save Arthur. But even as I told myself that, I remembered that I had told myself that before. But listening to my mother and watching her reaction made me realise that

I had loved Arthur once and had loved him for a very long time. I had sacrificed my entire way of life and my relationship with my father for him, and I was not about to give up on him now. We had our children to think of. It was time to make Arthur realise that.

Chapter 58

Jean

Thursday 24th September 2020

"Edith was the ultimate optimist," Brian said.

"I don't know about that. Let's face it, what choices did she have? What choice did any woman have in those days. That saying, you make your bed, you lie in it, has been around forever, and always directed at women."

"Imagine saying that to one of our girls. I know what they'd tell you."

I laughed at the image Brian had conjured in my head. Thankfully the world was changing. My girls would never have to depend on anyone other than themselves. They were independent, modern women with careers and relationships with men who treated them as equals. Having said that there's no sign of either of them settling down. We got very excited when Jenny brought Zack to meet us. They seem to be in a serious relationship but there's no sign of them moving in together or anything like that. Certainly, no hint of a ring. As for Sinéad, she's enjoying the single life immensely.

"Are they still all okay for tomorrow?"

"Yes, Brian. Don't worry. It's all arranged. They'll be here.

Even Sinéad, although she said she had to create murder to get the day off."

"Speaking of murder, do you feel up to reading the latest?"

"Another murder?"

"Here, read this."

Henry's journal was open on the next entry, and I placed it gingerly in front of Jean, anxious that she wouldn't have to touch its pages. That none of the evil contained within them would contaminate her.

Chapter 59

Henry's Journal

Dover: September 1921

It was her hair colour that caught my eye at first. That flame red that shouts Irish, or maybe Scottish. Liquid fire framed pale skin dotted with freckles and dark hazel eyes. I felt her gaze on me as she left the pub with a sailor. He could barely walk, bow-legged and toothless and full of rum. I wondered why such an attractive girl would leave with a man like that. She looked too clean and healthy to be a prostitute, but that was what she was, fresh off the boat and earning her way to London.

The next time I saw her, she was sporting a shiner. Her right eye was nearly closed, and it looked like her eyes had leaked out, snaking her skin with hints of green amongst the black and purple. A warning, I would imagine, to stay away from the established patch of one of the regulars meted out by her pimp.

It made her easy prey. No one was looking out for her. I charmed her into bringing me back to her room in a dodgy boarding house and had fun with her, but I was not expecting her to fight back. When I started to tighten my grip on her throat, I saw the fear in those expressive eyes of hers, the realisation that I wanted to extinguish that flash, that spark.

I got quite a shock when I felt the jug crash over my head. It shattered into a hundred pieces and soaked my head and shoulders with tepid water. The shock of it heightened my senses, and my grip loosened, but only slightly. She pummelled my chest with her childlike fists, and I felt my passion rising.

Power surged through my veins as I pounded myself into her, my hands getting tighter and tighter around her neck until I heard the snap at the exact second of release. My heart raced and I struggled to normalise my breathing as the light in those beautiful eyes died, fading from hazel to drab grey. I lifted a shard and cut her throat as she fell. A torrent of blood shot out of her like a final encore.

Chapter 60

Jean

Thursday 24th September 2020

I closed my eyes and took a deep breath trying to settle the churning in my stomach. "Oh my God, Brian. That's deplorable."

"I can't read any more of it. Yet I feel if I don't read on, maybe those poor women will never get justice. All three journals have to be tied together in some way, so I'm hoping one of them will give me answers."

"Well, keep reading. Let me know if you want me to help. Maybe later. I have to get a shower now. This shift work is killing me. I tell ye, I can't wait to retire."

Brian nodded. I know he has reservations about retirement. Unlike me. I can't wait. He loves the military life, loves living in the camp. You would think he was the one that was born and bred here, instead of me. I'm leaving behind the only life I have ever known. At least Brian was brought up in Waterford. He still retains the accent, for God's sake.

"It'll all work out, Brian. We've worked long and hard for too many years. It's time for a new beginning, a fresh start. We're going to be so happy in Waterford."

"I know you're right, love. I'm just...I don't know." Brian

266

broke off, struggling to put into words how he was feeling. My husband is a good man but sometimes he finds it hard to articulate his fears, especially if he is uncertain about something. He is accustomed to laid down plans and regulations. Anything outside of his normal comfort zone unsettles him. It's not so much the move, it's more to do with leaving the army, finding a new normal for himself. I put my arms around him.

"It's the right time, for both of us," I said.

"I don't know why I have these niggling doubts. If I'm honest with myself, I think it's wondering how I'll fill my days. I've seen soldiers who couldn't cope with retirement. Men who didn't play golf or follow the horses. I fall into that category. The army's been my career, but it's been my hobby as well. What will I do with myself when I don't have a uniform to don every day, a certain standard of fitness to maintain, a set of goals?"

I took my husband's face in my hands and looked directly into his eyes. "You need to find something to motivate you. Find a routine to stick to in retirement. Your life has been disciplined for so long. You need discipline. There's something out there that will get you out of bed in the mornings in retirement. You just need to look for it."

I left Brian sitting in the half-light while I went for a shower. He needed some alone time to gather his thoughts. He had no choice about retiring. Brian had served the maximum number of years. He knew that. We had been planning this move for over six years. Our new home was waiting on us to move into. Once the stand-down parade was over, Brian would put his military career behind him, and we could move on to the next phase of our lives. I was looking forward to genuine leisure time and I knew Brian would too once he put his mind to it.

He smiled when I returned. Two steaming mugs of cocoa sat on the table at each side of Edith's journal, opened to the next page.

Chapter 61

Edith's Journal

Ireland, 1922

I did not know how much more I could cope with. It had felt good to be back in India, see my mother, and show my children where I was born and raised. But I was no longer part of that life. No, I was a sergeant's wife, a drunken sergeant. The events in Jullundur were traumatic for him. I understood that. But why he always fell back on alcohol to deal with his problems is beyond me. Were we not enough for him? I did not love him anymore. Not this Arthur anyway. This alcohol-fuelled shell of a man was not the man I married in India. I needed my Arthur back, but how could I reach him?

The previous night was the proverbial straw that broke the camel's back. I did not know where the blood came from, but his shirt was soaked in it. There were cuts and scratches on his torso and on his face, and I visualised long red fingernails. The water in the basin I soaked his shirt in was dark pink, and I could not control the shudder that ran through me as I wondered if it was all Arthur's blood.

We could not continue that way. I had hoped that the

move to Dover would settle him somehow, but how could it? He was still a Connaught Ranger, no longer "The Devil's Own" but the outcasts in the empire, the men who mutinied, the traitors. Arthur was horrified, traumatised by the events. One part of him sympathising with the Irish men he served with, the other fully supportive of the actions taken by the Crown Forces. He struggled to reconcile the two.

Helen had called earlier with her news. They intended moving to Ireland, and I found myself remembering our years on the Curragh Camp with great affection.

"James will enlist in Richmond Barracks in the capital. This new Irish National Army is crying out for professional soldiers. It seems Ireland has descended into civil war, and the newly formed government are recruiting men like our husbands."

"That sounds great, but after everything that they have been through during the war, are you not frightened for him."

"He is a soldier, Edith. That's what they do."

"You are right, of course. I just wonder how much more death and destruction they can take. Their minds are frazzled as it is. I miss India. Life was so peaceful there when I was a girl. It is my country of birth, where I was raised, and where my firstborn is buried. I visited his grave while we were there. My ayah is dead, but my parents are still there. I thought I could make a new life here in England, but it is not working out that way. Mind you, my parents' thoughts on that are that I have made my bed, and I must lie in it."

"Oh, Edith. Maybe you could talk to Arthur. After what happened in India, the Rangers will be disbanded. I heard that *all* the Irish regiments are to be disbanded. Arthur needs to transfer to another regiment. If he chooses wisely, he could be shipped back to India, and you could go home."

"I have tried. He will not listen to anything I say. They

should never have executed that Private Daly. That day changed something in Arthur. It changed the way he felt about the army. The Connaught Rangers are family to Arthur, more so than the children and me. The unit is in disarray, and Arthur has become unhinged. I am at my wit's end, Helen."

I was completely honest with her. I needed to talk to someone in fairness, but now that she was moving away, threads of what could only be described as panic ran through me. I would have no one. Although there were thoughts I could not even share with Helen. Only my diary knows my innermost thoughts.

That day was the lowest I had ever been. England was so foreign to me. Strange is it not – an army brat who married a soldier. I have been supported my whole life by men who served king and country, and I felt like a foreigner in the country they served. Did that say more about me than them, I wondered. Who was I really? Who was Edith Torrington?

If I had been asked that question at eighteen, I would have said British, of course. Yet here I am, aged forty-two, living in Britain and feeling like a foreigner. Life in India is so different. We brought our traditions out to India, but we adapted them to life in India without even realising it. We assimilated Indian traditions into ours and called them our own. My mother, for all her stiff upper lip, would never survive in Britain. The thought made me laugh out loud as I imagined her trying to survive without the multitude of servants she surrounded herself with.

The children arrived home then, disturbing my thoughts. I put my worries away for another day, busying myself with preparing the evening meal. Arthur had not been home in four days, and I did not know when to expect him. I went about my daily business as if our lives were completely normal. The girls and I were chattering about their day at school when we heard the key turn in the door and Arthur's footsteps in the hall. I froze as the children stopped and fixed their eyes on me, like miniature statues frozen in time.

It was still bright outside, late afternoon, with the heat of the sun lingering on the red-brick buildings. The only sound was the neighbour's dog, barking woodenly at the solitary cloud in the sky. We stood like statues as Arthur walked into the kitchen and spoke.

"What's for tea?" he asked as he ruffled Imogen's hair.

I do not know what surprised me most, the fact that he was home before dark or the fact that he was sober.

It had been a while since we had witnessed Arthur, the loving father. Longer still, since we had seen sober Arthur and none of us knew how to react. Conscious that the children were watching for my reaction, I decided to treat Arthur's entrance as if that were how and when he came home every day.

Rose and Imogen relaxed and smiled. Luckily, a large pot of soup simmered above the fire, and I told the girls to finish setting the table. The bread I had made earlier had cooled on the windowsill, and I cut great slabs of it and placed it in the centre of the table. The waft of fresh bread filled the kitchen as I ladled out large bowls of soup for my family.

I could not bring myself to smile at Arthur. It was too late for that. He spent all our money on beer and whiskey, out gallivanting every night with God knows who. If it were not for the few pennies I earned, mending and making do for the officer classes, me and the children would starve.

I looked across the table at him as he ate his soup and questioned the girls about school. He could not have a loving conversation with them, for he did not know them. They spoke to him politely, like the stranger he was to them, and the sadness of it all broke my heart.

"Edith."

I raised my chin and looked at him.

"There is something I need to tell you."

He cleared his throat, and I could see Colour Sergeant Torrington come to the fore.

"I have resigned. I have enough years under my belt to qualify for a small pension, but it will not be enough to keep us, for we must move out of quarters."

"When?"

"Next week."

"Wha..."

He raised a hand to silence me. "I have found a place for us."

"But where, Arthur?"

"Ireland."

"Ireland?"

"Yes, Ireland."

"What about the children? They have school."

"It's time Rose went out to work anyway, and as for Imogen, there are schools in Ireland, Edith. They went to school when we lived there before."

I just sat there, shaking my head while he talked on and on.

"It's a new start for us. I have signed up with the new Irish National Army. They will take me on at the same rank, and we will have married quarters in the Curragh Camp. Maybe even the same place we had last time."

My mind was racing. We had been happy in Ireland, but that was years before. So much had happened since then. Arthur's drinking, the war, the death of my precious son George. If we moved to Ireland, I would be cut off from the friends I had made here in England. But most of them were moving away as well.

The end of the war and the disbandment of the Irish regiments meant significant changes. The war had changed lives entirely and not just the men who had fought there. The lives of the women left behind to keep the home fires burning: the women who had to deal with these men who came back from war, damaged from experiences that were unimaginable to us.

A tiny flicker of hope sprang up in my heart, and I allowed myself to believe that maybe, just maybe, this change would be a change for good in our lives. If Arthur left the Connaught Rangers, he might just be able to leave all that baggage behind him. Forget about the war; forget about the mutiny.

"But there is fighting in Ireland. Will it be dangerous, for you, for the girls?"

"It will probably be rough for a little while, but it cannot be as bad as Mesopotamia, or France for that matter. The war in Ireland is over. There has been a truce with Britain, and Ireland has been partitioned. The new Irish government is split over accepting the treaty, but the ones in power are hiring soldiers like me, experienced soldiers from Irish regiments. My accent might be English, but I...am as Irish as the rest of them."

"And have they said we will be in the Curragh?"

"Yes. I spoke to the recruiting officer today. He says he cannot guarantee anything, but he will try his best to get us placed there. The Curragh Camp will be empty, the British army has moved out, and there are not enough soldiers in the new National Army to fill it."

That evening I tucked the girls up in bed and made my

way downstairs. Arthur was still in his armchair, staring into the embers of the fire as if searching for answers.

"Arthur..." I hesitated, unsure of how to proceed but sure in my own mind that I had to say something. "Arthur."

He looked up at me, and I could see the vulnerability there, the remnants of the old Arthur I had loved over so many years.

"This is the first time I have seen you sober in a long time."

Arthur winced, and I gulped back any reluctance.

"We cannot continue this way. You talk about a new life for us in Ireland. But...unless you quit drinking, then it will not be new. It will just be a repeat of what we have here, only worse. I cannot do that to the girls."

Arthur rose from his chair, and I took a step back, suddenly fearful. His face crumpled, and he reached out to me.

"Oh, Edith. I will not hurt you. I am so sorry, so sorry."

Arthur wrapped me in his embrace and buried his face in my hair. I could feel his sobs rack his body as he held on to me, and my heart melted. Despite everything, I still had some feeling for him, some remnant of love buried deep within me. While I do not think I can ever forget how he has treated me, maybe there was room in my heart for forgiveness. Perhaps the move to Ireland was just what we needed. A fresh start, a new country, a different army, a new way of life.

Within a week, we were packed up and ready to go, across the sea to Ireland and our new lives with Arthur, a soldier in Ireland's National Army. We were allocated the same house we had left before the war. Arthur's shed still stood in the backyard. The view from the front room window looked the same. The only difference was the tricolour flying from the top of the water tower instead of the Union Jack.

Arthur was sworn in, and true to their word, he had the same rank.

Even the Sandes Soldiers' Home was still there. I reckoned Ms Elsie Sandes, who ran the homes all over the empire, was more interested in meeting the soldiers' needs in her care than which flag they fought for. It was a relief to me, for Arthur needed the Sandes Soldiers' Home. It was their help and guidance that kept him sober, and for that, I felt nothing but gratitude.

Chapter 62

Brian

Thursday 24th September 2020

"Wow. I didn't see that coming," I said. "What was Arthur thinking of moving to Ireland during the Irish Civil War?"

"Poor Edith. I suppose they had no choice, really, for England was in a bad way after the First World War but talk about going from the frying pan into the fire." Jean tutted.

"Arthur probably thought life in the Curragh would be much the same as when they left it. He was in for a rude awakening. Six thousand British soldiers down to a few hundred Irish."

The Curragh Camp would have been a vastly different place. Most of the Irish regiments in the British army were disbanded at that time.

"I've no doubt quite a few of those soldiers found their way into the Irish National Army. Most of them were Irish born. It made sense in a way, that they would join the new Irish army."

"But Brian, Arthur wasn't. Arthur was English. Edith was born in India to a British military family. How were they going to survive in anti-British Ireland?"

We were both hooked. The last of the packing could wait. I lifted Arthur's journal and opened it between us. We had to find out what he thought about the Curragh Camp post rebellion.

Chapter 63

Arthur's Journal

Sandes home, Curragh Camp: 7th August, 1924

Henry is by my side constantly today. Goading me, calling me a goody two shoes, a loser. Maybe I am, maybe he's the smart one. I'm finding it so bloody hard. Edith has changed. She is not the woman I married. Constantly harping on at me. What more does she want from me? I gave up the drink for her and abandoned Henry, my oldest friend, or so he keeps reminding me when he whispers in my ear. Why can't Edith see just how much I have sacrificed for her. I can't give up the Sandes home as well.

Curragh Camp, 1923

I was sorely tempted. Only the influence of the mother in Sandes Soldiers' Home kept me sober. To have served king and country for thirty-five years with the backing of the traditions of the Connaught Rangers and then move to a fledgeling country with a fledgeling army was a massive change.

The horror I saw in Ireland. The sheer brutality of it all. It was as bad, if not worse, than anything I had seen in France or Mesopotamia. I was based in the same barracks I was in when I served with the Rangers. Except now, the camp was like a ghost town. When I came here in 1908, it was the largest camp in Ireland, in the British Isles for that matter. There were over six thousand men stationed here, now the numbers are in the hundreds. I thought that I identified with these Irish men, that to be Irish was how I was meant to be. But once I lived here, wearing the uniform of the state, serving the republic, I did not know who I was.

I demanded respect from the men under me. My rank demands respect. They saluted as I approached, but it was the uniform they respected. I ruled with an iron fist. It was the only way to survive. I was a limey in their eyes. They distrusted my English accent and my British ways, but they knew better than to cross me, and I intended to keep it that way.

The war here was over, but the repercussions will be felt for generations. I was glad I did not have any sons alive to witness what was happening in this country. At times it felt like the bitterness seeped from the very soil around us.

When I wasn't in the barracks, I spent as much time as I could in the Sandes Soldiers' Home. The mother there took me under her wing, so to speak. Maybe she saw a kindred spirit in me; what did I know? It was her who advised me to write this journal, to try and exercise my demons as she put it. What demons inhabit this body of mine, I wondered. What demons dragged me to drink? What urged me to imbibe whiskey and forget the horrors that occupied my brain.

I have been sober since I came back to Ireland. I promised Edith, my lovely Edith. She has suffered so much. Losing George was hard on her, on both of us. For now, with my sons dead and buried, there is no one to carry on my name. For what that is worth. Why would any man want to carry the name of Arthur Torrington, soldier and drunkard, son of a drunkard and a prostitute? Some legacy to pass on to any man. No, I think it's best that the Torrington name dies with me. The end of the drunkard line. My lineage is not fit to pass on to any man.

Henry tapped me on the shoulder today again. He said he heard I was a regular in the Sandes Soldiers' Home and that I was writing a journal about my military life. It was good to hear from him, yet his presence filled me with terror as well as joy. Henry was with me during the horrific parts of my military life. My partner, my brother in uniform.

We have been through so much together, and I do not know if I want to remember it all. Some things should not be spoken about, nor should they be written about. Some things are too horrible for the human mind to bear without shattering into a million pieces. Are they the type of memories that Henry and I share? How many more of our battalion share those memories, but they just get on with their lives. They go back to wives and children and become whole again.

Sandes home, Curragh Camp: 7th August 1924

Why is it just me, me, and Henry, who struggle, who drink to cope, who drink to forget, or are there large groups of soldiers just like us? I do not mean the ones that came back shell-shocked, as they called it. No, not the mad ones, for that is what they are. They will never go back to families, never lead normal lives.

The army sends them to centres dotted around the coast.

There they rest and try to heal their broken minds. My mind is not broken; it is just damaged, always was damaged. But to the outside world, I am completely normal. I have my wife and my family and my military career – an upright member of the military circles, a respectable member of the community.

Chapter 64

Brian

Friday 25th September 2020

Arthur's journal left me thinking. Ireland was a different country in 1923. Still reeling from the horror of the civil war. I suppose I always knew that many of the first soldiers in the Irish army had previously served with the British army. After all, the country had been ruled by Britain.

At one stage, something like forty per cent of the British military were Irish men. The War of Independence and the Civil War changed all that. It's only in recent years that we as a nation have started to recognise that indisputable fact and, for the first time, honour the Irish men who died in the First World War.

Arthur and Edith were different though. Neither of them were Irish born. Arthur may have had Irish parents, but there was nothing Irish about his upbringing. All he knew about the Irish was what he learned in his years in the Connaught Rangers.

My eyes met Jean's. She looked heartbroken.

"That poor woman. I hope it worked out for her. She had such hope, although was she mad to even consider moving to Ireland during the civil war. Imagine a British woman reared in

India, in a British military family; it must have been awful for her. She would have been so isolated here in the Curragh, in this house."

We looked around us as if expecting to see Edith walk through the door. A door slammed upstairs, and we jumped then laughed at each other.

"I've never felt this house to be haunted, and I'm not about to start now with only days to go before we leave."

"It's always been a happy home for us."

"That it has, my love. That it has. Come on. Time to put these journals away. We have a stand-down do to get ready for tomorrow, and we both need a good night's sleep."

It was my last day on the job. My last day to wear the uniform. There would be a bit of a fuss, a presentation, flowers for Jean, a gift for me. I had my photograph taken professionally, in full dress uniform, courtesy of the men in my unit. They had it framed, and they would present it to me as a gift, a memento of my army career. I was looking forward to hanging it in our new home in Waterford.

I knew Jean couldn't wait to move, but I was apprehensive. The house is lovely. We took our time building it and put only the best into it. Jean spent hours poring over brochures and searching the internet for ideas, and she had done a brilliant job. It was everything we could want. In a way, I was glad of the distraction of the journals over the past few days.

They had taken my mind off the fact that after tomorrow I wouldn't have to don a uniform every morning. I wouldn't have to go into the barracks, issue commands, or take orders. I would be my own boss. Boss of what, though. The army has been my life.

I never got around to taking up a hobby like some of the men I know. Golf has never appealed to me. I was of the Churchill persuasion that golf spoils a good walk. The new house was close to the sea, and that was something I was looking forward to, swimming in the ocean every day, but once that was done, how was I going to fill my days? The future loomed endlessly in front of me.

The next morning, I stood in front of the mirror, checking my appearance. Jean appeared behind me.

"Nervous?"

"Nervous of what?" I asked her.

"Your stand-down. Your last day in uniform. It's a big deal for you."

"It is, but it's been a long time coming. Onwards and upwards, my love. Our future awaits. At least we have a future. Arthur and Edith should never have come back to this house. I don't understand how Arthur even contemplated bringing Edith here after the civil war."

"He probably didn't realise the depth of ill-feeling against the British, Brian. He was a soldier, first and foremost. King and country and all that. I read an article recently about the men who returned from the First World War. They were mistreated in England as well, you know. It was a hard time for everyone. Maybe he thought that they had been happy here once and that they could rekindle that."

"More fool him."

"Maybe, but let's forget about them for today. Today is about you, C.S. McElroy, and might I say that you look very handsome in that uniform. Very handsome indeed."

Jean wiped an imaginary piece of lint from my shoulder and stood back to admire me with a radiant smile.

"You don't look so bad yourself."

Jean looked amazing. Her hair was tied back in an up style that showed off her elegant neck. The dark pink of her dress suited her colouring, and the full skirt shimmered as she walked. A horn sounded outside, and we hurried downstairs to greet our adult children. The house seemed so much smaller with them inside. When we moved in, they were young children and the house felt huge. They had spent their formative years under that roof – the same roof that sheltered Arthur and Edith and countless other families over the generations.

"You look really smart, Dad," Conor said.

All I could do was grin. While wearing the dress uniform felt good, having the three of them home for this event meant everything to me.

I had told Jean the truth about not being nervous. For me, there was nothing to be anxious about. The beauty of military functions is that everything is planned and rehearsed. For the stand-down parade, I knew exactly where I was expected to stand; when I was expected to salute, I knew exactly to the last second when everything was going to happen.

Failure to plan is planning to fail. That maxim had been drummed into me for years, and I, in turn, had drummed it into those I had trained. That's the army way, and I had been part of it for forty years. Wearing your country's uniform is something to be proud of, and I wore mine with pride that day. It is a fantastic feeling to be acknowledged by your peers with your family and friends present to witness it. I was immensely humbled by the whole experience whilst remaining incredibly proud.

After the parade, we retired to the hospital mess, where another presentation took place, a less formal one but more heartfelt. If I had retired a year earlier, the room would have been full of friends and family and comrades, but the coronavirus restrictions meant the numbers were limited to close family and friends. As I looked around me, I realised how lucky I have been in my career and private life. There were stories told and lots of laughter that lasted long into the night.

The next morning, I sat at the kitchen table surrounded by

my family. The radio was on its lowest setting as Morning Ireland grumbled away in the background with the latest bad news that none of us wanted to hear. Jean served up enough sausages, rashers, and eggs to feed an entire platoon. Sinéad was still the joker, teasing the other two, and I was transported back to when they were teenagers, fighting over toast and how bad the newest boy band was. Except now, they were adults with their own lives to be getting on with. Jean caught my eye and smiled.

"Penny for them?"

I grinned at her and raised my coffee cup.

"Here's to the next stage. Roll on Waterford."

Conor raised his cup. "Cheers. Here's to Mam and Dad."

Jenny and Sinéad were staying for the weekend, but Conor was staying on for a few days to give a hand with the move, even though I told him there was no need, but he insisted, and part of me was glad. It would be good to spend some time with him.

Although they were all heading over to the outlet centre at Kildare Village after breakfast. A shopping mecca that the ladies loved. I declined, offering to clean up the breakfast dishes and let them off before the traffic got too heavy.

Jean blew me a kiss as she ran out the door, the girls in front of her and Conor sauntering out after them, waving the car keys, for he was driving them.

With the kitchen cleaned up, I made myself a fresh pot of coffee and sat down at the table with the journals. I reckoned it was time to find out what Edith thought of Ireland during our bloody civil war.

Chapter 65

Edith's Journal

Ireland, 1924

Arthur told me he was writing a journal. Every evening, after supper, he goes across to the Sandes Soldiers' Home. He writes his journal and drinks tea and speaks to Mrs Magill. I envy her sometimes. My husband leaves my side and goes to her and talks to her; in a way he would never converse with me. What was it about her that allowed him to open up to her but not to me?

Arthur rarely speaks. He has always been quiet, happy to work in his shed, to read to the children, but he was not one for long chats. If I wanted to know something, I had to ask him outright, and he would answer me, but he would only answer the question. There was no embellishment. No idle chatter. I had been told that when he was drinking, he could be the life and soul of the party in the wet canteen. He was known as a storyteller. A man who could spin a yarn, usually some story about life in the army: that was Arthur the drinker. The sober Arthur was a different person.

Do I still love Arthur? I do not know is the honest answer. Do I regret marrying him? Again, I do not know. If I had not met my Arthur, I would not have had my children, and my girls are my life now. My sons are dead and buried, and there will always be a place in my heart for them. A hole actually for sometimes my grief visits me, unexpectedly, like a thick fog that descends on me, pulling me down until I feel like a blob, a massive blob of flesh, stuck to the floor as if the pain has metamorphosed into stones, barrels and barrels of stones that pour down on me and keep me pummelled until I can take no more.

And then it passes, and I pick myself up and go about my day as if nothing happened. I sometimes wonder whether people can see the bruises, the invisible bruises that make me what I am. Arthur cannot. There again, Arthur has not seen me in a long time. When he first told me we were going back to Ireland, I made him promise me that he would not drink anymore. He has kept his word, for he does not touch alcohol. I thank God and the Sandes Soldiers' Home for that small mercy.

When Arthur was drinking, there was a badness in him that came to the fore, which was not in my Arthur. It was as if he was a different person. But this new Arthur, this non-drinking Irish Arthur, is not the man I married either. He is a closed book to me. There is no fun in him, no sparkle in his eyes, no hint of charm.

It was the sparkle in my Arthur's eyes that I fell in love with. Those crystal-blue eyes that won my heart. I know in my heart and soul that it is not the fact that he is now a teetotaller that has changed him. It is something else. Something has died in my Arthur, that part of him that loved me and loved life. That part of my Arthur has died and has been replaced by a man who has no tolerance, no joy.

Maybe it was the years of war that did that to him. We all have heard the stories of men who came back from the war unable to function. Arthur was not one of those, but maybe the effects of the horrors he has seen just took longer to manifest in him.

The Curragh Camp is a different place than it was under the British. I no longer fit in. The other wives look at me with distrust. While there are many ex-British army men in the National Army, they are primarily Irish born men, and their wives are Irish born. Me. I am an army brat, daughter of a decorated colonel of the empire, brought up in India, with British ways. Everything about me is British, and they refuse to tolerate me. They make my life a misery. When I try to greet them, they ignore me. If I try to make eye contact, they look the other way.

Only last week, a local woman spat on the ground as I walked past. I stopped walking and stared at her. She met my eye with a "what you going to do about it" expression, her right hand poised on her hip, a sly grin across her reddened cheeks. I lifted my skirt and walked past. They were wittering behind me "English bitch" "Snobby cow", but I chose to ignore them. I have given up trying to win their trust. Let them talk about me. I do not care.

I tried to speak to Arthur about it, but he did not understand. He listened to me, then told me to ignore them and that they would get used to me eventually. One night he even told me to try to lose my British accent, that if I spoke with the same accent as the natives, then maybe I would fit in better.

"Don't be ridiculous, Arthur. How can I possibly change the way I speak?"

"Edith, you could make an effort. After all, you should try to understand the locals, and how they feel about the British. Your accent reminds them of the ruling classes."

The next day I was in the bakery, and two women were

there ahead of me. One I knew to be the wife of Sergeant O'Connor, a fiery red-haired man from the west of Ireland. We had met in India at a function in Wellington barracks. She was a pleasant enough woman. While we had not been friends in India, we had been thrown together socially on several occasions. I took a deep breath and said my good mornings, only this time I tried to tone down my accent, tried to emulate the Irish lilt I had always admired from Mrs O'Connor. What a mistake.

It was disastrous. She laughed, her companion laughed, the baker joined in, and I found myself wishing the ground would open up underneath me and swallow me whole. My face flaming, I turned and ran out of the building with their derisive laughter in my ears.

Once back to the comparative safety of my hearth, I fell into my armchair and cried sore. Not just for myself but for my girls. They fussed around me, making tea, and offering platitudes until they too succumbed to tears.

Arthur found us there when he got home. Sitting around the hearth drinking tea, red-eyed and despondent.

"What's happened, Edith?"

He touched my hand, and his concern touched my heart, but not for long as I poured out my story.

"A few women laughed at you," he repeated as he stood up and looked down his nose at me.

"You're sitting here like this because someone laughed."

He banged his fist on the table. "What is wrong with you, woman? Why are you making this so difficult? They are army wives, just like you. You do not have to live with them, cook or clean for them. No, you are my wife; you are supposed to look after my needs. Where is my tea? Is a man supposed to come home from a hard day and cook for himself? I might as well stay in the barracks, move in with the single men. Then your women friends would have something to talk about, wouldn't they?" He swept out of the room and up the stairs.

I was not surprised by his reaction. Annoyed yes, upset yes, but surprised, no. I got up from where I was sitting and set tasks for the girls while I started to prepare the evening meal. My husband has no concept of how miserable we are. I miss England. I miss India. Anywhere would be better than here.

I worry about my girls. They are isolated, unhappy, teased and derided by the locals for their accents and their ways. They cannot find work. In fairness, there is none to be had. The Curragh Camp is a ghost town compared to the busy centre it had been ten years earlier. Shops and businesses in the nearest town closed with no British to buy their wares. We are totally dependent on Arthur and praying that he stays sober.

I shudder as the thought enters my head that I wished my husband dead. Then I despair as I realise that if that happened, I might have his widow's pension, but me and my girls would have nowhere to live. Where would we go? We could not stay in an Ireland that detests everything British, including us. England holds no appeal to me.

In my forty-three years on this earth, only seven of those were spent in the country of my heritage. No, my heart belongs in India, but there is no one left in India to claim me. My parents are gone, their bungalow assigned to another Colonel. My father died on the day he retired, and my mother followed him a few short months later. They are buried in India. My brother looked after the funeral. He lives there now. I have not seen him in years, probably would not recognise him if I did see him. There is no place for us in India. It, too, is a foreign land to me.

Arthur attends the Sandes Soldiers' Home every night

working on his journals. I had hoped that he would find solace in his writing. I really did. I prayed that he would find the person he once was, and perhaps, just perhaps, he will remember how we loved each other once. Enough to defy convention. And maybe, just maybe, he would come back to me. That sweet blue-eyed man I fell in love with all those years ago. But it wasn't to be. I fell in love with an illusion.

Chapter 66

Arthur's Journal

Sandes home, Curragh Camp: 21st August 1924

I am unsure what else I have to write down. Mrs Magill said that writing it all down would excise my ghosts. That in reliving my past I can seek forgiveness for my sins. It hasn't worked out that way. Maybe if I were still a Connaught Ranger, life would be different. We were respected, feared even. The Devil's Own they called us. Every other unit looked up to us. A Connaught Ranger was the ultimate soldier.

Here, in Ireland, in this National Army, I am like a fish out of water. An Englishman in the army that threw the English out of Ireland. My Edith hates me for bringing her here. As for my daughters, they are so very like their mother in everything they do. They must have happy memories of when we lived in the Curragh Camp before the war. Imogen was born here and spent the first five years of her life enjoying the freedom of the Curragh Plains. They were good years for all of us.

Well, other than the time my wife found the body of that young girl. That was a horrible time for everyone. I was drinking heavily. My memories of those years are a little shaky. Who am I kidding? There are large parts of my life that are a complete blur.

I made a promise to myself as a young snapper that I would never become a drunkard like my da. I failed miserably at that, breaking that promise time and time again over the years. Somewhere in the deeper recesses of my brain, I argue that I had my reasons, that my life was so hard I was pushed into drowning my pain in alcohol. But at the end of the day, there is no excuse. I failed my wife. I failed myself.

But now, thanks to the Sandes Soldiers' Home I am back on the wagon. I haven't touched a drop since I signed up for the Irish National Army. Why then, do I feel so broken? In giving up my crutch I thought I would become a better person, happier, content with my lot in life. It hasn't worked out that way. I don't know who I am. I know where I came from. I recognise the forces that shaped me. The person I don't recognise is the face I see in the mirror every morning. Who is Arthur Torrington?

Chapter 67

Edith's Journal

21st August 1924

It was a warm autumnal evening. In the forest at the bottom of the hill, the trees were still heavy with leaves and cast dappled shade for the sheep who had taken shelter from the earlier sun. When Arthur left for the Sandes Soldiers' Home, me and the girls walked out as far as Donnelly's Hollow.

We enjoyed a pleasant stroll, arm in arm, making the most of the last of the sun before the onset of autumn. We chatted and planned our project for the long winter nights, a large quilt we planned to sew from old dresses no longer fit for purpose. When we returned, the girls went up to the attic to open the old chests from India and rummaged through what materials we could start with.

Downstairs I lit a small fire from the last of the seasoned logs I had stacked in the shed. It was an extravagance, but I wanted to take the edge off the night chill that always descended once the sun went down. My armchair beckoned, and I took up my mending, more at peace than I had been since we came back to Ireland.

Engrossed in my thoughts, I did not notice the time passing. The girls retired early, and the house quietened. The only sound was the tick-tock of the mantel clock, and I must have dozed, my mending in my lap until a loud bang woke me.

The kitchen door burst opened, and there wavered a dishevelled, broken Arthur. My heart sank under the waves of alcohol that emanated from him. He stumbled his way across the room and collapsed into his armchair. His clothing was dirty, his fly undone, his knees caked with dust and grime. There was a long thin scab across his cheek, and the buttons on his shirt were missing. The drunkard Arthur had returned, and my first fleeting thought was, "Be careful what you wish for". I sat perfectly still, barely breathing, like one of those mannequins in the shop windows.

"What you lookin' at?"

His speech was slurred, the words running together and slamming into the defensive wall I had put up around me.

"You, with your nose in the air. Think you're too good for me, don't ya?"

He struggled to stand, but his jelly legs would not hold him, and he collapsed back into the chair, with one finger in the air as if to admonish me and drool running down his chin. I did not answer him, could not answer him. What would be the point? I put my mending back in the basket at my feet and rose from my chair. Even though I tried to avoid coming within touching distance of him, he managed to grab my wrist as I tried to leave the room. His grip pulled me to the floor beside him. Arthur twisted my arm and brought his face close to mine. There was hatred in his eyes, hatred and contempt as I struggled to free myself.

"Please, Arthur, please let me go."

His laughter startled me into silence. It was a manic laugh

that tapered off to a growl, the likes of which only an animal could emit, and my heart pounded at the threat contained in it. Suddenly I was pushed back onto the floor as he flung me away from him. He stood unsteadily and grabbed me by my hair, forcing me upright. I did not have time to react before he slammed my face against the kitchen wall. Pain exploded in my right cheek, and I slid down the wall to the floor like a rag doll, dazed and sobbing.

I saw his boot leave the floor and I braced myself for the onslaught, but the movement unbalanced him, and he fell. Seizing the opportunity, I jumped to my feet and ran upstairs, closed the bedroom door behind me and pulled the heavy dresser in front of it, praying that it would keep him out if he decided to follow me. But there was silence, no heavy footsteps on the bare wooden stairs, no hammering on the door, and I prayed that the alcoholic haze had descended on his brain and sent him to sleep.

I slept fitfully that night, waiting on him hammering on the bedroom door, but it never happened. When I heard the girls moving around in their bedroom, I made myself pull back the dresser and go downstairs. Even though I was frightened, I did not want the girls to witness their father in that state. I should have known, of course. Arthur was sitting at the kitchen table, drinking a cup of tea, his uniform pristine, his boots shining. The only hint of the previous night was the long scab down his cheek.

"Morning, Edith," he said, his steely eyes waiting for my reaction.

Anger crawled up from my stomach and spewed out my mouth before my brain had a chance to engage.

"Morning! You promised me, Arthur. You said if we came back to Ireland, there would be no drink..."

"Shut your mouth, woman," he growled.

I did just that. There was no remorse present in the Arthur that sat at my table. No pretence, no pity, no compassion, for the Arthur I had loved was gone, replaced by this cold hard fish. I sat heavily as waves of despair washed over me. Arthur left before the girls made an appearance downstairs, and for that, I was grateful. I just did not know what to do next, for I had no choices. Nowhere to run to, and no money to run with. We were trapped, my girls and me, and our future looked bleak.

Chapter 68

Edith's Journal

21st September 1924

My Arthur is dead. I am both aghast and grief-stricken. I do not have the words to communicate my horror at the events of the last few weeks. I saw his mind shatter into a million pieces in front of me, witnessed the horror on his face, in those blue eyes I had once adored when the truth of his past crashed with his present.

Looking back at it, when Arthur gave me his journals to read, he knew that there was something that he needed to face but could not. By telling me to read them, he was asking for my help. It was a glimpse of my Arthur, the man I had fallen in love with, back in India. The handsome man with the twinkle in his eye who swept me off my feet. They say the eyes are the mirror to the soul. Well, on that day, what I saw in Arthur's soul frightened me to the core.

Arthur had not been home for over a week. I presumed he had gone drinking and I went about my business, praying that an Irish republican would take offence to his accent and his attitude and make me a widow.

Eight nights later, I sat in my chair by the fire with my mending in my lap, praying for guidance, for divine intervention of some sort. I was surprised to hear the front door open and even more so to see a sober Arthur in front of me. His eyes burnt into my soul, and I swear he knew the evil thoughts that were running around in my head all day.

"I am going to the Sandes home. I just wanted to leave these here."

He placed two books on the dresser.

"You can read them if you want." He hesitated. "Actually, do read them. It's important."

I nodded, afraid to say anything in case I provoked him, once again, into violence. He turned, his polished heels squeaking on the linoleum, and strode out of the house. It was as if the air settled again on his departure, and I let out a sigh of relief, not realising I had been holding my breath. My legs felt weak, jelly-like, and I gripped the sink to steady myself. The kettle whistled, and I made a cup of strong tea.

The journals called out to me. One red with his name, rank and serial number printed in Arthur's neat script on the front. The other one was green in colour and had the word PRIVATE across the front, and as I flicked through it, there was page after page of scrawling childlike writing.

The house was silent, and I took my seat at the table, picked up Arthur's journal and started to read. That red journal taught me so much about the Arthur I fell in love with back in India. My heart broke for the child who witnessed his mother's violent death at the hands of his father. For the first time, I understood the demons that possessed him when he drank alcohol, even though I could not condone it.

After reading about his time with Eamon and Mary, I finally understood what had attracted him to the Connaught

Rangers. Most of all, I understood why he was so happy there in that life. The accounts of our life together brought a smile to my face, for I caught a glimpse of how happy we once were. Arthur loved me. He loved our children. There, on those pages, in shades of indigo, was a testament to his love for us. Arthur had been so happy once.

The thought struck me. Was it I that had failed him? What changed my Arthur, the man I fell in love with, into this solemn morose man. I know the war had its effects on our men. They had seen horrors that no man should ever see, committed horrors in the name of king and country, and that sits heavily on a man's conscience. But it was more than that with Arthur. There was darkness in his makeup, a darkness in his soul that surfaced when he drank but now circled just below the surface.

I flicked back through his journal. There were considerable gaps in his accounts of his daily life. He had documented his early years in quite a lot of detail, yet there were years unaccounted for in his adult life. I thought that maybe it was when he was drinking heavily that perhaps he could not remember. Or did not want to.

On closer examination, I saw where pages had been ripped out. Had Arthur purged something onto paper then did not want anyone to read it, so he ripped it out and destroyed it? Or was it simply that he had made mistakes on those pages, spelling or inkblots and had ripped them out and started again. It is a pity that it is impossible to do that with our lives. Start afresh with a clean sheet.

I put the red journal to one side with a sigh and a heavy heart, and I picked up the other. What I found inside frightened me, horrified me. All thoughts of Arthur fled my mind in abject horror, and several times I had to run to the outhouse to be sick. Yet something drove me to go back and reread more, time and time again until I got to the last page.

It took me a while to make the connection. I swear my heart missed a beat as I matched that first loose page inside the green journal to one of the missing pages in Arthur's. The clock on the mantel seemed louder somehow in the deafening silence that engulfed the room. In that second, I think I may have even stopped breathing as that flash of recognition of the truth struck me.

I went back and forward from one to the other, trying to deny the awful truth that was staring me in the face. But every page, every line, confirmed the evil twinning, and my heart sank into my boots as I read and compared. They were interlinked, two sides of the same coin.

The following day, I sent the girls on an errand to Newbridge to get them out of the house. I did not want them anywhere near the evil contained in those journals. Arthur had not come home, and I was glad in a way. It gave me a chance to think, for I did not know what to do. When he returned that morning, I was still reading, flicking from one journal to the other. Even as I placed them in front of him, side by side, he did not seem to know the significance.

"Who is Henry?"

Those crystal-blue eyes that once had shone with love for me, sparked ice-cold daggers straight into my soul.

"You know who Henry is. We have served together since the beginning."

"The journal, Arthur."

"What about it? Have you read it?"

"Yes, yes, I have."

My tongue stuck to my mouth, and I took a long gulp of water. My hands were shaking, and beads of sweat ran down my back as I struggled to find the right words.

"Tell me about Henry, Arthur."

"Tell you what? What is there to tell? You hate Henry. You blamed him for my excessive drinking, and I suppose, looking back on it now, we were a bad influence on one another. We joined up together, went through recruit training...Malta. He was in India when I met you...in Ireland...Aldershot...Mesopotamia...Dover. Henry is the closest I have to a brother, and you have always hated him."

Arthur's voice broke into a sob. The ice melted in his eyes and poured down his face. My Arthur was broken. I could see it in the tilt of his head, in the slump of his shoulders. Yet, I pushed him further.

"Look, Arthur." I opened both journals and pointed it out to him.

Moving from page to page, I showed him what he did not want to see. The simple fact is that both journals were written by the same person.

He looked puzzled at first, then the realisation of what he had done crept down his features and into his hands. Holding them out in front of him, he stared at them as if they belonged to someone else. Sweat broke out in a line on his brow, and he started to shake.

Somewhere all those years ago, Arthur Henry Torrington had split into two people. In his mind, Arthur and Henry were two separate entities: two separate people, and now, with the evidence in front of him, they collided, merged back into one. Arthur Henry Torrington's mind could not cope with the horror, and he snapped.

"I couldn't...My God...Henry is me...I am Henry."

An anguished howl erupted from deep within his soul and reverberated around the house. My heart broke for him. The memories he had buried in the segment of his brain that he had labelled Henry broke free and haunted him, chasing away all the goodness and light from his mind and replacing it with darkness and blood-drenched dead women. I cowered in the corner of the room, my hands to my ears to block out his anguish, but nothing could mask the pain that emanated from him. He lifted the chair and fired it against the wall with a curdling scream.

Tears blinded me, and I curled into a ball beneath the table, willing myself to become invisible, afraid of his pain, of his anger. I felt a whoosh of air as he upended the heavy oak table. Fear nailed my knees to the floor, and I could not move. My body trembled as he lifted me to my feet and shook me like a rag doll. His eyes were on fire. Those crystal-blue eyes I had once loved shot daggers of ice-cold rays while the rest of him burned with rage. He put his hands around my neck and squeezed.

"Arthur..." I started to plead with him, but it was as if the sound of my voice touched a switch in his brain and the rage stopped. Burnt out. Depleted. Something died in his eyes. He dropped me like a sack of potatoes on the floor, turned and walked out of the room. I heard his heavy footsteps on the stairs as he dragged himself up to the bedroom.

My legs turned to jelly as I slid to the floor, my heart beating in my throat, and there I stayed, for how long I do not know. I went over and over everything I had read. My Arthur and Henry were the same person. My stomach turned, and I retched violently. Then I heard the shot.

There was silence as if the whole world had stopped, breath paused, as it waited for the ripple effect of the gunshot to dissipate. Slowly I became aware of the hiss of the fire in the grate and the sound of voices outside. I was afraid to go up the stairs, fearful that he would be waiting for me, to shoot me, to put an end to us all, but he was not.

The stench of blood met me on the landing, and I gagged as I opened our bedroom door. He was half lying across the bed, his feet on the floor, the gun on the bed beside him, his head a bloody mess. My Arthur was dead. But there again, the Arthur I loved had been dead for a very long time.

Chapter 69

Edith's Journal

30th September 1924

The banging on the front door brought me downstairs, and I opened the door to neighbours who had not spoken to me until that minute. I allowed them to take over, lead me to the kitchen, fetch my daughters, and give us tea and sympathy while they gossiped in the hall. They meant well. At least I believe they tried to look after us as best they could, for we were strangers to them.

The military police investigated, of course. By then, I had hidden the journals. Put them in the steel cabinet that Arthur kept in his shed and locked the door. The investigating officer was an Irishman from the west of Ireland, an ex-Connaught Ranger, and he knew Arthur. He remembered me, remembered that I was the colonel's daughter and treated me with a mixture of contempt and respect that puzzled me. It was as if he could not make up his mind whether to like me or loathe me.

It did not matter anyway. All that mattered was that they decided that Arthur's gun had gone off accidentally while he was cleaning it. That was good news for the girls and for me.

It meant we got a pension. We had an income, enough to get us away from this awful place.

I got in touch with my brother in India. He has settled there, working for the East India Company. He is willing to accommodate us until I find somewhere. My small pension will go further there and hopefully give my girls and me a decent standard of living. And I will finally get to make a permanent home. This evening I have packed up our belongings for the last time. This next move will be the last one for me and my girls. I have one son buried in India and one in England. My girls and I deserve this last chance at happiness, and I swear I will grab it with both hands. They must never know of the evil that inhabited their father. That part of our lives I am leaving behind. The cabinet has been moved to the furthest end of the attic and hidden under blankets, hopefully never to be discovered in my lifetime.

When they do emerge in the future, and I sincerely pray they do, I hope that whoever reads this will tell the story and find justice for the victims of my husband's crimes. But I also want them to know this indisputable fact. Arthur Torrington was not a bad man. Evil was not in his nature. It was introduced there by the evil that was done to him by his parents and others he met along his path in life and by the horrors he endured during the war.

It was fuelled by the effects of alcohol. He struggled with that part of himself and managed to keep it at bay for many years. I witnessed the sweet side of his personality, his loving side and I will always love that part of him. It is the evil part I cannot bear, and I hope that by leaving these journals here, I can somehow only remember the good aspects of our life together.

Whoever you are, please think kindly of my girls and me. We had no clue, no idea of the evil behind my husband's façade. If I had known, I would have stopped him. I found the body of one of his victims, and the memory of what he did to that poor girl's body will haunt me forever.

Please find justice for her and for the others. I cannot do it. I cannot expose him, for if I do, I will lose my pension, my only income and what would happen to my girls? They are the innocents in all of this.

Chapter 70

Brian

Saturday 26th September 2020

I was stunned. How could I fulfil Edith's wishes? For I was determined to do just that. I wondered if Conor could help with this. He had recently been assigned to work with a Cold Case Unit. It was a great relief to Jean and me, for it meant he wouldn't be "on the beat" so to speak, but in an office.

He might know who could help find justice for Gráinne Delmer and the other women who had died at the hands of Arthur Henry Torrington. I could speak to him over the weekend. We were due to move out of this house on Monday. Any belongings we were taking were packed in boxes ready to go. The van was booked, ready for pick-up at eight am.

Movement outside signalled the family's return. We were going out later, into Newbridge, for a meal together in the hotel restaurant. Our last one together before Jean and I moved to Waterford, our first one out together as a family since before the Coronavirus restrictions started last March.

Our favourite restaurant hadn't reopened after the lockdown. Many businesses failed, unable to remain viable after a series of lockdowns. When they were allowed to open, the social distancing restrictions meant they couldn't have the same number of tables. Smaller premises just didn't have the floor space to cope. Others couldn't seat enough people to cover their overheads. Covid-19 has changed the way we socialise, probably permanently.

"Brian, we're home." Jean's sing-song voice called out from the front door.

My family filled the kitchen with shopping bags and laughter, and I put the journals away. Gráinne Delmer had waited over a hundred years for justice; she could wait a few hours more.

It was fun having the kids at home even though it was temporary. The house was full of noise and laughter, and once again, I felt nostalgic for the days when they were young. Until a pillow hit me on the side of the head, shaking me out of my reverie. Jean's eyes were twinkling, her still beautiful full lips turned upwards in laughter.

"I know what you're thinking, Brian McElroy," Jean said. "Don't you even think about getting all sentimental. It's great to finish out our last weekend in this house with our family at home with us. It feels like the closing of the circle, letting us move on to the next stage."

"Now who's sentimental?" I said as I wrapped her in my arms.

Conor's voice echoed up the stairs, "Are ye ready yet?"

Conor, the designated driver for the evening, had a habit of punctuality inherited from me, I have to say. It was only a short trip to the hotel. Every table in the discreetly lit restaurant was filled with diners. Our table waited, resplendent with tapered candles, silver cutlery and dazzling glassware. It was dark outside, but the extensive gardens were illuminated with twinkling fairy lights.

The girls ordered champagne and toasted Jean and me. Any nostalgia we felt for the past dissolved in the bubbles. Our future looked bright. Looking around the table, I think we both felt pride in our children, mixed with gratitude for our lot in life. When I raised my glass to toast our kids, they reciprocated before falling back on our usual wisecrack banter. Over the course of the evening, I found myself telling my family Edith's story.

"That poor woman," Sinéad said. "Imagine carrying that around with you for the rest of your days."

"Although it sounds like she went through hell on earth as it was with that man," Jenny replied. "He beat her; he drank all their money. She did right to take his pension and get out of here."

"Do you suppose she got to live out the rest of her days in India?" Jean mused.

"I hope so. Edith and her girls deserved some happiness. Is there any way of finding out, I wonder?" I raised an eyebrow at Conor.

"Don't know, Dad. I would imagine there would be shipping records. They would have been listed on the ship manifest. If she was getting a pension from the British army, then they would have records, but you might have to go to Kew in London to get them."

"What about Gráinne Delmer? We have a handwritten confession in that journal. Finally, the mystery of who murdered her is solved. Who do we go to with that information?"

"I don't think the Cold Case Unit will be interested, Dad. The crime itself goes back to before the formation of the state. You have a confession. Does she still have family in the area?"

"I don't think so, Conor," Jean said. "She had two brothers. One was killed in the First World War, and the other went to America, as far as we know. But I'll ask my mother again. She might know of another relative of Gráinne's, but I doubt it."

The idea of the identity of Gráinne Delmer's murderer remaining hidden after all didn't sit right with me.

"So, that's it then. What about the other murders?" I looked around the table for answers, but no one had any.

"The murders are old, Dad, and in different jurisdictions." Conor shrugged. "I'll ask around. Maybe the British Cold Case Unit might investigate the murder in Dover in 1921, but it's still a hundred years old. They might be able to match the confession to an unsolved murder case, but the older ones…"

They were right. Jean asked around, but Gráinne Delmer's family were dead and buried. The whereabouts of the older brother was a mystery. The Cold Case Unit sent the information to the British authorities. In due course, they matched an unsolved case of a young Irish immigrant to Henry's handwritten confession. The girl with the flaming red hair and hazel eyes had a name, Blánaid Fitzsimmons, just fifteen when she was found, raped, and butchered in a cheap boarding house in Dover. At least that was some sort of closure.

While the information was sent to the relevant authorities in the other countries, the murder victims could not be traced. Nazareth was in Palestine at that time, and law and order were non-existent. There was a full-scale world war going on. The murder probably wasn't even reported. It is part of Israel now. The British Empire no longer rules India, Egypt or Malta.

The relevant authorities were unwilling or unable to trace the unsolved murders. In one way, who could blame them, for it had all happened so long ago that no living person could possibly have any memory of the women who were murdered? It doesn't make sense to waste valuable resources on solving those crimes when no one would benefit. But still, Edith's plea niggled me.

Chapter 71

Brian

November 2022

I held on to the journals. Why? I don't know. I sent photocopies to the relevant authorities, but the original journals came with me to Waterford. For months they lay unopened, in a box, in the garage. Our first few weeks were spent settling in. We already knew the area well, for we had holidayed there for years. We swam, walked; I even played some golf badly, but at least I tried. It was as if we were on honeymoon. I suppose we were in a way. The honeymoon period of the new stage in our lives, and we enjoyed every second.

As the winter drew in, the dark nights and cold weather kept us indoors. I began to get bored. It's easy to say relax and enjoy your retirement, but it's hard to change the habits of a lifetime. For years I had got up early, exercised daily, worked hard, and did my duty as a member of the Defence Forces.

I was surprised by how much I missed the social aspect of work. If it wasn't for Jean, I wouldn't speak to a soul from one end of the day to the other, whereas I interacted with people all day long when I was working. I missed the camaraderie, the craic, and to be honest, the testosterone-fuelled chat. The manner in which men speak to each other is very different when members of the opposite sex are not around. I am not an alpha male by any means, but I missed the male companionship.

"Why don't we join the local Tidy Towns committee. They do great work in the village, and it would get you out and about," Jean suggested.

I contacted them and attended their next meeting, but there wasn't a lot of hard, physical work to do during the winter months. The meeting was very positive though, and I met a lot of new faces. Buoyed up by the prospect of a busy spring, I called into the local shop to pick up a bottle of wine. I figured I should celebrate my new role as a volunteer in the Tidy Towns workforce.

As I left the shop, a woman I had never seen before walked straight into me, knocking the flyers she was carrying out of her hand. They fluttered to the floor, and I promptly followed them while she apologised profusely.

"I'm so sorry. I was so busy checking the flyers I wasn't watching where I was going."

"Not at all, my fault." I grinned as I stooped to pick up another flyer. "Writers group?"

"Yes. I'm putting one up on the community noticeboard. Are you interested by any chance? It's a new group, only just setting up, really."

I was intrigued. Writing was something I had dabbled in occasionally over the years. Usually, they were short pieces about my experiences in the army. Now and then, I pushed myself into flights of fancy inspired by the people I had met along the way.

"I'm Louise," she said as she shook my hand.

"I'm Brian. Pleased to meet you."

The rest, as they say, is history. I attended the first meeting of the writers group and never looked back. Writing takes up every spare moment for me. When I'm not out swimming or walking with Jean, I'm out pulling weeds and planting with Tidy Towns, but no matter how busy I am, I always find time to write.

I have to say that, mostly, it is a pleasant pastime. But sometimes it is so frustrating, that I end up pulling out the little bit of hair I have left, but the meetings are always fun. We share our work, and the feedback is always encouraging. I know some of the stories I share with the group are complete rubbish, but I think a few good ones are among them. Well, I think so anyway, and the feedback from the group is constructive. It was during a general discussion one night about finding inspiration that I mentioned the journals I'd found in the attic.

"Wow. You have to write that story," Louise said.

"But it's not my story to tell," I replied, for, in fairness, I thought of it as Edith's story.

"But if you don't tell it, who will. Edith is long dead, her daughters too. When you think about it, Brian, it's your duty. It would be like getting justice for the girls who were murdered."

I laughed it off, but the seed was planted. Was writing about those murders a method of getting justice for Arthur's victims? When I told Jean, she agreed with Louise. So did Conor when he arrived for a visit shortly after Easter.

"That's a great idea, Dad. You should do it. Someone needs to tell Edith's story."

That was all the encouragement I needed. For the next year, I wrote and rewrote the story of Arthur and Edith. The writers group gave me great support and encouraged me to try to publish the finished story. My children took it in turn to read it and offer criticism and praise. I have agonised and typed and read and reread.

Finding a publisher was hard. After numerous rejections, I nearly gave up, but then, out of the blue, an email's ping gave a tentative maybe. More edits followed, rewriting and rewriting, but finally, I finished it.

So here it is. Edith's story is out there in black and white for the world to see. Arthur Henry Torrington's secret has been exposed. Justice, of sorts, for Gráinne Delmer, Blánaid Fitzsimmons, and for the other nameless victims. They may not have received justice in their time, but what happened to them has been recorded at least now. The shocking and brutal murders committed by Arthur Henry Torrington are finally in the public arena. You, dear reader, are judge and jury.

THE END

Acknowledgements

Where to start? I have been extremely fortunate to have the backing and support of so many people. The gem of the idea for this book has been lying dormant in the back of my mind since I first saw the Curragh Camp, way back in 1978. Little did I know I would end up living there, albeit for a short time, early in my married life. Built by the British as their main training camp after the Crimean War, it is filled with history. I was fascinated by the stories I heard from family and friends about the people who lived there. It would take another forty years for that first spark of an idea to come to fruition.

The staff of Newbridge Library were invaluable in enabling my research. I owe a debt of gratitude to James Durney, http://www.jamesdurney.com/ historian and author, who set me thinking about the Connaught Rangers. James gave me access to books and pointed me in the right direction. Thanks to Mario Corrigan, http://mariocorriganblog.wordpress.com for allowing me to study old maps of the Curragh area and for his generous support. Our local libraries are a valuable resource that we all should treasure.

Thank you to my friend, Comtd (Retd) Kevin McDonald, no relation I might add. When I told Kevin I was writing about the Connaught Rangers, he gave me a private tour of the museum in Dún Uí Mhaoilíosa (Renmore) Barracks, the main training depot for the Connaught Rangers from 1881 until 1922. Kevin then put me in touch with Joe Loughnane, military historian who gave me the grand tour of Galway and lots of insightful background information on the life of a Connaught Ranger.

Thanks also to military historian and musician, Damien Quinn, who is a fountain of knowledge on the Connaught Rangers. If ever you are in Galway city, catch his walking tour. Damien brings history to life. https://www.facebook.com/Galway-History-Tours-141375579225924/.

I mustn't forget to mention my friend, award winning author and journalist, Eamon Dillon for his advice, support and an excellent copy edit.

My friends in the Ink Tank Creative Writing Group based in Newbridge Library, are a wonderful group of people who managed to meet virtually throughout the lockdowns and came out the other side not only intact but stronger. They were the first readers of my work. Their encouragement and support has been amazing.

A special word of thanks to Aimee Dyamond, beta reader extraordinaire. Her insightful and very detailed notes were far more extensive than I could ever have imagined. Her appraisal was honest, encouraging, meticulous, and I have to say, invaluable in helping me shape my manuscript. https://aimeedyamond.wixsite.com/deved

Heartfelt thanks to my editor, Morgen Bailey, whose valuable knowledge and experience has helped me whip this manuscript into the novel you just read. I will be forever grateful for her expertise and her attention to detail. www.morgenbailey.com/editor

I cannot adequately express my gratitude to the team at Bloodhound Books. My thanks to Betsy Reavley, Tara Lyons and Hannah Deuce for turning my dream into a reality.

Last but not least, my sincerest thanks to my family. My little fan club, consisting of my adult children Kevin, Paul, Eilís and Gearóid, not forgetting their lovely partners, Aislinn, Sarah Louise, Giovanni, and Suzan, my dad, siblings, in-laws, and of course, my husband. Gerry has always been my greatest cheerleader. His encouragement and support kept me writing at times when I wanted to quit. Thank you, Gerry.

Author's Notes

The Sandes Soldiers' Homes

The Sandes Soldiers' Homes were founded by Ms Elsie Sandes in 1869. Born into a wealthy Anglo-Irish family in Tralee, Ms Elsie Sandes was an evangelical Christian who was concerned for the welfare of young soldiers. She saw them as vulnerable lonely young men, some as young as fifteen, who needed a good feminine influence to keep them away from the dangers of alcohol and loose women.

She first invited these young soldiers to Bible study in a room in her parents' house, but it became so popular that within a few years she opened a large centre in Cork City. By 1913 there were thirty-one soldiers' homes, all situated in or near garrison towns, twenty-two in Ireland and nine in British India. The aim of the Sandes Soldiers' Homes was to provide a social place for soldiers where alcohol and gambling were prohibited. Each home had a woman in charge, known as the mother. Every home had a reading room and religious literature was available but not obligatory. The homes offered Bible study for those who wanted and taught others how to read and write.

After the Anglo-Irish War only three Sandes homes remained open, Cobh (formerly Queenstown), Dublin and the Curragh, although not for long. The exception was the Sandes Soldiers' Home on the Curragh which remained open until the 1980s, although not under the auspices of the founder. Ms Elsie Sandes moved her operations to Ballykinlar Camp in County Down. She died in 1934 and was given a full British military funeral, one of only two women to receive that honour. Her legacy remains to this day. www.sandes.org.uk

The Shelbourne Hotel

Situated opposite St Stephen's Green in the heart of Dublin city this historic five-star hotel is beloved by Dubliners (even if they can't afford to stay there). Its guests have included the Clintons, The Obamas and the Irish Rugby Team. www.theshelbourne.com

The Connaught Rangers

An Irish infantry regiment of the British army, formed by the amalgamation of the 88th and the 94th Regiment of Foot in July 1881. They quickly gained a reputation of being fierce fighters earning them the nickname of The Devil's Own. The Connaught Rangers were one of eight Irish regiments raised mainly in Ireland. They were based in Galway, recruiting in the west of Ireland. The regiment served all over the British Empire from 1881 to 1922. Arthur's postings are based on those of the 2nd battalion of the Connaught Rangers.

After the First World War they were posted to India, away from the war for independence happening in Ireland. In July 1920 they mutinied over the treatment of their loved ones by British forces back in Ireland. Seventy-six rangers were convicted of treason and sent to Dagshai prison. One of them, Private James Daly, was shot by firing squad, the last British soldier ever to be executed for mutiny.

After the mutiny in India the Rangers were posted back to England and disbanded in June 1922, along with five other Irish regiments. Many of those seasoned soldiers went home to Ireland and joined the newly formed Irish National Army.

For further information https:// connaughtrangersassoc.com/

http:/nam.ac.uk/explore/connaught-rangers

http:/maltaramc.com/regmltgar/88th.html

Ayah

In British India, the wealthy upper classes employed local women to rear their children. These nannies were known as ayahs. Some households moved back to England during the hot Indian summer and hired an ayah to look after the children on the sea journey. These women were then abandoned in England until the household was due to travel back to India.

Ayah, Caregiver to Anglo-Indian Children, c. 1750–1947 | SpringerLink

https://scroll.in/article/820022

A note from the publisher

Thank you for reading this book. If you enjoyed it please do consider leaving a review on Amazon to help others find it too.

We hate typos. All of our books have been rigorously edited and proofread, but sometimes mistakes do slip through. If you have spotted a typo, please do let us know and we can get it amended within hours.

info@bloodhoundbooks.com